"A true detective novel, *Game, Set and Murder* builds its case layer by layer, unfolding every step as D.I. Angela Costello uncovers the mystery surrounding a tennis star found dead on Court 19 on the opening day of Wimbledon. Readers share the journey as Angela learns the deepest secrets of all the players in her charming, understated way. What a delight to read a murder mystery filled with people one really enjoys knowing!"
DONNA FLETCHER CROW, author of *The Monastery Murders*

* * *

"A witty and intriguing whodunnit, set in the glamorous and fiercely competitive world of international tennis, featuring a young female Detective Inspector on her first big assignment."
CINDY KENT, Premier Radio

* * *

"*Game, Set and Murder* is a complex and thoroughly entertaining mystery, set in the vividly portrayed Wimbledon tennis fortnight, that will keep the reader guessing until the dramatic conclusion."
DOLORES GORDON-SMITH, author of the *Jack Haldean* murder mystery series

* * *

"Elizabeth keeps the aces coming chapter by chapter!"
TONY JASPER, author, broadcaster, actor

GAME, SET AND MURDER

Elizabeth Flynn

LION FICTION

Published by Lion Fiction
an imprint of
Lion Hudson plc
Wilkinson House, Jordan Hill Road,
Oxford OX2 8DR, England
www.lionhudson.com/fiction

ISBN 978 178264 072 1
e-ISBN 978 178264 073 8

First edition 2013

A catalogue record for this book is available from the British Library

Printed and bound in the UK, September 2013, LH26

Acknowledgments

As is well known, there is a very famous tennis club at Wimbledon, and it holds a Grand Slam tournament each year. I have used these two facts as a backdrop to this story but would like to stress that this is a work of fiction, as are the characters depicted as club personnel. Equally, there is no Catholic parish of the Immaculate Conception in or around the Richmond area in Surrey.

Writing might be a solitary occupation but getting published is a group effort and I can't let this opportunity slip of acknowledging the debt I owe to various people who've helped in the process of bringing *Game, Set and Murder* to birth.

To continue with the obstetric analogy, I'm very grateful to Tess and to Ali Hull, joint midwives to the book. Tess encouraged me to get back to the story once I thought it had died and Ali licked my prose into shape in no uncertain manner and helped present it to the publisher.

I'm very grateful to Tony Collins and the team at Lion Hudson for all their help and advice, and to my copy-editor Sheila Jacobs for her encouragement. I'd also like to add a special word of thanks to Donna Fletcher Crow, Dolores Gordon-Smith, Tony Jasper and Cindy Kent who kindly endorsed the book.

Gordon Berry, Ann Murphy and Dave Howard of the Brent and Harrow coroner's office were always very kind, and patiently answered my questions about police procedures, even when they were up to their necks in cases – thanks, guys. However, any errors on this front are, of course, my own.

There are others, of course; friends and family members who've supported and encouraged me. I couldn't possibly mention you all but, believe me, I know who you all are and I'm very grateful.

Prologue

Early May

Petar Belic raised his racquet high in the air, his body arched back in the service motion recognizable to thousands of tennis fans around the world. His long, evenly tanned legs stretched upwards taking his feet off the ground. The sun glinted on his gold bracelet as his arm came over his head. His opponent had just enough time to register that it was going to be a smash as the racquet bore down. A nanosecond later the ball whizzed past him in a fluorescent yellow blur, crashed onto the service line and bounced out of court.

What the heck, thought Danny Moore. *I'm hot, I'm tired and I want a drink*. He went forward to the net and shook hands with Petar. "Well done, mate," he said. "You win. Again."

Petar laughed. "You weren't trying; not on that last point anyway. You were just thinking about that pint of beer waiting for you."

"Ah, you know me so well," replied Danny as the two men entered the pavilion of the exclusive Surrey tennis club to which they belonged. Twenty minutes later, showered and changed, each with a drink in front of them, they relaxed into the leather upholstery of the club's pavilion bar. They gazed out across the array of courts as they listened to the rhythmic "thwacks" of games in progress, while the sun began its lazy descent towards the western horizon.

They sat for a while, each with his thoughts. Danny nursed a pint of beer while Petar sipped a Scotch on the rocks. The sound of Petar's mobile phone ringing interrupted their companionable silence. He pulled it out of his pocket, glanced at the screen and rejected the call. Danny looked at him with raised eyebrows.

"Vinni?"

"How did you guess?"

"Doesn't give up easily, does she?"

Petar gave a humourless grin. "Lavinia never gives up. She always thinks if we just go through it all one more time the whole thing will be hunk-dory again."

Danny nodded. "Hunky-dory," he corrected absently. He cast a sideways glance at his friend. "Does she know you've got other fish to fry?"

Petar's eyebrows shot up.

Danny looked pleased with himself. "I've got my spies."

Petar laughed. "Of course, I should have guessed."

"You and Una giving it another go?"

"Yes," he replied after a moment. "It's gently, gently catching the monkey, as they say – but, yes, we are trying again."

Danny didn't bother to correct the idiom this time. "I bet the kids are delighted."

"Oh, you can be sure," began Petar, but just at that moment they were interrupted by a discreet cough. They turned to see a man in his mid twenties, wearing jeans and an anorak, waiting for an opportunity to speak. Petar and Danny stiffened slightly, wondering if the anorak pockets held a notepad and a recorder. They'd both been in the limelight long enough to recognize a journalist.

"Mr Belic? Petar Belic?"

"Yes, who wants to speak to him?" answered Petar.

The young man came closer. "I'm Greg Thompson from *The Herald*. We're hoping to do a series of pieces in the run-up to Wimbledon."

"How did you get in here? You're not a member, are you?" asked Danny, displeasure clouding his amiable features.

Petar turned to him. "It's OK, Danny. I am cool with this." He turned back to the journalist. "What kind of piece do you plan?"

"Well, with you, Mr Belic, the article would be two-pronged. You've been a great champion in your own right, of course, and I'd like to cover that. And then there's the fact that you're the coach to Stewart Bickerstaff, and since you've started working with him he's become the British number one. Obviously a lot of people will be watching very closely to see how he does this year."

Petar nodded as he considered the matter. "Do you have any of our cards on you?" he asked Danny.

"Yep." Danny fished in his pocket and brought out a couple of business cards for the Bel-Mor Sports Agency, their joint business venture.

Petar took the cards and gave one to Greg Thompson. "Call this number," he said kindly. "Tell the secretary I am willing to see you. Make an appointment."

Beaming with delight the journalist took the card, thanked Petar profusely and made his getaway.

Danny gave a rueful smile as he gazed at the disappearing back of the young man. "I'd still like to know how he got in here."

"A determined journalist will squeeze himself between the narrowest of cracks."

"Or bribe one of the staff."

"Or that, yes," conceded Petar. He turned the remaining card between his fingers as the silence lengthened. After some moments, Danny took a sip of beer and put the glass down resolutely.

"I've got something I need to discuss with you, Pete, about the business."

"Yes."

"You knew?"

"Yes."

"You didn't say anything."

"No, I wanted you to come and tell me of your own free will."

Danny leaned back in his seat, his cheeks suddenly flushed. "It's scary, having someone know me as well as you do." He sat up and took a deep breath. "I've been a bit silly with our company finances."

"More than a bit, I think, my friend."

Danny took another deep breath and spread his hands. "Very silly."

Petar's eyes searched his friend's. Danny felt the gentleness of his gaze. "Talk to me."

Danny leaned in close to Petar and began to speak.

Chapter One

He looked in good shape. The cream linen designer suit couldn't hide his taut thigh muscles or the pectorals, honed to perfection. He probably had an impressive six-pack hidden under the hand-finished shirt. His blond-streaked hair fell away from his handsome, Slavic face and the whole picture screamed – *fit*. This man is fit.

Except he was dead.

His body had been found on a lawn. Not just any patch of grass. This was a Wimbledon tennis court, and the Championships would be starting in just a few hours.

Detective Inspector Angela Costello gazed down at the body. She gave a long, regretful sigh as a weight of sadness settled round her heart. She didn't need a formal process to identify this man. A tennis fan since childhood, his images had taken precedence over those of pop stars on her bedroom wall for most of her teenage years.

She raised her head and took in the whole of the scene around her. She loved this place. The sights and sounds, the battles and emotions, the excitement of the Championships were essential components of the summer as far as she was concerned. Sunshine. Health. Vitality. But this had never been part of the picture.

Oh, Petar, what on earth's happened? she thought.

She looked up at the three men who had been standing nearby since she had first arrived.

"Local CID?" she asked.

The nearest of them nodded: a solid, heavily built man. Under his tie she could see his shirt straining across his chest. "D.I. Coombes," he said. "We didn't like the look of it, not here, not today of all days. Thought the best thing to do was to get straight on to you lot in Homicide."

Angela nodded. *D.I. Coombes. I'm a detective inspector as well.* The reality was still a novelty to her. *I know the fact that I've only just been promoted doesn't show,* she thought, *but I still feel as though I'm carrying some sign saying "wet behind the ears".* She took a few seconds, allowed herself a deep breath and gave a tight smile.

"Not a problem, Inspector," she said. "We can deal with it."

Coombes nodded. "We'll get out of your way, then. The official handover can be sorted out later."

"Yes, thank you. Before you go, who found him?"

Coombes stood aside and Angela found herself gazing on what looked like a boy dressed in a policeman's uniform. She blinked and looked again, taking in the slight build. She noted the smooth face and the clear, innocent eyes under the peak of a hat that, like the uniform, seemed slightly too large. Goodness, was she getting so old that the new recruits looked like kids to her?

"What's your name, Constable?"

He cleared his throat. "Martin, ma'am. Martin Pearse." Angela found herself resisting the temptation to ask him if his mother knew where he was.

"OK, Martin. Did you discover the body?"

"No, ma'am." He was unable to hide the note of disappointment and, aware that she knew this, he blushed.

She smiled in sympathy. "OK, Martin, put me in the picture."

"I was on crowd control outside when one of the groundsmen came running out of the club and asked me to come in. This is what I found."

Angela nodded. "So, did you call the station?"

"No, ma'am." She waited. Anxiety crawled across his face as he tried to remember all the training school procedures for such an incident, worried that he'd plumped for the wrong action. Eventually he risked: "I... er... I felt for a pulse."

"Well done, Martin. I presume you didn't find one."

He relaxed. "No, but then I'm not good at that sort of thing. I sometimes can't feel my own pulse. Fortunately a doctor came along just at that moment and he examined the.... him... the body. And he declared him dead."

"That was handy. Was the doctor just passing?"

"I'm not sure. When he fetched me, the groundsman mentioned that he'd sent for one. I presume in a place like Wimbledon the medics are never very far away. I've got his name and contact details when you're ready, ma'am." Confidence rang in his voice as he said this last sentence. He knew without any doubt he'd ticked the right box this time. "And I've called the station," he added. "They're getting in touch with the coroner's office."

Angela nodded. She wondered if her husband would be the one to take the call. Patrick Costello was a coroner's officer. "Thanks, Martin. So what strikes you about this scenario, then? Do you know who he is, by the way?"

A look of genuine regret passed across Martin's face. "Sorry," he replied. "I know he's something in tennis."

He'd got that right. "He was one of the best tennis players of the twentieth century, Martin. His name is Petar Belic." A shaft of grief shot through Angela and she stopped speaking; "*was*" – *his name "was" Petar Belic*. She cast her eyes about, looking for a distraction. These lawns were amazing, like velvet. Rye grass, that was it; somebody had told her once that they used rye grass here, not wheat grass. She tuned in to the young constable again.

"Ah, well, I'm more of a rugby man, myself," he was saying.

Angela allowed herself a fleeting image of young Martin getting flattened in a scrum. She glanced across to the far bulkier D.I. Coombes, who was waiting patiently. "Right," she said. "Well, what we've got is a very odd sight."

"Yes, ma'am."

"Hmm…" Angela looked silently beyond Martin to the perimeter of the court. She felt acutely aware of people passing, some dressed in their uniforms as stewards or line judges, their heads drawn as if by a magnet to where she stood, each somehow finding a reason to make a detour by Court 19. Ideally she would like to keep the lid on this, but didn't for one moment imagine that would be possible. She could already anticipate the buzz of speculation rapidly spreading to every corner of the club.

"OK, Martin," she said. "That'll be all for now. Hand in your report of the event before you go off shift, OK?"

"Yes, ma'am," he said, and followed D.I. Coombes away from the court.

Angela caught a movement out of the corner of her eye and turned to see Detective Sergeants Rick Driver and Jim Wainwright and Detective Constable Gary Houseman hurrying across the grass towards her. She had arrived with them in the Homicide Assessment Team car but got out at the club gates so she could get straight to the court.

"So, what have we got, then?" asked Rick.

"Not too clear at the moment," replied Angela, "but the locals thought they'd better call us in, given what's going to be happening here for the next two weeks."

Jim looked puzzled for an instant and then his brow cleared. "Oh, yeah," he said.

Angela, resisting the temptation to roll her eyes at Jim, nodded at the third man, Gary Houseman. His brand new suit and nervous expression made her suddenly remember that for him this was also the first day in a new job. She gave him a smile.

"Sorry, we'd barely been introduced when the call came through. Welcome to the team."

"Thanks." He returned her smile and she thought he relaxed a little.

"You've struck lucky, in a manner of speaking. There are worse places to start off."

"Yeah," grinned Rick. "It's downhill all the way after this." He turned his whole attention to the body. "All looks very neat and tidy, doesn't it?"

"Yep," added Jim. "Hmm… nice threads." He squatted beside the corpse. "Kept himself in shape."

"Yeah," agreed Rick. "You'd think twice before taking a pop at him, wouldn't you? He looks like he could handle himself."

"Didn't this time, though, did he?" Jim's expert gaze took in the details. "Nice clean hands. Manicured nails."

"Yep," said his partner. "No obvious sign of struggle."

"Know anything about him yet, Angie?" asked Jim.

"You bet I do," she replied. "Petar Belic, ex-champion. During my teenage years I was one of his biggest fans." She looked from one man to the other and could almost hear their minds calculating. "It wasn't *that* long ago," she added, hoping it didn't sound like too much of a protest. "You should have seen him. He caused a real sensation the first time he played here. He was just this skinny boy from the wrong side of the Adriatic back then."

"You what?" asked Jim.

Angela glanced at him impatiently. "Look it up," she said. "Anyway, nobody noticed him at first and then all of a sudden, there he was in the quarter-finals with everybody scrabbling around trying to find out something about him. They couldn't even pronounce his name. By the way, make sure you get it right, won't you? You say it 'Beleech', which isn't what it looks like."

"Oh yeah, I remember now!" Light dawned for Rick. "Big-time champ; my mum was his number one fan. When we were young, whenever he came on the telly we had to get our own tea. She was that keen on him."

Ouch! That's right, make me feel old, thought Angela.

Jim shrugged. "Don't look at me," he said. "If it doesn't involve a round cork board that you can throw pointy things at I don't know anything about it."

Each to his own, Angie thought, casting a glance at Jim's chunky figure. She'd always assumed he was just built that way, but she now wondered if his girth had anything to do with standing around in pubs and consuming beer while waiting for his turn to throw the darts. Rick, she knew, had a fondness for road racing, a hobby to which his spare, muscular frame bore ample witness. As the pause lengthened she realized, with a small stab of nervousness, they were waiting for her to speak. "OK," she said briskly. "We've got to seal this place."

"If this turns out to be murder it'll be your first case as a D.I.," remarked Jim. Angela wondered if he was deliberately ignoring what she had said, or just following his own train of thought. She mentally noted the possibility that he might even be trying to needle her. She hadn't realized until they'd turned up just how nervous she was about her first outing as a detective inspector but she was determined not to show it. *Take a deep breath, Angie,* she said to herself. *OK, so Jim applied for promotion at the same time as you did and didn't even get an interview. That's for him to deal with.*

"Will you find whoever's responsible for the games to be played on this court today and explain it will have to remain out of bounds, at least until the scene of crime officers have done their stuff?"

"Will do," said Rick.

"And find out how to get the undertaker's van to this court – preferably not through the main gates."

"Check."

"And don't forget to apologize for the inconvenience caused."

Jim looked puzzled. "For what? They've got an unexplained death in their club."

"Yes," she said patiently. "But they've also got a very high-profile international event beginning in a few hours and a little diplomacy goes a long way."

"That's their problem," he replied, a little truculently.

Angela saw Rick making a great study of his shoes. "Just be polite, Jim," she said. "It's better to have their cooperation than not."

There followed the merest of pauses. They were all equal colleagues a short while ago and now Angela was giving them orders. *It probably feels as awkward to him as it does to me,* she thought.

"No probs," replied Jim after a moment. "You're the boss."

Angela gave a sigh of relief as she watched them move away. She looked back down at Petar's body as she remembered something else. Surely it was on this very court that he had achieved his first victory?

She turned and hunkered down for a closer inspection, careful to touch nothing. This man had seen her through a pivotal stage in her development. She had spent her adolescent years dreaming of what she'd do if she ever got the chance to meet him, and now here she was, leaning in close over those beautiful cheekbones. She found nothing and rose a few moments later. It was best left to the scene of crime officers who had now appeared beside her and were ready to get on with their job.

"SOCOs," announced one of the men unnecessarily, casting an appraising glance at the body.

Angela nodded. "I'll leave you to get on with it." She took one last look at the dead man's features, perfect in death. *Well, Petar,* she thought. *It's the big question. Did you fall or were you pushed?*

Chapter Two

Jim and Rick were hovering a short distance away as Angela left the court.

"Did you find out who's in charge?" she asked.

"Chap called Burrows. He wants to see you," said Jim, with a distinct lack of finesse. Angela wondered if he was still smarting from their earlier exchange and let a beat pass while she made a business of fishing in her bag for her notebook. Jim had never been known for his delicacy of touch, so it was hard to tell if he was trying to goad her or just being himself; either way, she couldn't afford to let his attitude get to her.

Fortunately, Jim was partnered with Rick, who had no chip on his shoulder and was a bit more savvy. "Mr Burrows asked if he might have a word with the officer in charge, Angie," he offered in placatory tones, "so we said we'd bring you to his room as soon as you came off the court."

Angie nodded curtly, rewarding him with a small, tight smile. "Righto then," she conceded. "Lead the way."

Rick was careful to outpace her as they went into the club and along a passage, so as to pull open the door to let her pass, in punctilious courtesy. Jim strolled along behind, his hands in his pockets.

Mr Burrows' door opened quickly to Angela's knock. She found herself confronted with a smart man of military bearing. His impeccable blazer and sharply creased flannels accorded well with his tidy, organized office. From the chart on the wall to the separate pages hanging from clipboards and the spreadsheet on his computer screen, Mr Burrows could clearly have told you at any moment what should have been happening on all the courts for which he was responsible.

The relief in his face at her arrival betrayed the fact that he hadn't yet fully come to terms with the unscheduled event of that morning. He stood back to let her enter.

"Please sit down, please sit down, er, officer," he began.

"I'm Detective Inspector Angela Costello, Mr Burrows," supplied Angela, sitting down and balancing her notebook on her lap.

"Ah yes, Inspector. I see, thank you. Well, well, well, what a dreadful thing to have happened. Poor Petar, poor Petar." He was genuinely distressed. Angela was cheered that his first concern was for the dead man and not the logistics of having his court available on schedule. She warmed to Mr Burrows.

"Indeed," she agreed. "Do you have any idea what happened? Did you see anything?"

"Nothing whatsoever. I was checking out the courts when I came across the... him, and sent one of my assistants for a policeman and another one for a doctor." He gazed down at his desk shaking his head. "Poor Petar; what a terrible thing to happen."

"Did you realize he was dead?"

"Well, I wasn't sure, and obviously I was hoping he'd merely had some sort of – I don't know, seizure, perhaps. I was just wondering if I should get something to cover him, to keep him warm, you know, when the doctor came and certified him as dead."

"Right," said Angela, making a note. "Did you know Petar Belic personally?" she asked.

"Oh yes – that is, not closely, you understand, but in the way one gets to know the players here. We were nodding acquaintances, if you like, and we'd met many times over the years. That was about it. He was a very nice man. He always remembered our names; the regulars, that is. He never seemed to get too big for his boots, and goodness knows he had reason enough. But he was always the same, even when he was at the top of his game." Burrows chuckled. "Of course, he was playing in the days before players could legally dispute points and ask for a call to be properly verified."

Angela grinned. "You can*not* be serious!" she exclaimed with an attempt at an American accent.

Burrows laughed. "But you didn't get any of that with Petar. Not one single tantrum, as far as I recall."

Angela paused. She was aware of a strong temptation to reminisce. *Come on, Angela; stay on track,* she said to herself. *What was happening more recently in Petar's life? In fact, what was going on last night?* "I'd like to know everything you can tell me about him. We don't know yet how or why he died. The people he mixed with and the things he did recently might throw light on the matter for us."

"Of course; I understand you have to ask these questions. I do see that." Burrows picked up a pen and fiddled with it. "It's just that it's all so distressing," he replied with a sigh. He lapsed into silence as he gave the matter some thought. Angela waited patiently.

"He was always very friendly with Danny Moore and Helmut Wolf," said Burrows eventually, "and from what I hear they've remained in touch. I think Petar was Helmut's best man a couple of years ago."

Angela smiled. "Helmut Wolf. Do you remember when you could guarantee that Petar, Helmut and Danny would always be three of the last eight?"

"Indeed I do." The official realized that he was talking to someone who knew their tennis, and relaxed slightly. The pen went back into its holder. "Helmut generally comes over for the tournament, so I would normally expect to see him about the place and chatting away somewhere or other with Petar during these two weeks."

"But you haven't seen him yet?"

"Not so far. Mind you, I could have missed him; it's a big place. I'm kept very busy," he added with a touch of pride.

Angela nodded. "What about Danny Moore?"

"Ah, well that's a completely different kettle of fish. Danny runs a sports promotion agency that handles some of our players and I would expect to see more of him. He's been about quite a bit during the last week; in fact, he was here yesterday. I know I saw him and Petar together at one point. I think they are – were – on very friendly terms."

"Was that the last time you saw him?"

"Yes… yes, I think so. They were having a drink together at one of the bars."

Angela looked up quickly from her notepad. "What time would this have been, Mr Burrows?"

"I think – I didn't look at my watch, but it might have been late afternoon, half past four, five? Thereabouts, anyway. To think that that would be the last time…" He blinked, a look of distress evident on his face.

"Right. Can you think of anybody else who was seen around with Petar?"

"Well, there was a… er… lady friend."

Angela suppressed a smile at Burrows' old-fashioned delicacy, but she'd seen quite a bit in the gossip columns about Petar's girlfriend, Lavinia Bannister, and suspected that she was up to speed on the "lady friend" situation.

"What about Stewart Bickerstaff?"

"Ah yes, well, I saw him with Stewart. You'd expect that, of course, with Petar being his coach. And then there are some of the other players who are Stewart's pals on the tour. There's a little group of them that seem to stick together quite a bit, Philip Turnbull for one – and I hear Philip's been seen out and about a bit lately with that American player, Tessa Riordan."

"Did Petar mix much, socially, with Stewart and this little… er… group?"

"From what I hear he went for a meal with them now and again. Petar was a great one for nurturing up-and-coming talent and I should imagine a bit of socializing went with that."

Angela thought for a moment. "I'd better add Joanna Clarke to this gang, hadn't I?" she asked, pleased with her knowledge of the game.

"Ah yes; Stewart and Joanna have been an item for a long time, haven't they, yes… mind you…" His voice tailed off and Angela cast a puzzled glance at him. "Well," he continued, "it's just that that other American player, Candy Trueman, has been with them a lot lately as well. Once or twice recently I've seen her leave the club with Stewart when Joanna's stayed on to practise."

As she added the name to her list, Angela remembered seeing a picture of Candy and Stewart out together at a Mayfair restaurant recently, looking very much like a couple. She looked up to catch a carefully noncommittal expression on Burrows' professional face and wondered if she was being told that Joanna was on the way out and Candy on the way in.

"Well, thank you for your time," said Angela, shutting her notebook. "I think that's all for now. At the moment this is an unexplained death and we have to proceed on the basis that it could become a murder enquiry; in which case I might need to speak to you again. But let's hope it doesn't come to that."

"Indeed."

"It might also be necessary for us to speak to certain of the players and members of the staff. Obviously we'd want to do this in private and I believe there's a police room here."

"Oh yes. In fact, you have two rooms here – well, the police have, that is. There's a control room and another room which isn't really designated for anything. Happily we don't have a huge amount of crime, but you know how it is: there's always some pickpocket around wanting to take a chance. If the police want to question anybody, I've noticed in the past few years that they're more likely than not to take them to the local station. So this second room doesn't get much use these days. It would be ideal for your purposes. I'm sure any of your junior officers know how to find it."

Angela stood up. "Thank you very much, Mr Burrows. I do appreciate your cooperation," she said. "And I'd like to assure you that we'll free up Court 19 just as soon as we can."

He gave a bleak smile. "That's the least of our worries at the moment, Inspector. The tennis world has lost a truly great champion."

"Yes," said Angela.

There was a moment of silence. They exchanged sympathetic glances as Angela moved out into the corridor. Just at that moment her mobile rang, and she sighed as she glanced at the screen: her boss, Detective Chief Inspector Stanway.

"Good morning, sir," Angie said as she let the door close silently behind her.

"Morning, Angie. I hear you've got an unexplained death at Wimbledon."

"Yes, sir, Petar Belic," she responded as she made her way along the corridor to the nearest exit. "I'm sure you remember him."

"I certainly do. I've got meetings for most of today but I've no doubt the post-mortem will be tomorrow. I'll attend that, and catch up with you later in the office."

Angela frowned. She hoped he wouldn't be breathing down her neck too much. She wanted to flex her newly promoted muscles. Even as the thought came, she recognized its childishness but found it difficult to shake off the feeling. "OK, sir, see you then," she replied, making a huge effort to keep a peevish note out of her voice.

She looked up to see a harassed-looking woman of about thirty waiting for her as she emerged into the grounds. Angie scanned her plastic lapel badge – Janina Duncan, Press Officer. Noting the look of mild panic in Janina's eyes and the flush rising up her neck, Angela wondered if the press officer, like herself, was also new in post.

Janina gave Angela a tight smile. "Are you the police officer in charge here at the moment?" she asked.

"Yes, Ms Duncan. I'm Detective Inspector Angela Costello." At that moment a small group of stewards passed between them, and it was clear there might be other interruptions. "Shall we go somewhere more…?"

"Absolutely! I know a spot that will be nice and quiet at this time of the morning." She turned hastily and led Angela by a couple of pathways to where some picnic tables stood in the inviting sunshine. "Obviously… er… um… we want to cooperate fully with the police. Well, naturally, of course we do, yes," she said, once they were both seated and Angela had taken out her notebook. Janina's eyes darted about in a nervous manner.

Being in the company of someone even more nervous about the situation than herself helped Angela to relax. "Thank you; as we do with the club, of course."

Janina nodded and steadied herself. "It's just such a terrible thing to happen. Everybody's so shocked."

Angela noted the "everybody" and imagined the many that must have flowed past the court even during this short visit. The SOCO team would have sealed the place now and set up some sort of cordon to keep the curious at bay, but you couldn't stop people talking.

"It's going to be impossible to keep the lid on this, of course. But there's no reason for us to get carried away," Angela grinned. "We can safely leave the press and the public to do that. I think at the moment all we need is a statement to the effect that the body of an as yet unidentified man has been found in the grounds, and the club is cooperating fully with the police in the investigation."

"That sounds about right," agreed Janina. "Er, re identification…"

"Yes, do you know whom we can call on? I've been quite a fan of Petar in my time but I wasn't clued up on his domestic arrangements. I've seen him in the glossies, of course, with Lavinia Bannister, the publicist that he's been with for a while." *And a very odd couple they made too,* she thought. Most publicists contented themselves with obtaining publicity for their clients, but pictures of Lavinia Bannister, skimpily clothed with a glass of champagne in one hand and a cigarette in the other at some glamorous function, featured in the media on a regular basis. More recent photographs had betrayed Petar's ever-increasing discomfort with this arrangement.

Janina broke into Angela's reflections. "I think your best bet is to call his wife."

"His wife?"

Janina correctly interpreted Angela's tone. "The word is that they were getting back together again, or at least trying."

"Did he split up with Lavinia Bannister, then?"

"I don't know but I don't think so, or at least, not quite," replied Janina. She shrugged her shoulders. "I think everything was a bit fluid but I got the impression he was happy to be seeing Una again. They weren't actually divorced, you know, which means that she's his next of kin. I heard Una fielding questions about Petar the other day on some radio programme. She was very cagey, as you might expect, and wouldn't give any information about the possibility of a reconciliation, but she did say that they just hadn't ever got round to divorcing."

"Hmm. Still married. That's very interesting," said Angela taking out her notebook again. *It's very simple, Angela,* she said to herself as she wrote. *If a couple split up but don't get divorced, perhaps it's because, deep down, they don't want to.* She smiled at Janina. "OK, I'll leave the press release with you. Would you give me the contact details for Mrs Belic? We'll need to ask as soon as possible if she's willing to do the identification."

Angela was back at the court in time to see the undertaker's van drive away. Rick and Jim appeared at her side.

"What do you reckon, Angie?" asked Rick.

"We'll have to wait for the post-mortem, of course, but given the place where he was found, my gut feeling is that it's not a natural death. I hope I'm wrong."

"Would you go as far as to say murder?"

Angela paused for a moment. "Yes. I think I would."

"It's a very odd place to leave a body, though," said Rick.

"Very."

"I suppose he could have been on the court for some legitimate reason when he was taken bad," suggested Jim, whose voice had lost its earlier edginess.

Angela shrugged. "Until we get the results of the PM we can't take it any further. I don't know about you, but I've got a desk piled with paperwork."

Fifteen minutes later saw all four back in the car. Angela drove; Jim shared the back seat with Gary. They edged their way along Church Road as fast as the heavy traffic allowed. The sun streamed in through the open windows along with the noise from several hundred excited tennis fans snaking along the pavement, all eager to be courtside. A holiday atmosphere pervaded everywhere. They passed Constable Pearse, back at his post near a group of women all wearing bright T-shirts of the same colour. A memory stirred: Angela realized she'd seen this group, or one very like them, at the Queen's Club tournament recently. She could only see them from the back but she was sure each of them wore a letter on their front, which together spelled out the name of the player they supported – Stewart Bickerstaff in this case. She smiled as she passed. She could see Martin looking at the group with undisguised longing. She wondered if he fancied one of them in particular or all of them in general.

She turned the car radio on. They still hadn't cleared the crowd before she heard the announcement: *News has just come in that somebody has been found dead at Wimbledon. Police were called to the scene very quickly, and an investigation is underway. We'll update you on this story as soon as we have more information.*

The announcer then segued into the tournament. *The world's most famous tennis tournament starts today. Two of the main contenders for the ladies' title, Tessa Riordan and Candy Trueman, flew in from America several days ago and have spent the last week getting used to playing on grass. Tessa's a hard-working girl from the Mid-West who likes to keep her private life to herself, but California girl Candy has taken breaks from practice a couple of times since she arrived and has been seen about town with the British number one, Stewart Bickerstaff. The couple were snapped leaving a Mayfair nightclub just a couple of days ago. Hopes are high for Stewart to do well, and British fans will be watching him closely during this year's tournament.*

The number two Brit is Philip Turnbull. His game has come a long way in the past year and he's thought to stand a good chance of making it through to the second week. Flying the flag for the British ladies is Joanna Clarke. Her game has been inconsistent lately. She got to round three in the French but didn't get past two at Eastbourne. Let's hope she finds her form very quickly and can put up a good show here...

"Didn't say anything about foul play," said Gary.

Angela nodded. "I don't think they'd dare at this stage." She switched the radio off and left the tennis crowds behind.

Chapter Three

Several hours later, Angela entered her home in Richmond. Closing the front door behind her, she kicked off her shoes and stood for a few moments in the hallway. Angie loved this moment of the day. Bright evening sunlight streamed in through the glass panels above the front door, sparkling everywhere it landed, giving an added shining welcome to the house. She could hear Patrick pottering about in the kitchen just a few yards away. He was usually home before her, and she gave thanks to be married to a man who loved to cook. Through the door she could hear the faint sound of a CD playing. Patrick liked cooking to music. It inspired him. The Three Tenors tonight.

She pushed open the kitchen door.

"Evening, sweetheart," he said without looking round. Angela moved nearer and put her arms round him from behind. Holding aloft a peeled onion in one hand and a kitchen knife in the other he wriggled round in her grip, a wide grin of welcome on his face; they kissed. A moment later he drew back and looked down at her. She grinned up at him happily and buried her face in his shoulder. It amazed her that after two and a half years of marriage his smile could still cause her heart to flip.

"What are you thinking about?" he asked.

"I was thinking how glad I am that I've got a flipping heart."

He laughed; they'd had this conversation before. "I'm very glad about that too, darling. I must say, I thought you would come in all preoccupied with today's events." Angela raised her eyes to his face. "I didn't take the initial call but I heard all about it, obviously," he said. "Was it very traumatic, finding your first love dead this morning?"

Angela moved over and perched herself on a high stool just out of the way of cooking operations. She gave a rueful smile. "Not traumatic as such. But it was sad all the same. He was such a big part of my growing-up years. And do you know, Pads, he looked so damned healthy and vibrant lying there."

He gave a short bark of laughter. "Yes, I know what you mean." He was silent for a while as he finished chopping the onion and poured some oil into a pan. "Did you catch any of the news bulletins?" he asked once the onions were sizzling gently.

"No," she answered. "Well, only an early one as I was coming away from the club."

"Hmm. By the midday news broadcast there'd been a positive identification from his wife. So they announced his death and gave a brief summary of his career – you know how they do – and there was a minute's silence at the opening of the tournament."

"Oh, that's a nice gesture," Angie responded. "I didn't catch any of the bulletins today. I just got stuck into some paperwork. It occurred to me that it wouldn't be a bad idea to clear my desk while I had the chance. I suspect this might be murder and I'll be on the case. At least I hope I will be," she finished, unable to keep a note of chagrin out of her voice.

He shot her a puzzled look. "Why wouldn't you be, Detective Inspector Costello?"

"Call me paranoid, but D.C.I. Stanway rang me this morning and said he would go to the post-mortem tomorrow. So I immediately thought I might not get to run this investigation – he'd be breathing down my neck all the time…" Angela's voice tailed off.

"Well, he is in overall charge, sweetheart."

"I know."

"If anything goes wrong, it's his head on the block."

"I know."

"You're paranoid."

Angela laughed. "Yeah, I know that too."

"McKenzie is the pathologist on tomorrow and he's an old pal of Stanway, so I expect he actually wants the opportunity for a bit of a chinwag. You'll be heading up the investigation, no question."

"I didn't know McKenzie and Stanway were pals. Sounds like you've got inside knowledge. Is there anything else you're not telling me, Mr Coroner's Officer?"

He spread his hands. "I know *nutzing*. The PM will be first thing in the morning so all speculation is suspended for the time being. But I was at the public mortuary when the body was brought in along with the details of how he had been found." Angela nodded and a comfortable silence ensued between them while Patrick gave his attention to his mixture in the big copper frying pan. As the onion gradually became translucent and started to brown, he added garlic and ginger. "We had a tricky moment when Una Belic came in to ID the body," he said, glancing back over his shoulder.

"Oh? Really?"

"Yes, the viewing room wasn't quite ready, so they asked me to show her to the waiting room and then fetch her when things had been set up."

"Oh right. What's she like?"

"Seems a nice lady; well turned out. She had two kids with her – teenagers – a boy and a girl. I presume they were her and Petar's children."

Angela nodded. "Yeah, probably; they have three altogether but I think there's a bit of a gap between them and the youngest."

"Right." Patrick added a selection of spices to the pan. "Anyway, I explained the situation to them and left them to it for a bit. When I went back about ten minutes later, somebody else was in there and, my goodness, you could have cut the atmosphere with a knife."

"Who was this other person?"

"Well, I didn't know at first but she looked familiar. She was as thin as a rake and she was wearing the shortest skirt I think I've ever seen. Her gestures were kind of jerky and her face was just the tiniest bit haggard, and I couldn't for the life of me think where I knew her from. It turns out she was Petar's girlfriend, Lavinia Bannister, though she called herself his partner. And then, of course, I knew that I'd seen her in the papers."

"Yes," said Angela. "And she's forever in the glossies."

"Hmm, I'm not surprised," answered Patrick, getting a packet of prawns from the fridge and adding them to the pan. "I must say, that airbrushing stuff does wonders, doesn't it? Anyway, she was demanding to know why she hadn't been called in officially to ID him. She kept casting these glances across at Mrs Belic and the two kids. They kept their cool admirably, though – Mrs Belic and the kids, that is."

"What an awful situation. What happened?"

"Well, I explained to Ms Bannister that Mrs Belic had been called in because, as his wife, she was next of kin and we needed a positive identification. She got a bit hysterical then and starting shouting that she was his partner, she'd been with him for the past two years and she should be the one to ID Petar, and she carried on in that vein for a while. She was quite hyper, really. I was very impressed with Mrs Belic, though. She kept absolutely calm and suggested they both view the body; one after the other. Long story short, *La* Bannister seemed to realize that she wasn't going to win so she calmed down a bit once separate viewings had been suggested, and that's what they did. Mind you, Ms Bannister was holding fast to what she must think should be her place in the scheme of things, because when she came out of the viewing room she made a point of going over to John Marshall, who was handling the identification, and saying, 'Yes, that's him.'"

"Good grief."

"You're not kidding. But I must admit I did feel a bit sorry for her." Patrick scooped some rice from a sieve where it had been draining and added it in with the other ingredients.

"Biryani?"

"Yes."

"Oh, goody. So why did you feel sorry for her?"

"Well, if I had to choose between those two particular ladies I know which one I would opt for, but this Lavinia Bannister is kind of left out in the cold. The proper protocol means that we have to refer to the wife. Which is what's happening. Una Belic is contacting the various family members and setting the funeral in motion – once the body's released, that is. And I expect it's she who'll eventually take his property, as soon as forensics has finished with it." He looked at her. "His property, by the way, didn't include his mobile phone or car keys. Did the SOCO team find them anywhere near the scene?"

"I don't believe they did but I'm not absolutely certain of anything at the moment. Odd, though, if they're missing."

"Police work is full of oddities. Right, Mrs Costello, I've just got to add the water and simmer for about twenty minutes and we're all set." He pulled two trays from the side of the fridge in readiness and smiled at her. "Dinner in front of the telly for the next couple of weeks, I think, don't you?"

"You betcha," grinned Angela.

Patrick always left for work before Angela and she was touched, the following morning, to see that he had popped out to get a couple of tabloids to accompany their usual newspaper and had left all three by her breakfast plate. She went through them as she sipped her first cup of coffee. The heavy broadsheet that they normally took gave a restrained account of the death on the front page but didn't make it the leading story, directing readers to the obituary column for a resumé of Petar's life and career.

The tabloids, however, were doing what they did best. *Petar Belic Dead at Wimbledon* and *Champ Belic Dead on Court* were the headlines and they both put as much spin as they could on the sparse information they had been given about the finding of the body. A great deal of space on the inside pages was given over to Petar's life story and a rundown of his most famous victories. Some enterprising photographer had managed to get Una Belic and Lavinia Bannister into the same frame as they left the public mortuary at the same time. Una and her two eldest children had kept their heads down and turned away from the camera but Lavinia, getting into a taxi a few yards away, was shown full-faced and tearful.

Another photograph of Lavinia accompanied an interview with her in both papers. She talked about how shocked and devastated she was. *The grieving partner of Petar Belic, publicist Lavinia Bannister, sat in her luxury Holland Park flat wondering how she was going to face the future without her soulmate. "I'm distraught. He was everything to me," she told our reporter, her eyes filling with the tears which have hardly stopped flowing since the tragic news was first broken to her. "I've got an extremely important business lunch today and I really don't know how I'm going to cope. But I have to be strong for Petar. I owe it to him. I know he would want me to be brave and carry on."* Angela looked again at the photograph. This one hadn't been airbrushed: Bannister looked convincingly haggard.

She flicked over to the back pages. Her television viewing of the previous evening had already shown her that Stewart Bickerstaff and Philip Turnbull had both won their first-round matches. Their faces gazed at her from the sports section. By the time they had both come off court, the news of Petar's death was official and a statement had come in very soon afterwards from Stewart: *I dedicate this victory to the memory of my friend, mentor and coach, Petar Belic, who was found dead so tragically this morning. Petar, wherever you are, this one's for you.*

She continued her trawl through the papers and was just finishing her second cup of coffee when her mobile rang, Patrick's name on the display.

"Morning, Paddy," she said. "Thanks for the extra papers."

"My pleasure, sweetheart; I knew you'd want something a bit more lurid than normal this morning."

"Yes, indeed. Has he had his PM yet? Have you got any news for me?"

"Well, yes and no. The PM wasn't able to establish a cause of death, so we've got to wait for the results of toxicology and histology screening. However, the body has a puncture mark, as if from a syringe of some sort, in the back of his neck."

"The back of his neck?"

"Yes. A very strange place if you're injecting yourself but all too plausible if being injected by someone else. It's bruised as well, which indicates that whoever gave the injection wasn't very experienced at it."

"Gotcha."

"So, given the facts, how the body was found, the puncture mark and the lack of obvious cause, the whole case has now been upgraded and gained what you might call a forensic urgency. The blood and other tests will be rushed through but you know as much about forensic turnaround times as I do, and we probably won't have any results for a few days. Anyway, my darling, we are looking at what is now, officially, a suspicious death."

Angela swallowed and was silent.

"Are you still there, Angie?"

"What? Oh yes. I'm just thinking about this puncture

mark. Were there any other signs of a struggle? I mean, there didn't seem to be from what I could tell when I was looking at the body, but…."

"The report doesn't mention any."

"But you don't just sit there quietly while somebody injects you with a lethal substance and…"

"You're getting ahead of yourself, my darling."

"OK… yes. You're right; we don't know if the puncture mark had anything to do with his death."

"What are you going to do now?"

"I'll take a couple more deep breaths and go in to the office."

"That's the ticket."

"I'm glad I cleared my desk yesterday."

"You were wise to do so."

Angela wasted no time in finishing her breakfast and getting in to work. She hadn't been there long when she received the call she knew would come, summoning her to the detective chief inspector's office.

As she entered, D.C.I. Stanway swung round from the window where he had been watering his beloved miniature roses. His round face lit up in a smile, which Angela knew from experience was not the signal to relax.

"Ah, Angela; do sit down! You know why I've asked you to come."

"Yes, sir. Well, I presume it's about the death of Petar Belic at Wimbledon."

"You presume correctly."

Stanway put the watering can down on the floor behind his desk and sat up, looking at her, his hands steepled in front of him. Angela was expecting him to launch into procedural details and instructions but was taken aback by his next words. "This is the most awful shame, Angie."

"Sir?"

"I've dealt with many suspicious deaths, as you can imagine, but there's something about this one that touches a chord; such a fine player in his day and a credit to the game."

"I had no idea you were a follower of tennis, sir."

A small smile appeared around the corners of Stanway's mouth. "Not just a follower, Angie. I was county standard at one time. I had a killer of a forehand drive, even though I say it myself." He patted his all-too-visible paunch. "Those were the days."

"Indeed," agreed Angela, not knowing what else to say. She was having a little difficulty with the image of the chief, young and slim and dressed in white shorts. "You're right though, sir. Petar Belic was a credit to the game, by all accounts."

"Yes… yes." Stanway gave himself a little shake. "To business; have you seen the pathologist's report yet?"

"Not yet, sir, but Patrick rang me and gave me the gist."

"Ah yes, of course. The gist being?" You had to sing for your supper with Stanway.

"No obvious cause of death as yet, but a bruised puncture mark on the back of the neck, sir."

"So what do we make of this, Angie, hmm?"

"Well, the injection of a lethal substance is my first guess, sir, possibly administered by someone not used to handling needles. But we won't know for sure until we have the histology and toxicology results."

Stanway nodded and looked at her for a long moment. "OK, Angela," he said eventually. "This is where you get your wings. Are you ready for this?"

She caught her breath as a flash of either panic or elation shot through her, and let her stomach settle before replying.

"I am, sir."

Stanway smiled. "OK, you know what to do; get on with it. You can have Wainwright and Driver, and a couple of D.C.s

I'm very mindful of what a high-profile case this will be, but I haven't got any other sergeants available at the moment."

"Not to worry, sir; we'll manage." *What a bummer,* she thought to herself, *but I hope I know better than to get promotion one day and whinge about staffing levels the next.*

"Good-oh. You can have that new man Houseman with you as well. At least he's got a pleasant location for his first outing with us. Keep me updated throughout and if you feel you're getting tangled up, let me know."

Angela stood up. You always knew when an interview was at an end with Stanway.

"I will. Thank you, sir."

She was back in her own office before she allowed herself to exhale.

Chapter Four

The gleaming Lexus glided smoothly to a halt in front of the players' entrance and the people inside allowed a small pause to elapse before opening the doors and stepping out. A smartly dressed middle-aged couple emerged first. They gazed around with satisfaction. One crowd of tennis fans, contained some distance away, were waving and calling greetings to the new arrivals. Another group, in the street on the other side of the fence, were also eager to see which of the stars had just arrived. This second group included a couple of young women with large, lurid initials appliquéd to the fronts of their T-shirts. Having successfully managed to jostle for positions at the front, they had already recognized the couple as Stewart Bickerstaff's parents.

"Ooh, he's here, he's here," breathed one of them in a tone that came close to awe. She brought her hands up to her mouth, squashing the "A" on her frontage as she did so.

Her companion, a "W" stretched across an ample bosom, preferred a more forthright approach. "Oh, Stewart! Hi, Stewart!" she called.

The offside rear door of the car now opened and the remaining occupant got out and stood up. He paused for a moment, took in the crowd and bestowed a special nod and smile in the direction of the women with the initialled T-shirts, knowing from previous tournaments that the letters of the whole group spelled out his name.

"Good luck in your games, Stewart," called the "W" girl as Stewart collected his kit from the boot. Her cry was taken up here and there and several calls of "good luck" echoed from different parts of the crowd. Stewart raised a hand to acknowledge the good wishes and went into the club as the car pulled away.

A young man and woman in a car immediately behind had waited patiently for the Lexus to move off so that they could advance.

"Stewart's got a lot of fans," said the man, Philip Turnbull, as he watched his fellow player disappear.

His companion looked across at him with a grin. "Well, at least eighteen," she remarked in an attractive Mid-Western drawl.

Philip cast a quizzical glance across at Tessa Riordan. "Eighteen? What d'you mean?"

"Eighteen letters in his name."

Philip laughed. "Oh yes, I see. But there are lots more." He waved an arm vaguely in the direction of all the waiting tennis fans.

Tessa Riordan smiled. She'd recognized the choreographed entrance of the Bickerstaffs for what it was. She glanced affectionately across at Philip. She knew she was falling in love with him but she was doing so with her eyes open and had already recognized the mildly naïve strain running through his personality. For her, it added to his charm. "The rest of them aren't Stewart's fans, specially," she said. "He knows how to work a crowd, that's all."

"You're probably right," said Philip as he put the car into gear and moved forward.

The women with the initialled T-shirts made their way back to where the rest of their friends held their places on the centre court. At first they were silent; a row two days ago had left a lingering frostiness.

Then: "Love that warm-up suit," said Chloe, of the letter "A".

"It must be new," replied the "W" girl, Michelle Davies, who had been a devoted fan of Stewart for a good while longer than her friend and considered herself something of an authority figure in the group. "He wasn't wearing it at Queens the other week."

"It looks good on him," said Chloe. A brief pause followed and then she spoke again, allowing appeasement to creep into her voice. "Was he wearing it, you know, when…?"

Michelle considered getting on her high horse but changed her mind. After their row she'd stormed off and while separated from the group had, wonder of wonders, managed to get a precious glimpse of Stewart. She'd rushed hurriedly back to the tent she shared with Chloe only to find that her story wasn't believed. At least Chloe said she didn't believe it. This led to an accusation of jealousy, which brought forth a counter-charge of showing off and resulted in an uncomfortable silence in the tiny tent. Michelle had nursed her sense of grievance for a further twenty-four hours but now she smiled suddenly at her friend. She didn't want to continue the row. And she really did want to revel in the details of her sighting with a fellow devotee. Perhaps, if she discussed it, what she had seen wouldn't seem so strange. She leaned into her friend and they bent their heads together and chatted as they walked.

Nursing a hot cup of tea, Angela sat on the edge of a desk in front of a huge whiteboard in the incident room and faced her newly formed team. In spite of the tea her mouth felt dry, she had butterflies in her stomach and she felt sure everyone in the room could see her nervousness as they waited for her to begin the first briefing. *Come on, Angela, you're a big girl*, she told herself sternly. *Get on with it.* She put the cup down.

"OK, folks, so what have we got?" she said to no one in particular.

For an answer, Jim held up a copy of a tabloid newspaper he had been leafing through. She glanced at the bold headline: *Petar Belic Dead at Wimbledon.*

"Thank you, Jim. You have a very firm grasp of the obvious." This was greeted with a couple of nervous chuckles from some of those present and Angela let her gaze roam over the room. As Stanway had promised, apart from Rick and Jim she had two detective constables, Derek Palmer and Leanne Dabrowska, and the new man, Gary Houseman. He wore the same new suit as yesterday with an almost snazzy tie, and looked alert and intelligent. She couldn't ask for much more at this stage.

"Right," she said. "I've now gone through the PM report. Petar Belic died between 11 p.m. Sunday night and two o'clock Monday morning. The cause of death has not yet been established, but the circumstances are suspicious and that's why we're here. As you know, he was found lying on Court 19 and there is a puncture mark in the back of his neck, quite possibly made by someone unused to handling a syringe."

"We'll cross all the known druggies off our list then, Angie," murmured Jim with just the merest hint of hesitancy in his voice. A tiny wave of uncertain laughter went through the room.

Angela considered glaring at him to put him in his place but she very quickly realized that this was a mark of her own nervousness. *Lighten up, woman*, she thought. *Get over yourself. A little levity in a team is a good thing, right?* She found herself able to grin at him. "Yeah, but keep the snorters and pill-poppers in the frame for the moment though, Jim," she said. The laughter in the room was heartier this time and there was a definite relaxing of the atmosphere. "OK," she continued. "We know the first three questions we have to ask, don't we?" She formed her mouth into the shape necessary for saying "M".

"Motive, means and opportunity." Rick was right on cue.

"One brownie point for you, Rick; this leads us, of course, to all the "W"s – who, what, when, where, why and how. And the person who tells me that 'how' doesn't begin with a 'W' will be doing the tea run the entire time we're on this case."

This was met with an open guffaw; more, in fact, than the weak quip warranted, but it signalled that the ice had been broken. Angela breathed an inward sigh of relief.

"Right, it's about time we had some information on the board. Leanne, what's your handwriting like?"

"Not too bad, guv," answered Leanne, going over to the board and picking up a marker.

"Petar Belic, natch," said Jim. Angela noticed that the moodiness of yesterday seemed to have completely disappeared.

"Yep," she nodded. "Let's keep our focus. Stick him at the top, Leanne. Have we got any photographs?"

"Yes, here," came the voice of Derek Palmer. He came forward with a picture cut from a magazine.

"Well done, Derek," said Angela as the image of Petar appeared beside his name. "We'll get proper stills as we go along but this is good enough for now."

Within ten minutes a small collection of names and the relationship each had had with Petar had been written up for all to see. Stewart Bickerstaff, after a brief discussion, was listed as a pupil/player. Una Belic and Lavinia Bannister were marked as wife and girlfriend respectively. Angela stood looking at the board with a thoughtful expression. "Danny Moore," she said.

"Who's that?" asked Rick as Leanne wrote the name up.

"Ex tennis player and very good friend of Petar."

"Oh, right. Do we know anything about his last known movements?"

"Not a lot so far. Petar was having a drink with Danny Moore in one of the bars at about half-four or five Sunday afternoon, but in a place like Wimbledon he must have been seen by any number of other people. Leanne, stick 'security staff' up and 'ground staff' and…" she turned round to face the room. "Sorry, everybody, but we have to add 'crowds'."

A groan went around the room.

"We'll need to check it out first," she said. "Keep them in the picture until we've got a clearer idea of how Petar's body got to where it was found. As far as I'm aware there aren't any campers out in the street any more. They keep to the park."

"Actually…" began Gary, then stopped as he saw that all eyes were suddenly on him.

"Yes, Gary?"

A slight blush came and went very quickly on the new boy's face. "Well, I don't know if it's worth following but I've got a mate in uniform and he's working with the crowds there. He told me there's a particular group of fans that support Stewart Bickerstaff. They camp out, apparently. Several of them wear T-shirts with letters that spell out Bickerstaff's name. My mate's been talking to one or two of them and they're very keen – well, you know, it's just the same as being a pop star's fan and hanging round the stage door hoping for a glimpse. They'd be looking out for Stewart and they might have seen something."

"It's Petar's movements we've got to track," began Jim, but Angela cut across him. She'd seen where Gary was coming from.

"You're thinking maybe that at tournament time, where Stewart is, Petar couldn't be far away?"

"Yes, guv, something like that."

"That's good thinking, Gary. We'll cover that angle. This friend of yours – he's not Martin Pearse by any chance, is he? The constable that was called in when the body was found?"

"Yes, guv, that's the one."

"OK, tell him to stay alert." She nodded at Leanne, who started another column on the board. "We need to find his car. You get on to that, Derek. Try all the car parks there first and if you draw a blank get back to the guys here to put out a general alert. As well as that, it's probably a futile exercise, but given this puncture wound we've got to look for a syringe of some sort. That means a search of the lockers. I'll sort out the warrants for that. Rick and Jim, you get started on the security and ground staff. Leanne, you go with Derek; you can take the crowds. I think Gary's idea is a good one and you shouldn't have too much difficulty. From what I've seen, Stewart Bickerstaff's most ardent fans are instantly recognizable."

"OK," said Derek.

"And we'll need to check whether or not he left a will." She made a note. "Leave that with me for the time being." She looked up at the board. "It would be helpful to have a map of the club and grounds. Derek, before you do anything else, can you get on to one of the uniforms at the club and ask if they can get us one? Gary, you wait here, please; I think I might need you. OK, everybody, you all know our starting point."

"Last known movements and who he was sharing them with," said Jim, ambling past her, crushing a paper cup.

Just at that moment the telephone rang, and Angela picked it up. "D.S. – *oops* – D.I. Costello," she answered.

"D.I. Costello, excuse me, ma'am. It's the control room at Wimbledon here. I believe you're the officer dealing with the case of Petar Belic."

"Yes, I am."

"I'm sorry to bother you, but there's a lady here at the club who's demanding – er, she's wondering why nobody has interviewed her yet."

"That's because we're barely off the starting blocks, but don't tell her that. Who is she?"

"The name's – er…" There was a brief pause and Angela could hear the rustle of paper as a notebook was consulted. "Lavinia Bannister."

"Ah, right." Angela remembered Patrick's account of Lavinia Bannister's behaviour at the coroner's mortuary and thought that "demanding" was probably an apt word. "Will you please tell Ms Bannister that I'll be at the club shortly and will contact her in due course."

"Thank you, ma'am."

Angela finished the call and looked across at the names on the board. Still gazing at it, she said, "Right. Gary, of the people closest to Petar, one of them is at the club now and waiting for us."

Gary looked up at the board. "Stewart Bickerstaff will be there, I s'pose."

"Actually I was thinking of Lavinia Bannister; she's there and creating a fuss about not having been interviewed yet. I'm not sure where Stewart will be because he's not playing today but we might be lucky and catch him at practice." She looked at Gary. "You've drawn the short straw, I'm afraid."

He met her gaze; no hint of a blush this time. "Guv?"

"You get to ride shotgun with the boss."

He smiled. "Great. Thanks, guv."

He seemed able to combine confidence and modesty. Angela was impressed. "Come on, then," she said. "Let's get started. I hope you're good at taking notes."

The second day's play was in full swing by the time Angela drove back into the club, and despite the seriousness of the circumstances she couldn't repress a feeling of pleasure at the prospect of her licence to come and go freely during the tournament. She asked the first constable they came across for directions to the police room; the journey there meant weaving through a constantly shifting throng of excited, chattering tennis fans dressed in summer clothes and clearly enjoying themselves enormously.

Once in the room, she sat behind the desk and made herself comfortable. "Will you go and see if you can track Stewart Bickerstaff down, please, Gary? Start with the practice courts."

"Oh, OK. You're not worried about Lavinia Bannister, guv — since she's been making a fuss, I mean?"

Angela smiled up at him. "I'm fully aware of my position as a public servant. But that doesn't mean that when the public says 'jump' I have to ask how high."

Gary grinned and set off on his mission. Within ten minutes he was ushering someone into the room.

The tall figure of Stewart Bickerstaff appeared in the doorway and paused. Angela had the impression that he did so in order to give her the chance to register that a celebrity was standing there. She reasoned that his life must be full of people seeing him, doing a double take, and wondering if it was really him before approaching and asking for an autograph.

Gary, behind him, obviously couldn't see why he was held up from entering. Being the shorter man, he raised himself on tiptoe to see into the room. His puzzled expression peering over Stewart's shoulder made Angela want to laugh but she kept her face straight.

Gary tucked himself into a corner with his notebook open on his lap as Angela introduced herself. She indicated the chair on the other side of the desk, studying Stewart as he arranged himself in the chair. His expertly cut blond hair framed an unlined face in which the points of colour – deep blue eyes and generous red lips – showed well against his light tan; a smooth, handsome appearance overall. He wasn't Angela's type – she liked her men a bit craggy – but it was no surprise that he'd attracted a coterie of followers who were prepared to wear T-shirts spelling out his name.

"Congratulations on your win yesterday," she began. "It must be a relief to get the first-round match out of the way."

A set of perfect white teeth flashed into a smile. "Thank you. Things have improved among British players in recent years but we haven't completely lost our reputation for falling at the first fence. So yes, I'm glad to be through to the next round. And as I've already said to the media, after the tragic circumstances of yesterday… well… I wanted to win for Petar." Stewart turned a candid blue-eyed gaze on Angela. "I'm not a religious man, Inspector, but I like to think there's something 'out there'. And I truly hope that Petar is in a better place now."

Angela nodded at this speech and let a moment pass.

"When did you last see him alive?"

"Sunday evening. We had a meal together in a restaurant near here."

Ah, thought Angela, *this beats a late-afternoon drink.* "Just the two of you?"

"No, we were, let me see…" Stewart narrowed his eyes. "There was Vinni – Lavinia Bannister, that is – but she went early." There was the merest of pauses. "Candy came with us, and Joanna and Philip. Tessa joined us later. All in all we had a very pleasant evening."

Angela noted the order he used. He mentioned Candy first and almost made it seem as if his official, long-standing girlfriend, Joanna, was actually there with Philip Turnbull.

"So there were – what – seven of you altogether? But not everybody was there all the time?"

"That sounds about right." Stewart crossed his legs in a relaxed manner. "I dare say you want the name and address of the restaurant."

"Yes, please."

"It was *Le Grand Accueil* in the high street," he said, his faultless pronunciation indicating a good all-round education. "I think I've got their card in my locker."

"Thank you, I'm sure we can find it. I'd also like to know, if you remember, exactly what time Lavinia Bannister left and what time Tessa Riordan joined you."

The dark blue eyes narrowed again as Stewart thought about his answer.

"Vinni flou… Vinni left about half past nine and Tessa arrived… oh, gone ten, I think, but not much after. She just joined us for a coffee."

Angela considered this. Given the gossip she had already heard this opened up interesting possibilities.

"How long had Petar and Lavinia been going out with each other?"

"I'm not entirely sure when the relationship began, as such," he said. "What I can be certain of is that they met two years ago, shortly after Petar became my coach. I know that because I was the one that introduced them."

"Oh, really?"

"Yes, Vinni's family and mine have a friendship stretching back to before I was born, so I grew up knowing her. We socialize a fair bit on and off."

Angela made a note. She thought Lavinia was in her mid to late thirties and knew that Stewart was twenty-two, so whatever socializing they did at anything other than family parties would probably only have happened once Stewart had reached adulthood.

"Neither of them told you that they'd started going out with each other?"

"Well, not really. The relationship took a while to get off the ground; I got that impression, anyway. I thought that Vinni was very keen from the beginning, but I didn't like to ask. Of course, I was younger then. She might be a bit more willing to confide in me if it was happening now. Anyway, after about six months they were definitely going to parties and restaurants and stuff as a couple."

Angela nodded. "Did you leave the restaurant together – those who were still there at the end of the meal, that is?"

"Yes, we all did. We didn't go on to a club, though, and our cars were parked just outside on the road."

"Right. Did Petar drive away on his own, or was someone with him?"

"He was by himself."

"May I ask who you went home with?"

He hesitated and a definite suggestion of embarrassment appeared on his face before he answered. "I took Candy home," he said. Angela nodded and let a silence develop. It bore fruit. "It made most sense," he continued after a moment. "Candy lives on my way back, but Joanna is in the other direction – so she got a lift with Tessa and Philip."

Ah, so Philip's with Tessa now, is he – not with Joanna after all? thought Angela, "About what time was this?"

"Eleven-ish."

Angela nodded. "So you dropped Candy off and went on home?"

Stewart dropped his gaze to his hands and paused before answering. "No. No, I stayed with Candy."

"The whole night?" Angela had long since got over any embarrassment she ever felt at asking potentially awkward questions.

Stewart met her gaze this time. "Yes, the whole night."

Angela made another note. So Stewart was happy to dine at the same table as Joanna but went home with Candy. It was looking very much like yet another fluid situation.

"Do you know if Petar was involved in anything that would have made him enemies?"

Stewart gave a short burst of unbelieving laughter. "Petar, enemies – it doesn't compute, Inspector."

Angela nodded. She hadn't really expected anything else.

"How long have you known Petar?" she asked.

"About two and a half years. After my success in the juniors, my parents and I – we're quite a tight-knit family – were aware of the need for a coach who could take me on to the next level. We approached Petar and he was happy to work with me. It turned out to be a good decision as he's guided me through some gratifying wins on the satellite circuit. I've had a good year, in fact, which is why I've been given a wild card for this tournament."

"Oh, really? That's a step up; you'll get a seeding next," she said, aware of a lurking temptation to get stuck into a conversation about tennis.

"I hope so."

"OK, well, I think that's all for the moment, Stewart. Thank you for your cooperation. It might be necessary for me to speak to you again but I'll try to keep the questions to a minimum."

"Not at all," said Stewart. "Mind you, I'm certain you'll discover the cause of death to be perfectly natural. I can't believe that anybody would want to kill Petar. Not only was he a good friend but I've lost a darn fine coach. I don't know how I'm going to find someone who can help me as he did. It's going to be quite a problem."

After he had left the room, Angela turned to Gary, raising her eyebrows. "Did you get all that, Gary?"

"Yes, guv."

"I'll be interested in seeing the transcript later. He almost made it sound as though Joanna was with Philip Turnbull at the restaurant – at the beginning of the meal, anyway."

"Yes; I'd heard that Stewart and Joanna are splitting up and he's getting it together with Candy Trueman."

"Well, spending the night together might seem pretty conclusive evidence, but you can't always tell these days, can you?" replied Angela, considering this morsel. Then she looked at Gary with a quizzical expression. "You're very up on tennis circuit gossip. Is it coming from your friend in uniform?"

"Martin, yeah. He's quite keen on one of the fans."

"Oh, one of the T-shirt wearing ones?"

"Yeah, he's been bending my ear about her and bringing in all the gossip he's picked up on the way. The fans have been hanging around a fair bit because the players are in and out of the club quite a lot in the week before the Championship, and he's listened to all the talk. They seem to have all the low-down on Stewart's private life. It makes you wonder how they know."

"I see. And what sort of things were they saying?"

"Just what I've said really, guv; they're Stewart's fans so he can't do any wrong for them. They were all for him needing to move on in his life. They seemed to think that Joanna's holding him back. She's been a bit of a drag recently, according to them, looking downcast and worried all the time. Her game's been off, apparently."

Angela nodded, remembering the commentary she'd listened to on the car radio the previous morning.

"OK, Gary, this meal on Sunday evening means a rethink on the order in which I was planning to see people, as we'll need to speak to all those who went to the restaurant. We'll do Lavinia Bannister next. I've kept her waiting long enough."

"Yes, guv." Gary was nearly out of the door when Angela called him back.

"Oh, and Gary –"

"Yes, guv?"

"Keep pumping your friend for all the gossip."

Chapter Five

Angela found it strange to be sitting in this room when there was so much tennis going on a short distance away. Knowing that a place in the inside of this world might never come her way again, she decided to step outside in case any famous faces passed her. *Just for the novelty of it*, she told herself. As soon as she stepped through the door, a noise on her left made her turn. A flash of black, red and blonde was tearing towards her in a fury and ready to do battle.

"Ah! Miss Bannister," said Angela, stopping abruptly to avoid cannoning into her.

"Are you the person in charge?"

"Yes indeed, I – "

"I was Petar's partner." Lavinia drew her head back, raised a pair of imperious eyebrows, and seemed to be trying to give the impression that she was looking down on Angela from a higher perspective. It didn't work. "Why haven't you been to interview me yet? I've been waiting for ages."

Angela kept her tone neutral and pleasant. "I've just sent one of our officers to find you," she said. "Would you come in here, please?"

Lavinia pursed her lips and waited a moment before following. Once inside, she gazed disdainfully around before sitting on the chair in front of the desk. Clearly she thought Angela should go to her for the interview, not the other way round.

Angela called Gary and asked him to come straight back. "Sorry about that," she said, keeping her tone bright as she finished the call. "Just waiting for one of our chaps to come and take notes." She leaned back in her seat. *Start off as you mean to go on, Angela. You're not going to be intimidated by her and she has to realize this.*

She studied Lavinia as best she could without actually staring. She was about Angela's height with an immaculate cut and coloured chin-length bob. Her Versace top just met the slender diamanté belt adorning tight Tommy Hilfiger denims, and a pair of Jimmy Choos on her spray-bronzed feet added the finishing touch. About a thousand pounds' worth of bulging bag – Gucci? – hung from her left shoulder. Surveying the under-eye bags, the hollow temples and fine lines etched around her mouth, Angela thought Lavinia had lived on salad and not much else for a very long time. Vinni raised her hand to push back her hair with a nervous movement, reminding Angela of Patrick's comments about airbrushing.

"I'm really not very impressed. I've been distraught," said Lavinia with a disdainful sniff as she ran a hand jerkily through her hair.

"Yes, I saw that," replied Angela, deliberately making her voice mild and gentle. She hoped the other woman would take her comment in the sympathetic manner intended, but Lavinia obviously didn't because she stiffened immediately, fixing Angela with a look of suspicion.

"Are you taking the mickey?" she asked.

Angela allowed a beat to pass before speaking. "No," she said, keeping her voice quiet and kind. "I saw in the papers where you said you were distraught. And let's face it, it's hardly surprising."

"Oh yes." Lavinia sank back, somewhat abashed. She seemed to need something to do with her hands as she constantly clenched and unclenched them. Eventually she pulled her shoulder bag onto her lap, took out a gold cigarette case and held it out on her palm as if in query.

"Please do," said Angela. She didn't smoke herself but had no objection to witnesses doing so if it helped them to relax.

No doubt club rules forbade this but she wasn't about to tell. Lavinia took out a cigarette with one hand and was still riffling through her bag looking for a light with the other when the door opened and Gary came in. He settled himself on the seat in the corner and got out his notebook. Angela coughed and sat up straighter to indicate that they should now start talking in earnest. But suddenly Lavinia threw her bag to the ground, dropped her head forward into her hands with an angry, almost violent movement and let out a gasp of anguished frustration.

"No light?" guessed Angela. Lavinia raised her head and looked at her. Tears glistened on her eyelids and her face crumpled.

"He's dead," she sobbed. "She's killed him." She burst into a paroxysm of weeping.

Her sobbing was the only sound in the room as Angela and Gary exchanged glances over the thin shoulders and shaking mass of perfectly coiffed hair.

After a couple of moments, Angela stood up and went round to the front of the desk. She sat on the edge of it and waited until the sobbing had subsided to a series of sniffs before she spoke in a gentle voice.

"Are you OK to continue? Would you like us to get you a cup of tea or coffee or something?"

"No, no." Lavinia shook her head and, glancing at Gary who was rising from his chair, waved away the offer. She pulled a tissue out of her bag and brought it up to her eyes. "It's OK. I'm OK... I'm OK." She dabbed at her eyes before looking Angela full in the face. "It's OK. I can talk."

"Well, then," said Angie, still speaking calmly and quietly. "How about we start with the bombshell you just dropped. Who are you accusing of killing Petar?"

Lavinia sniffed again and opened her eyes wide. "Well, isn't it obvious? His bitch of an ex-wife, that's who!"

"Ah." Angela went back to her chair and sat down. She decided not to bother pointing out that Una Belic wasn't an ex. "What makes you think Mrs Belic killed Petar?"

A hint of panic appeared behind Lavinia's eyes. She opened her mouth but, seeming to find nothing to say, snapped it shut again on another sniff. After a few moments she tried again.

"It's a case of 'if I can't have him nobody will'," she said finally. "She won't let him go and can't bear the thought of him being happy with anyone else." There was a pause. "At least I'm being interviewed by the police first. See how she likes that!"

Angela was very aware of Gary raising his eyebrows at this. She looked carefully at the woman facing her. *Late thirties*, she thought, *but aiming at twenty*. She ran over in her mind what she knew of Lavinia from the media. The words "party animal" and "glitterati" came immediately to mind. But she funded that lavish lifestyle somehow, and Angela had no reason to suppose that Lavinia wasn't a clever publicist with a full client list. The fact that her face was as well known – and maybe in some cases better known – than her clients was just one of those things. There was no law that said a publicist couldn't enjoy the limelight.

"OK." There was nothing for it but to play the whole thing straight. "Do you have any evidence to suppose that Una Belic killed Petar?"

Another sniff. Lavinia dabbed at her nose. "Well, that's your job, surely. You'll find that, won't you? There must be some."

Angela suppressed a sigh. "Oh, I can assure you that we'll be looking for evidence. But I would like to know the reason behind your accusation." Angela kept her voice low.

Lavinia blinked, put her unlighted cigarette in her mouth and took it out again. "He was going to come home with me. But he texted her from the restaurant and then he changed his mind about me and… and… well, now he's dead." She looked with a kind of defiance into Angela's face as if to say "so that just proves it". Angela directed her gaze towards Gary so that Lavinia wouldn't be in any doubt that the conversation had been properly recorded. Gary seemed to sense her eyes on him because when he had finished he looked up and nodded.

"Got that, guv."

Angela nodded and turned back to Lavinia. "Thank you, Miss Bannister," she said. "I can assure you we will be looking into it."

Passing on her suspicions, or at least her hopes, seemed to settle Lavinia a little. She put the cigarette back into the case and almost relaxed.

"Can you tell me, when was the last time you saw Petar?"

"Sunday evening; we had a meal together."

"Where was this?"

"That French-type place in the village – welcome, The Big Welcome." She focused. "*Le Grand Acceuil.*"

Angela knew the answer to the next question but asked it anyway. "And this was just the two of you?"

"Well, er…" Lavinia subsided a little in her chair. "No," she said finally, in a small voice. "Other people were there as well."

"The others being…?" Angela prepared to tick off the names in her head as Lavinia went through them.

"Er… Petar, of course; Stewart, Candy, Joanna – very odd that – and Philip."

"What was odd?"

Lavinia gave a derisive little smile followed by another sniff. "Well, both Candy and Joanna being there together like that. I've known Stewart for years and we're pretty good friends. He confides in me so I know for certain that he's broken up with Joanna but there she was in the restaurant. I mean, clinging on or what? Some women just don't know when to let go. She must have been taking lessons from Una."

Her tone grated on Angela, but she remembered how Patrick had had some sympathy for her and realized that Lavinia was probably just building herself up against the eventual reality that she was, indeed, out in the cold. She let it pass. "How come Joanna was included in the invitation?"

"Oh, I expect Philip invited her. He's a bit of a softy, Philip. He would want everyone to be friends. He also probably felt sorry for her. She's been going around lately like the weight of the whole world is on her shoulders and it's been quite a drag. I'm not surprised that Stewart split from her. And as for her game... I wouldn't be surprised if she finds herself back in the satellites soon; I mean, is it off or is it *off*?"

Again Angela declined to be drawn into the mean and pitiable disparagement. "How was Petar during the meal?" she asked.

"Just normal."

"Cheerful? Preoccupied? Quiet? Chatty?"

"Just normal." Lavinia's face began to crumple and she raised a tissue to her nose to deal with yet another sniff.

"I'm afraid I have to ask these questions."

Lavinia flicked her hand to and fro in a rapid gesture. "Yes, yes, I understand. It's OK."

"I believe you left before the end of the meal," she said.

Lavinia's eyes opened wide and narrowed again immediately, her gaze hardening on Angela's face. Angela glimpsed the sharp perspicacity that had built her sports promotion agency. "Yes. I had a headache."

"I'll need your address, please," said Angela, keeping her tone as neutral as possible.

Lavinia gave a derisive snort. "Yes, well I'm sure you've already gathered that it's not the same as Petar's," she snapped. "*She* saw to that, of course." Angela raised her eyebrows. "Managed to persuade him that it wasn't good for the children to see Daddy shacked up with another woman. That's how she kept her claws in him, through those whingeing brats. 'We need to think about Milan going into the sixth form, Petar', 'Lucija's very nervous about senior school, Petar'," Lavinia mimicked what Angela took to be Una Belic's voice. "They came round to visit him a lot and Mummy didn't want her darlings seeing my knickers about the place or my make-up in the bathroom cabinet. Ha! Can you believe that in this day and age?"

Angela could believe it only too well and was privately of the opinion that she would have felt exactly the same in Una Belic's position. "So you went back to your own flat. Did you take your own car, or a taxi?"

"I didn't have my car with me that day and the restaurant was quite near the underground. It wasn't too late, so I took that," said Lavinia. Angela nodded and hid her surprise. She had classified Lavinia as someone who would consider public transport beneath her. Her heart sank at the implications. If they had to verify a journey home on public transport it would be much more arduous than tracing a cab fare. They had nearly finished the interview now, to Angela's relief. Lavinia's wire-taut energy and venom sapped her will to live.

"And, just for the record, you spent the night alone?"

"Yes, of course!" spat Lavinia, apparently enraged at having to spell it out. She immediately seemed to realize that she was being unfair and qualified her answer. "That's why I didn't have my car. I had thought Petar would be driving me back to my place."

"Was that the arrangement between you?"

"What?"

"Had you and Petar agreed to do that?"

"Oh, I see what you mean. Well, yes, of course. What else would he have done? Of course he'd take me back home."

The silence in the room was suddenly very eloquent. It was saying, *But he didn't, did he? You left the restaurant before the meal was over.* "Silly me," continued Lavinia. "I should have known better. I've been spending most nights alone lately, ever since *she...*" She broke off and let her gaze linger for a long moment on Angela's wedding ring. "Well, anyway... what would you know about going home to a lonely flat?"

Angela had spent all of her twenties and most of her thirties as a single woman and suspected that she'd forgotten more about going home to a lonely flat than Lavinia had yet learned. But it wasn't relevant to the investigation and anyway, she was a police inspector, not an agony aunt. She thanked Lavinia for her time and cooperation, said she might need to speak to her again and breathed a sigh of relief when the door closed behind her.

"Phew," said Gary, voicing Angela's own feelings.

"I'll say. It's interesting, though, that she accused Una Belic."

"Wasn't it just hot air? Or maybe," Gary grinned, "wishful thinking."

"Or projection."

"Guv?"

"Well, she thought it an acceptable hypothesis that Una would kill Petar because she didn't want anyone else to have him. We could just as easily apply that reasoning to Lavinia."

"Ah yes, I get it. So she's in the frame, then?"

"Oh, most definitely; the distraught grief could be all part of the act – and she's got no alibi."

"Hmm, bit dodgy that, from our point of view; going home on the underground."

"Yes, indeed. I wouldn't give odds on our chances of finding a witness. Although you never know. She would stand out in a crowd and she's often in the papers." Angela took a deep breath. "Let's talk to the rest of the people who went to this restaurant. Will you see if Philip Turnbull's at the club and, if so, ask him if he could spare us a few minutes, please?"

Once Gary had set out on his errand, Angela sat and pieced together what she knew about Lavinia Bannister. She remembered Patrick's description of her coming to view Petar at the coroner's mortuary. "Hyper" – that's how he described her and, having met her, Angela felt inclined to agree. She had only a very fragile control of herself but her manner hid a sharp intelligence; no way could she be dismissed as an airhead.

"Well, that's Lavinia done. Now I need to meet the third person in this triangle," she said out loud to herself. She entered the number she had been given for Una Belic, thinking all the time about the contrast between the two women. "Oh, hello," she said, as the phone was picked up at the other end. "Am I speaking to Una Belic?"

"You are," came the answer in a soft voice carrying unmistakable undertones of the Emerald Isle.

Angela quickly made her request and was assured that Una would be at home the following day and would be able to see her at any time in the afternoon. Angela thanked her, finished the call and stared into the middle distance as she waited for Gary.

It was impossible to tell from such a brief telephone conversation, of course, but Una Belic sounded stable and well adjusted. Petar, by all accounts and her own observations, had been an upright, model citizen. It was very odd that he'd been drawn to the train wreck that was Lavinia. The whole business of the meal on Sunday was equally intriguing. Petar had been texting his wife while sitting in a restaurant next to his girlfriend. Did men usually do that?

Chapter Six

"I can tell I'll soon be able to lead guided tours of this place," joked Gary as he came through the door. Angela looked up and grinned. He went over to his chair and Angela watched Philip Turnbull's spare, lanky figure lope gracefully into the office. He had an attractive lopsided grin and a tumble of black curls.

"Congratulations on your win yesterday."

"Thank you," he said. "I'm always nervous at the beginning of a tournament. Stewart's always raring to go but I'm like, ooh-er, let's just get this first one over. I settle down after that. Well," he amended with a disarming smile, "that's always assuming I get through the first round."

"Well, I'm glad you did. It was a really good match."

He smiled, pleased at the compliment. "Thanks. I think I got lucky here and there because he's got quite a serve."

"Your return cancelled out his serve time and time again. You must have been working on that shot."

He shrugged deprecatingly. "Yeah; I'm pleased with the way it's come on."

"I wasn't sure if I would get you here today. I sent my detective constable out looking for you more in hope than expectation."

"Ah. Well, I came in to practise and stayed on to give the ladies a bit of support."

Angela was curious to note a delicate flush creep up his neck and across his face. It went as quickly as it came but she remembered Stewart's comment about "Tessa and Philip" taking Joanna home from the meal on Sunday evening. *Methinks he came to support one lady in particular.* There was a small pause. "Anyway, I haven't asked you here to talk about tennis, sadly."

Philip shook his head in sorrow and disbelief. "It was such a shock," he said. "I'm still having trouble taking it in, to be honest. I still think we're going to… I'm going to…" He paused, swallowed and a look of pain crossed his face. "You know, I still expect to see him arriving at the club tomorrow with Stewart. I still think he's going to be around."

"Yes, I know what you mean," responded Angela. She left a little space to acknowledge his sadness before making a gentle beginning on her questioning. "I believe you were with him on Sunday evening."

"Yes – yes, we had a meal, not far from here."

"Would you mind telling me who else was at this meal?"

"Um, let me see." Philip ran a hand through his unruly curls. "There was Petar; Vinni was there at the beginning but I think she'd gone by the time we got to dessert. Stewart was there, and Candy… and Joanna," he added. His eyes flicked up to meet Angela's and he looked away again. "And Tessa joined us later, when we were about to order coffee."

"How did the meal come about? Did one of you invite the others?"

"Oh no; well, I don't think so. We were all hanging around together after we'd been practising. I think somebody said they were hungry and one of the others suggested going for a meal. Tessa might say she was invited, though, because I asked her to come along."

"As a group, do you all see much of each other, socially?"

"Well, it depends who you're thinking of. Stewart and I were in the juniors together so we've known each other for years. I've known Joanna almost as long, I should think. We'd often make a foursome – Jo and Stewart and me and whoever I was dating at the time. Most people on the tour run into most other people at various times during the year, so we all know each other. But that's not the same as being friends, is it?"

"No indeed. What about Candy?"

"Well, as I say, I've come across her on the tour, but she's only recently – er, she and Stewart – er, um…"

"Have become close?"

"Yeah, become close." Philip grinned suddenly. "Oh, why am I mincing my words? They're an item. It's a full-blown romance."

"So he's finished with Joanna, then?"

"Well, I presume so. It's been a case of 'watch this space' – and Candy's the one who's inhabiting the space right now. It was rather odd, Joanna being at the restaurant as well. Well, not odd so much – I mean, we've had any number of meals together – but given the situation with Candy – I did mention it to him."

Ah, so you weren't the one that invited her, thought Angela. "Oh, really? What did he say?"

"He said he was sure she'd be fine, she would be able to deal with it, we're all grown-ups or supposed to be and there was no reason to exclude her from coming to a restaurant with us just because of recent history."

"That's how he put it, is it?"

"Yes."

"So, as far as he's concerned he and Joanna are definitely finished."

"Seemingly. It's just that nobody said anything. We've all been left to come to our own conclusions."

Angela thought she'd pursued this thread enough for the moment. "What about Tessa?" she asked and was intrigued to see Philip once again turn a very delicate shade of pink.

"Er, Tessa and I got talking in Australia in January and kind of found we've got some things in common. Then we ran into each other in Paris earlier this month at the French. We… kind of… we're…"

I think one or both of you made a very definite point of "running into" the other at the French, thought Angela. She grinned at him. "Stop mincing your words," she said and was rewarded when he burst into laughter.

"You're right," he said. "I'm being coy. It's just that Tessa's not like – well, Candy and Joanna are nice women, don't get me wrong, but Tessa's marching to a different drum. She goes to church and stuff and... well, we're taking things very gently. We want to get to know each other properly."

Angela nodded. Candy and Stewart could only have known each other for a month or so and were already sleeping together. Apparently this was not how Tessa liked a relationship to progress. Angela was impressed that Philip respected her principles.

"How much did you know about Petar getting back together with his wife?"

Philip shrugged. "I'd heard the rumours, of course; it would have been difficult not to. If it was true, I'm very glad for him." He smiled. "I'm a bit of a romantic at heart."

Angela could well believe it. "How did Petar seem during the meal?" she asked.

Philip hesitated. "He was fine. I mean, the same as usual."

"Not worried or preoccupied with anything?"

Philip found something on the back of his hand to attract his attention for a few seconds before answering. He frowned as if he'd found a blemish he couldn't account for. Then he relaxed.

"Well, it's not my business, but I don't think all was well between Petar and Vinni. I think Vinni wanted... what I mean is, I don't think she was happy about developments between Petar and Una. You can't really blame her for that. I think everything was a bit..."

"Fluid?"

"Yeah. At the beginning, when we were all looking at the menus and deciding whether or not to have drinks etcetera, they were having some kind of whispered conversation. It sounded a bit like an argument."

"Oh?"

"Yes, then it calmed down but you could tell that Vinni was put out. She didn't really join in the conversation around the table and it was rather noticeable because, actually, we all get on quite well and normally there's a good deal of banter and joking. And then she made some excuse and left early. She seemed a bit *hyper* to me."

"Yes?"

"It would be very easy to jump to the conclusion that it all had something to do with the rumours about Petar and his wife, but really the story's been going around for a few weeks now and I don't know any more than I'm telling you. It certainly didn't put Petar off his dinner, but I suppose whatever was up between him and Vinni must have been on his mind."

"Oh, really? Why is that?"

Philip shrugged. "I thought he seemed a bit distracted at one point early on. I heard him get a text and he sent one, presumably in reply."

"But when Lavinia left, he wasn't worried enough to go after her?"

"Well – no."

"And nothing else struck you during the meal?"

"No, I'm sorry. It was just a pleasant meal with a bunch of friends; I had no idea... It would never have occurred to me..."

"No, quite." Angela waited for a moment. "So what about after the meal?" she asked.

"After?"

"Did you all just come out of the restaurant and go your separate ways?"

"Er – yeah."

"Did you go straight home?"

"No, I dropped Joanna off and then I took Tessa back to where she's staying."

Time to find out if Tessa really is marching to a different drum. "Did you stay the night?"

Philip shook his head. "No. We had another cup of coffee, we chatted for a while… you know."

"What time did you leave her place?"

"I was only there for, well, less than an hour. I know I came away before midnight."

"Did you go straight to your own place?"

"Yes."

"Are you living alone?"

"Yeah, I…" Philip paled a little. "Oh no – no! I'm a suspect, aren't I? I can hardly believe it."

"These are routine questions, Philip."

"Yeah, yeah, I realize that, but…" He took a deep breath. "It leaves a very nasty taste in the mouth."

"Yes, I'm sure it does. Even so, just for the record, can anybody verify when you got home last night?"

"The man next door walks his dog at about midnight. I've seen him once or twice. I don't remember seeing him last night but he could have been around. I don't always notice him."

"OK, we'll check it out."

Philip left the room soon after that and Angela sat and doodled as she contemplated the empty doorway for several moments. The preliminary questions had gone very smoothly. But his reaction to her question about Petar's state of mind had resembled mild panic. And when he was speaking of Petar and Una she had formed the definite impression that he had picked up a piece of well-known gossip and waved it in her face in order to give a plausible answer. She blinked suddenly, and looked down at her pad. She'd written: *Philip Turnbull?*

"Hmm. Interesting," she said, staring into the middle distance. "Guv?"

Angela looked across at Gary who sat waiting patiently, not wanting to intrude upon her thoughts. "I found that very interesting," she said.

Gary flicked back through the conversation he'd just recorded. "Do you want me to go over what he said, guv?"

"Not at the moment, Gary. It'll wait till everything's typed up. In any case," she mused, "I was much more interested in what he didn't say." She stood up. "I think I need to stretch my legs a little. I'll just take a turn around the grounds and see if our ladies have had their matches yet. I'll let you know when I need you again. Thanks, Gary."

In truth she needed to step back for a moment. Ever since her promotion she'd known this kind of responsibility would be given to her at some point. Suddenly it had happened, and there she stood at the front in the incident room, sending junior police officers running around doing what she told them. She had faith in her own ability but she had to pace herself. The sense of being accountable, of being in the spotlight, seemed suddenly very daunting. Everyone looked to her to come up with the answers, and the Force judged her capable. Angela felt an overpowering need to give her mind a break.

Dismissing all thoughts of suspicious death, she opted to give herself a personal tour. She loved walking around and soaking up the atmosphere at Wimbledon, and took every chance to spend time here once the tournament began. On a few occasions she had even been fortunate enough to have tickets for the show courts.

On a day like this, so delightfully warm, Wimbledon teemed with life; the sunshine had brought everyone out. She ambled past hospitality tents and picnickers scattered here and there, then wandered between the outside courts letting the sights, the sounds and the glorious sunlight wash over and through her, stabilizing her again. Using the privilege her police pass gave her, she slipped into the centre court and was just in time to see Candy Trueman see off her first-round opponent, a player from Lithuania and the runner-up in last year's junior tournament.

Within the hour she was back in the now familiar office, with Candy Trueman – silky blonde hair, flawless make-up, an exquisitely designed tennis outfit and a California tan – sitting opposite her.

The brief respite had cleared her head. She felt relaxed and focused again. She hadn't been given the job for her skill at ticking boxes. She had imagination and they expected her to use it – to probe, even to push.

She started off conventionally, congratulating Candy on her victory and checking once more the details about Sunday night's meal. These corresponded in every respect with those already given by Stewart and Philip.

"So, Candy. How well did you know Petar?"

Candy raised her shoulders and let them drop again. "Not too well. I'd heard of him, of course. I mean, who hasn't? But I only met him properly a few weeks ago."

"How did that come about?"

Candy studied her fingernails as she spoke. "We were teamed together in an exhibition doubles match." She cast a brief glance at Angela before turning her attention back to her hands. "Joanna was due to play with him but she wasn't feeling too well and I was asked to step in." Given Joanna's poor form of late Angela wondered briefly if "wasn't feeling too well" was a euphemism, but the tennis fan in her let this interesting thread drop in favour of sticking to the point.

"So have you seen much of Petar over the past few weeks?"

"Kinda." Candy looked Angela full in the face and seemed to decide that a hurdle had to be dealt with. "Stu and I have been hanging out since that exhibition match, so I've seen Petar around a bit, yeah."

As hurdles went, Angela thought that this one had been crawled under rather than jumped.

"So, how did he seem to you lately? Did he seem preoccupied or worried about anything, fearful even?"

Candy looked blank. "No, he just seemed like always. It's really odd, him dying like that, but, well, it's just a sudden death... I guess."

"Dying like what?" Angela kept her tone very pleasant and level, yet a sudden flash of alarm appeared in Candy's eyes. It flared and disappeared immediately but it was there nonetheless.

"On the court, like it said in the papers." If she had lost her composure for a second she was in full command of it again.

"How did you first hear about the death?"

"Stu called me on my cell phone. He had an appointment to practise with Petar and he rang to say that he – Petar, that is – hadn't turned up, and he asked if he'd called me."

"Why would Petar have called you?"

"Oh, Stewart had realized that his cell phone had been switched off for a couple of hours so Petar wouldn't have got through."

"What time was this?"

Candy looked a little embarrassed. "Fairly early in the morning; I don't know if I ate something in that restaurant that disagreed with me but I woke up feeling awful. I couldn't get going so I'm a little hazy about the time. Anyway, Petar hadn't phoned. So we worked out, when we heard, that he must have been dead by then. It was a real shock."

"Yes, it must have been," agreed Angela with genuine sympathy. But the logic was not lost on her. Stewart would expect Petar to phone Candy to see if Stewart was with her.

The implication being that Petar would have expected Stewart and Candy to spend the night together – which they had, of course. She thought back over Candy's diffident use of the expression "hanging out" and reminded herself that she was a police officer and not a gossip columnist.

Candy left her office a few moments later.

Tessa Riordan quickly replaced her. She'd dealt with her first-round opponent in two businesslike sets and looked as though she hadn't even broken a sweat. Her interview, as Angela had anticipated, brought forth no further information. She studied the other woman for a moment before pushing a little harder. Tessa had chestnut brown hair, bright blue eyes and a slightly snub nose across which danced a band of freckles. Her friendly, open face smiled pleasantly at Angela, awaiting her next question.

"How well did you know Petar?"

"Well, we met here and there on the tour, of course, but not really as friends until recently."

"What's happened recently to change things?"

A delightful blush appeared on Tessa's face. "Oh... Philip and I have started a relationship."

"I see, and how did you find him?"

"We met first of all at the Australian – oh, I see, you mean how did I find Petar?"

"Yes."

"He was very nice. I liked him a lot. He loved the game, you could tell that – and not just from his conversation. I know he helped out with tennis clinics for kids from poorer backgrounds."

"That's good to hear."

"Yeah, he was a true sportsman. He hated for the game to be brought into disrepute. You're not going to find many people who disliked Petar." It was a spontaneous eulogy.

Angela nodded. "Do you know what his relationship with Stewart was like?"

Tessa bore no resemblance to Philip Turnbull, but for just a moment her response to this question put Angela in mind of him. Tessa raised a sudden finger to her brow to scratch an itch in what Angela could have sworn was a delaying tactic while she thought of how to answer. Everything about Tessa was open and honest. Dissembling didn't sit well with her.

"As far as I know they got on fine."

Angela quelled a sigh. She recognized that she couldn't take this line of questioning much further at this stage but she was sure the subject would be revisited. Right now, she thought, it would probably be a good thing to have Tessa Riordan completely off her guard.

"Thanks, Tessa. I think that's all for the moment, though I'm probably going to have to speak to you all again. Would you know if Joanna's finished her match yet?" she asked, making the enquiry as casual as she could.

Tessa had been in the act of rising and Angela sensed, from her body language more than anything else, her relief that the interview was over. She paused, relaxed about the innocuous question, which had been Angela's intention.

"She might be," she said. "She was doing well when I last caught any news of her match and that was about an hour ago."

Angela raised her eyebrows. Doing well? That exceeded expectations. Most sports commentators had so far been fairly polite about her and had tried to put the best spin on things, but the reality was that Joanna Clarke wasn't expected to get past the first round. If she had lost her match, the knives would no doubt be out tomorrow in the tabloids. As the door closed behind Tessa, Angela turned to Gary.

"I want you to do two things, Gary."

"Yes?"

"Find out if Joanna Clarke has finished her match, and if she has, ask her to come and see me. I'd also like to know the result before she gets here, OK?"

"No problem, guv."

Gary disappeared, leaving Angela staring once again into the middle distance. There was something being glossed over here, she was sure of it. Whether it had anything to do with the death, though, was another matter entirely. She frowned. She didn't like this no-man's-land between death and murder. Hopefully they would have the results of the tests tomorrow.

She rose. There was just time to get herself a cup of coffee.

Philip gazed across the large room, a popular gathering place for the players. On day two of the tournament most of those present were still contenders, keeping the atmosphere optimistic and cheery. The familiar hubbub of convivial chat, friendly banter and "shop talk" rose and fell on his ears. It suited him. The noise would provide cover for the conversation he needed to have with Tessa. He wondered where she'd got to. Then he saw her. A cup of coffee in each hand, her eyes scanned the crowded space. He raised an arm and waggled his hand around. Her face cleared as she spotted him and she moved forward.

"Smashing, thanks," he said, taking one of the steaming Styrofoam cups from her.

Tessa settled herself beside him and took a sip of coffee. "So, how did you find it?" she asked after a moment.

"A bit scary," he admitted. "I mean, she – the policewoman who interviewed me – was very pleasant and all that, but I think I must be a suspect."

Tessa put a hand on Philip's knee and squeezed gently. "Hey, don't worry. I'm sure that's standard. All of us who were in the restaurant are in the same boat. They've got to check us all out."

Philip smiled bleakly. "Yeah, but then she asked me about later."

"Later? What happened later?"

"Nothing, that's just it; after I left your place I went home and went to bed."

"So that's OK, then."

"Well, I hope so, but she asked if I had any witnesses – of me coming home, that is, and that gave me a really horrible feeling."

Tessa nestled closer to Philip and put an arm around him. "Hey, boyfriend! It's gonna be OK. From what I gather in the papers, they don't even know if it's really murder yet. In any case, they won't have any reason to suspect you."

Philip nodded and took a sip of his coffee.

A question appeared in Tessa's eyes. "They… they won't have any reason to suspect you, will they?"

"No, of course not," Philip assured her. But a second had passed before his answer and they were both aware of it. She felt a sudden chill. She was sure he wouldn't be involved in a murder but every so often she got the sense that there was something she couldn't quite place going on.

A slight commotion attracted their attention towards the door. Stewart Bickerstaff, his parents, his fitness trainer and his masseur had entered. Stewart's gaze travelled the room before he led his group slowly forward. Several heads turned in their direction before bending again to their own business.

"Team Bickerstaff has arrived," remarked Tessa.

Philip couldn't help laughing. "I see what you mean about him working a crowd. But I think he's wasting his time in this company."

"Yeah." Tessa nodded in agreement. She looked at Philip for a moment. "Let's go," she said.

"Go? Go where?"

"Any place. Let's chill, watch a movie or something."

"Good idea," said Philip, getting up. But one of the female players called out to Tessa.

"Oh, I'll just say 'hi' to Jenna, see how her injury is holding out. I'll meet you at the car."

Philip nodded and continued on his way. His passage led him towards Stewart, who had seen the seats vacated by Philip and Tessa. They drew level in the middle of the room.

"Philip."

"Stewart."

Stewart made a point of looking around and lowering his voice, an unnecessary gesture, given the buzz in the room. "Have the police spoken to you?"

"Yes."

"What did you tell them?"

Philip fought down a sense of irritation. "Tell them? There's nothing to tell. We went for a meal, we ate, we went home."

"Can you prove that?"

Philip stiffened, instantly defensive. "What gives you the right to interrogate me, Stewart?"

Stewart held up his hands, palms outward. "Hey, sorry! I didn't realize I was coming on so strong. I was only thinking, wondering, you know – if they start delving into the past."

Philip ran a tongue around suddenly dry lips. "Petar wasn't my coach. *Nothing* in my past has anything to do with him."

"No, of course not," said Stewart. He nodded at Tessa, who had just come up behind Philip. "Hi, Tessa," he said.

Philip turned to her with a brittle smile. "OK, let's go, then," he said abruptly.

"Sure," replied Tessa, in her easy way. She beamed at him and made much of putting her arm around his waist and smiling cheerily to Stewart as they went. She was aware, though, of the fragility of Philip's smile.

Chapter Seven

Joanna Clarke had amazed every tennis fan in the country as well as herself by winning her first-round match. She beamed with pleasure when Angela congratulated her.

"Oh, thank you, yes, it's such a relief to be through."

As soon as she'd finished speaking, though, a worried expression appeared at the back of her eyes and Angela wondered why. She was fresh from a win with nearly forty-eight hours till her next match. Most people would want to savour the moment. Of course, the indications were that she had just been dumped by a highly desirable boyfriend and that was enough to take the gloss off any sort of victory. Angela quickly took in the bitten nails and the pallor of an otherwise flawless complexion. Joanna wasn't very tall by modern female tennis player standards: about five feet five. She had light brown hair, hazel eyes and sat stiffly in her chair looking very much as though she wanted to be somewhere else.

"Right," continued Angela gently. "I'm afraid I've got to ask you questions about a much less pleasant subject."

"I understand," replied Joanna in a small, tight voice.

Angela launched herself into the now familiar preliminary questions. The times and details relating to Sunday's meal contained no surprises. After the younger woman had finished, Angela smiled in a friendly manner and relaxed back in her chair hoping that it would encourage Joanna to do the same, but the girl remained rigid.

"It must have been an awful shock when you heard that Petar was dead, Joanna," she began. She noted the sudden flash of sadness in Joanna's eyes.

"I'll say. I was really upset. I still can't quite believe it."

Angela nodded. "That's normal, especially with a sudden death. How well did you know Petar?"

"He was very kind to me."

"Yes?" queried Angela, hoping the question in her voice would invite further confidences.

Joanna kept her gaze fixed on the edge of the desk between them, but her voice wobbled a little as she continued: "He was just always nice to me. He was very positive about… things. He made me feel special." She started to flounder, and there was a pause. Then she seemed to get herself back on track and looked Angela in the eye, clear about what she wanted to say. "Petar tried to encourage me, to build up my confidence. I've not been playing too well lately; well, I know I've won today and I'm really pleased with that, but I've been a bit off form for quite a while now. Petar tried to help me; tried to point out things here and there that would improve my game."

"And did they?" asked Angela. She was intrigued. She had the definite impression that at first Joanna hadn't been talking about tennis.

"Oh yes," Joanna looked quite animated now. "He was fun to be around."

"So – he didn't seem to have any worries lately, anything on his mind?"

"No, I wouldn't have thought so. I think things were going well for him…" Joanna tailed off as if unsure about the appropriateness of what she had been about to say.

Blast, thought Angela and told herself very firmly to depart from the box-ticking exercise and take a risk. "I understand there was the chance of a reconciliation with his wife," she ventured.

Joanna looked relieved that the subject had been broached and visibly relaxed. "Yes. I think he was really happy with the way things were going. You could tell."

Joanna looked so manifestly glad about the new accord between Petar and his wife that Angela felt no qualms about probing further. "I gather that Lavinia Bannister wasn't too pleased about this development," she said.

A gleam appeared in Joanna's eye that might have been a distant cousin of malice, but it was gone in an instant. Her lip curled ever so slightly and then, surprisingly, she giggled. "It was a bit embarrassing really, and it was all Stewart's fault."

"Oh really? Are you referring to a particular occasion?"

"Yeah. It was when we were deciding to go for a meal on Sunday. After we'd settled on the restaurant I saw Petar walk off a little way and make a call on his mobile. I heard him say, 'Hi, Una' and then he went out of earshot. Vinni was at the club and I could see her talking to some people on the other side of the room. We were still kind of hanging around before actually leaving when Vinni came over to us and Stewart invited her to join us."

"Ah, that must have been awkward."

"It was. I pulled Stewart back and told him that I thought Petar had invited Una, but he just told me not to be silly, that Petar wouldn't do that when he was at the club with Vinni."

"Was Petar at the club with Lavinia, as such?" asked Angela. Joanna frowned as she thought about it.

"Well, to be honest I didn't really think so. Some of the publicity work she does is related to tennis and she represents a couple of players, so… I mean, she would have been there for her job anyway and I didn't see them talking to each other much. Mind you, it was quite crowded for a while. Stewart seemed convinced they were there together so I didn't argue."

Angela nodded. This was becoming interesting. "So what happened then?"

"I think Petar sent her – Una, I mean – I think he sent her a text. He was texting while we were all hanging about waiting for a table. In any case, she didn't turn up."

"Have you any idea how Lavinia felt about that?" asked Angela, thinking back over Philip Turnbull's account of a muted argument.

Joanna nodded. The amusement in her voice was unmistakable. "She was furious," she said.

"Really?" asked Angela, putting as much encouragement into her tone as she could.

"Oh yes! When we had sat down, Petar excused himself to go to the loo and he left his jacket over the back of the chair. She thought nobody had noticed but I saw her take his phone out of his side pocket and she just went through the menus as if it was her phone and she was checking something. I reckon she saw the text he sent to Una. She certainly would have seen her name in the call log. Her own handbag was on Petar's chair at that point and she made as if to put the phone into it but I saw her slip it back into his pocket."

"So she was keeping tabs on the prospect of Petar getting back with Una?"

"I'll say. She's been in denial about it for weeks, but now... well, she can't keep it up much longer."

"How has she managed to be in denial? Even *I've* heard the rumours."

Joanna grinned. "Her story is that Petar and Una have had to talk about the kids. Milan is going to be doing his GCSEs this year and they have to discuss where he's going to do A levels – at a sixth-form college or whatever. And Lucija is finishing junior school in the summer, and there's been all the business of choosing a senior school for her. But basically they are – were – getting back together again and you can tell that Petar's – was – really pleased about that."

"I gather Lavinia wasn't too happy during the meal, either," ventured Angela, reluctant to stop the flow.

"That's right; she wasn't. She's saying she was his partner

but she could never manage to persuade him to move in and lately she couldn't even get him to stay the night. Well, I don't especially like Lavinia but being dumped is no fun..."

She tailed off as a pink flush spread across her neck and face and she cast a brief, self-conscious glance at Angela. Angela nodded as if the answer and its rider were no more than she would expect. She didn't want Joanna to feel embarrassed, partly out of a sense of compassion but also because she would probably want to speak to her again and didn't want the younger woman to feel anything but comfortable in her presence. She guessed this well had far from run dry, but she already had much food for thought in what she'd heard so far, and felt it to be enough for the moment. Besides, Joanna's last remark seemed to have recalled her own situation and Angela could see that misery had descended on her. A mask of sadness settled across the young woman's features and her head and shoulders slumped.

Angela waited long enough to let her recover, thanked her for her time and let her go.

She felt acutely aware that it was getting late. Her team would be tired. It was time to get them in here, see what they had been up to and examine the information they had managed to find out.

Five minutes later, she gazed solemnly around at them all and sensed a collective hope that they would be sent home after this meeting – a desire with which she felt in total sympathy.

"OK," she said. "It's been a long day and we all want to go home so let's get on with it. Rick, Jim, what have you got?"

Jim spread his hands. "The invisible man, I think, Angie. We've spoken to the security guards who were on during the night. One or two of them saw him leaving the club with some friends for a meal, but not one of them saw him come back in again. The thing is, the gate is manned twenty-four seven so someone must be lying."

Angela cocked her head slightly and assumed a sardonic expression.

"And why would they lie?"

Jim grinned. "Oh, well now, that's a toughie." He tapped his lips and feigned puzzlement. Angela waited, humouring him. "OK, I've got it. If someone had popped out and was having a forbidden smoke or something like that, attention would be diverted, wouldn't it?"

Angela smiled, "When we get back to the incident room we need to put a large question mark in felt-tip pen by the words 'security staff' on the board. While we're on the subject of security – did all those questioned know Petar?"

"Yeah, they all seemed to know who he was, Angie," replied Rick. "He was a member here anyway and also, as a coach to Stewart Bickerstaff, he had a pass. Nobody said they didn't know him by sight." Angela nodded and made a mental note of what she had heard – "They all seemed to know who he was" and "Nobody said they didn't know him by sight". She would be willing to bet that Jim and Rick hadn't spoken to the men individually but had gathered as many as were available together and addressed them as a group. She conceded that they still didn't know if this would develop into a murder enquiry but even so she didn't want any cracks in the investigation through which possibly important witnesses could slip. She opened her notebook to start a list that she hoped wouldn't grow very long: *Follow Up/Go Over.*

"What about CCTV?" she asked.

"Sorting that out is next up on our list, Angie," replied Rick.

"OK, what about the ground staff?"

"Nobody around at that time," supplied Jim. "They put their lawns to bed for the night and went home." Angela nodded and wrote "keep an open mind" by the words "ground staff".

She brought everybody up to speed on the interviews she

herself had conducted during the day, then dismissed the team for the evening.

Patrick leaned across the bed and topped up Angela's glass. She thanked him and sank further back into the pillows piled against the headboard before taking a sip. "Mmm, that hits the spot," she said, setting the glass down on her bedside cabinet. "How's your day been?"

Patrick refilled his own glass and sat cross-legged on his side of the bed. He wanted to know all about her first day at running a case but could see she wasn't yet ready to talk about it.

"Pretty routine," he replied. "The most interesting thing happened just after I got home. I had a call from Martin."

"Oh, really?" Martin was Father Martin Buchanan from the nearby parish of the Immaculate Conception, where Angela and Patrick attended Mass. Angela found herself wondering idly where Tessa Riordan would be going to church during the tournament.

"Yeah," continued Patrick. "He wants me to take someone under my wing for a while. It's a man who's been lapsed for some years and has just come back to the church. I'm to introduce him around and, er…"

"Befriend him?"

"Yeah, that's it; just until he's found his feet. Martin says his idea of keeping a Lenten fast is to drink an inferior brand of whisky, but his heart's in the right place."

This made her laugh out loud, as he knew it would.

"That's my girl; you look a bit better now. I was worried about you."

"Really, darling?"

"Yes, you looked so pale when you first came in, and I thought you seemed strained."

"I think it must have just hit me as I walked in the door. I've been on good form all day."

"Hmm... running on adrenalin, I expect." He peered into her face, his eyebrows raised. "Do we have flight?"

Angela grinned. "Funny, that's just how Superintendent Stanway put it when he gave me the job. 'This is where you get your wings' is what he said."

"Congratulations, Inspector; how does it feel?"

"Well..." she was thoughtful for a moment. "I'm quite excited about it. I think it's going to be OK." She frowned.

"But what?"

Angela shook herself. "I've got a sneaky feeling that my biggest problem will be working with Jim and Rick. Well, no; actually, Jim."

"Ah."

"Mmm," she mused. "He's not slapdash as such and I don't think he'd actually cut corners. It's just that he's inclined to glide round them a little too smoothly. And Rick's a nice bloke but I don't think he's strong enough to contain his partner. The thing is, we have to work together and I don't want to have them becoming resentful if I point out elementary stuff about collecting information which even the most raw recruit could get their head round. Trouble is, Jim's a bit bull-headed. I had to hint to him that his attitude wasn't as helpful as it could be, and I don't think he liked it very much."

Patrick took a sip of his wine and studied Angela for a moment, his head cocked to one side.

"What?" she asked eventually.

"You get on pretty well with your colleagues, don't you, Angela?"

"Yeah, I think so," she answered, puzzled at the question.

"The thing is, you've been promoted because it's perceived that you're a competent officer. You have the intelligence and imagination necessary for the job. You haven't been promoted in order to be more popular."

Angela nodded. Before he had moved into the coroner's service, Patrick had been a policeman himself, reaching the same rank that Angela now held.

"Yeah, you're right. Thanks for that, Paddy. I'll deal with it as and when the situation demands."

"That's my girl," he said. They chinked glasses and drank in companionable silence for a few minutes.

Angela was aware, though, that Patrick showed no disposition to lean back against his own pillows. Eventually she spoke. "You've put my mind at rest, Paddy."

He looked at her. "That's good, darling. I'm glad I'm able to help."

"Perhaps I can do the same for you."

He turned a look of astonishment on her. "How did you…?"

She smiled. "We've been married a couple of years now, Pads. We'd be a bit thick if we hadn't learned to read each other at least a little in that time."

He gave a short laugh and nodded. "Yeah, you're right," he said, but the ensuing silence showed that he still felt awkward about proceeding and Angela knew she was going to have to help him out.

"Whenever you jolly me along or encourage me about something and I take on board what you've said, you usually say to me, 'That's my girl.'"

"Am I that predictable?"

"Don't worry, I like it." Angela moved over so that she could put her hands on his knees and look directly into his face. "The thing is, I'm not your only girl, am I? You have another one that takes up a lot of your attention."

"My goodness, you *have* learned to read me well."

Angela smiled. "So, what's happening with Maddie?"

When Angela had met Patrick four years earlier he'd been a widower for twelve years with a seventeen-year-old daughter.

Angela watched him take a deep breath before speaking, wondering why he was nervous about what he had to say.

"Her plans to share a flat with her two best friends from uni have fallen through."

Angela nodded.

"And she hasn't managed to get a job yet," said Patrick.

"Yeah."

He paused. "You already know?"

Angela laughed, and kissed him lightly on the mouth. "Linzi's accepted a proposal of marriage from that geeky bloke she's been dating forever and Gemma's had a very good job offer from America. Oh, and Maddie's applied to a couple of places in the City."

"Wow."

"You are dozy, you know, darling. You seem to think I don't have any communication with your daughter unless it's through you."

A relieved expression lit up his face. "So it's all right – I mean...?"

"As far as I'm concerned, this is her family home and she'll always have a place here." Patrick knelt up, grabbed Angela to him and held her close for a long time. "Mind you," she said, nuzzling into his neck, "we've got a bit of work to do. If you remember, when I moved in we just dumped a load of the stuff from my flat in her bedroom and shut the door on it."

Patrick released her and leaned back against the headboard. "That's no problem." He looked at her. "Dozy, eh? Oh, what the heck, you're probably right."

"That's my boy."

Chapter Eight

"OK, everybody, let's see what we've got," began Angela as she faced her team the following morning.

"Did you get the warrants for a search of the lockers?" asked Jim, as he strolled to a vacant chair.

"I'm in the middle of sorting that out," replied Angela. "Ah, thanks, Gary," she added, as the D.C. handed her a cup of coffee. Before Angela could take the meeting any further her mobile rang. It was Patrick. "'Scuse me, folks," she said, hurrying out to find a quiet place along the corridor where she could take the call.

"Angela," he said, his voice sounding brisk and efficient as it always did when he was at work. "There's a bit of a queue for the fax machine here which means the full report on Petar Belic from the coroner's office will be held up for a few minutes but I could just let you know the result anyway."

"You're a star, Paddy. I'll make it worth your while."

"Indeed you will, my dear," replied Patrick in what Angela called his suggestive voice. A broad smile stretched across her face as she listened to him. "OK, cutting out all the medical jargon about blood counts and sugar levels... blah, blah, blah..." he paused. "Petar Belic died from a massive injection of insulin."

Angela's stomach, which hadn't been completely relaxed since she'd got out of bed that morning, suddenly clenched itself into a tight ball and she felt cold. She'd known, of course; she'd known all along. Not in detail but in essence. She became aware that Patrick was speaking and there was a trace of concern in his voice. "Angela, darling, are you still there? Are you all right?"

"What? Yes, sorry, Pads. I'm here. I'm just – just…"

"Computing the implications?"

"Yes, I didn't realize the jump from suspicious death to murder would give me such a jolt."

"Take a deep breath, sweetheart; let it out slowly."

Angela did so. "Thanks, Paddy. I love you."

"I love you too, sweetheart. You going to be OK?"

Suddenly, inexplicably, all the tension disappeared. Angela's stomach realigned itself and she took a deep breath. "Yes, darling, I'm going to be just fine."

"Well, don't try to carry the burden alone. That's what your team and your superior officers are for. It's what I'm for as well."

"Bless you, Paddy. I'll remember. Is the inquest tomorrow?"

"Coroner's court, nine o'clock in the morning; it's already being set up."

Angela relaxed. The whole scenario became normal. She was investigating a murder. It was her job; it was what she did.

A few moments later, feeling completely in command of the situation, she strode back into the room. There was something about the way she planted herself in front of them in complete silence that made them all stop what they were doing and look at her. When she was sure she had everyone's attention she spoke.

"I've just received news from the coroner's office about the results of the tests on Petar Belic. He was killed by a massive injection of insulin and as of this moment this enquiry has been upgraded to a murder investigation."

There was a collective intake of breath and she could almost feel them all cranking their attitudes up a gear. She waited in the silence as they all digested the information.

Rick was the first to speak. "Insulin? That's a bit unusual, isn't it?"

"Yes, but not unknown," replied Angela.

"Was he a diabetic – an insulin-dependent diabetic, I mean?" asked Leanne.

"That's a point," added Jim. "Was he, Angie?"

"It's a good question," said Angela, noting with amusement that the team seemed to think she was an authority on Petar Belic. "I haven't ever heard that he was but then I wouldn't know. The coroner's office will be contacting the GP for his medical details, so we'll know soon enough. I suppose you're thinking that if he was, the perpetrator could have used his own supply to kill him."

"Just a thought, guv," Jim answered.

"Yes. Or the perpetrator might be diabetic." If true either way, that would narrow the field down considerably.

"Maybe the perp's a bit of a jerk," said Jim.

"I sincerely hope so," replied Angela. "That would make our job much easier. Now, insulin's a prescription drug, which means we shall have to consider access. Yes?" This last question was addressed to Derek, who had raised a tentative hand at the back of the room.

"You can get most things on the Internet these days, guv."

Angela smiled broadly at him. "You can indeed, Derek. And if that looks a likely route for us to follow, guess who'll get the job of trawling through the drug companies?" Derek grinned ruefully while Jim and Rick broke into muted laughs.

"That'll teach you to open your gob, Del-boy," said Jim. Derek blushed and appeared slightly discomfited. Angela regretted having spoken. It was no part of her plan that helpful, keen constables should be the butt of jokes on any team led by her and she stepped in to nip it in the bud.

"I know that sort of job can be really boring, Derek," she said in a matter-of-fact voice, "but it's often very necessary and there's many a case that's been blown wide open by something found through routine slog. We don't know how things will go in this investigation yet, but drugs companies have got to be on our radar. From the point of view of our perpetrator, there's one major drawback to buying prescription drugs on the Internet, though. Would you like to remind us what that is, Jim?"

Jim picked up her cue and the opportunity to move on from the awkward moment, and spoke in the same matter-of-fact tone. "You have to pay with plastic money."

"Exactly, and as we all know, plastic money is traceable. However, it wouldn't be wise to abandon the idea altogether. Leanne, will you make sure that we get another heading for this on our board?"

"Will do, guv," said Leanne.

"OK, folks, I know we've already been following all the proper procedures and lines of enquiry but this is where we 'raise our game', as they say on the tennis circuit. This is where we get our gloves off."

"They don't say *that*," quipped Jim. A gentle wave of laughter ran around the room and Angela grinned dutifully.

"Well, you've got an inspector here who likes to mix her metaphors," she said. "You'll get used to it. OK, I know we've been a bit gentle with people but we mean business now. We've got to go over all the ground, and I mean *all* the ground." She positioned herself so that she could see Jim and Rick out of the corner of her eye. "Everyone we interview now has to be spoken to individually – in person and alone." She caught them exchanging the merest of glances. "You don't need me to tell you that the trail in a murder enquiry goes cold very quickly and this one is now two days old so we're already behind. Right, let's get to work. Rick, Jim – we need to nail down the business of security. Petar left the club in the early evening on Sunday and came back – or was brought back – later that same evening or in the wee small hours of Monday. Did he drive? Was he on foot? If he drove, where is his car?"

"It might still be outside his own front door," said Derek.

"Exactly," replied Angela. "Or it might not; you and Leanne get on to that." She turned and looked at Rick and Jim. "Somebody must have seen something. Going through the CCTV footage has just become imperative."

"We'll sort it, Angela," said Rick. Both men were leaning forward in their chairs and looking very alert. *You two chaps have had a narrow escape*, she thought to herself. *I shall be keeping a very close watch on your reports and if you blow this, believe me, you'll find yourself in deep doo-doo.*

"OK," she said. "I've got to finalize the search warrants so I'll see you all at the club in, say, an hour and a half."

The warrants came together quickly and Angela found herself at the club with half an hour to kill. She bought a Subway roll and a coffee and found a patch on the sun-drenched grass. She let herself slip out of her professional persona and become a tennis fan again.

For as long as she could remember, the sharp crack of racquet hitting ball had been the metronome of her summer, the natural percussion of late June and early July. She expanded her field of consciousness to encompass the restless sea of people endlessly coming and going, fluctuating, interweaving, the cries and applause and incisive thwacks emanating from the outer courts. "*Let!*" She smiled and watched the tide of passers-by.

Even ten minutes later, as she brushed the crumbs from her lap and tossed her empty cup in the rubbish she could still spare a moment to linger; so she allowed the drift of the crowd to carry her along to the practice courts, where the first person she spotted was Joanna Clarke, training hard with her coach.

She saw Angela as she was running, rather fast, for a ball and was heading straight for the net post. Angela gasped but just at that moment Joanna managed to pull herself up with a shriek and avoided a collision with the post. She stood still, panting and looking a little shaken as her coach came rushing over to her, asking if she was all right.

"Yes, thanks. I'm fine," she assured her, then broke away and came trotting over to where Angela stood on the other side of the fence. "Hello, Inspector. Did you want to speak to me?"

"No. I'm sorry if I startled you, Joanna. Are you OK? You nearly gave yourself a terrific whack just then."

"Yes, it could have been nasty."

"You're not kidding. I'm just taking the air before starting work again. When I'm not wearing my policewoman's hat I'm a mad keen tennis fan."

"I see." Joanna smiled, slightly embarrassed. "Have you found out anything about Petar yet?"

"Well, the investigation is going ahead. I'm afraid I can't say more than that at the moment."

"No, of course. Well, I suppose I'd better get back to work." Angela nodded and watched as Joanna turned round and walked back up the court. She couldn't imagine what it must be like, playing tennis and doing her job being the same thing.

Joanna was now conferring with her coach. Angela glanced at her watch and turned away. Time to head across to the police room.

As she went, the germ of an idea sprang to life in her mind. She thought about it as she continued walking. She decided to sleep on it and see if it survived the night.

A short time later, the searches of the lockers got underway. Angela had no hope they would find anything germane to the case and she was soon proved correct. As the lists of contents came in it became clear that there was no point in pinning any hopes of a clue, much less a breakthrough, on the predictable mishmash of sweet-paper wrappings, half-eaten sandwiches and dried up sausage rolls, mingled with bottles of water or juice, cans of drink, books, newspapers, betting slips and lottery tickets.

A few less generic effects revealed interesting glimpses of individuality behind the players' famous personas. Stewart Bickerstaff and Philip Turnbull both liked to amuse themselves between matches and training with Wiis but a half-completed cryptic crossword also lay exposed on a badly folded copy of *The Times* among Philip's things.

They found an iPod in Tessa Riordan's locker and a copy of *The Imitation of Christ*, whereas Joanna's locker revealed a penchant for pulp fiction. A length of delicate, soft white wool was doing duty as a bookmark and some needles and a ball of the same wool indicated that reading wasn't Joanna's only pastime. The neatly worked needlepoint nestling under Candy's iPod and BlackBerry displayed a surprisingly traditional outlook. The haul of personal property hardly varied from one locker to the next apart from these occasional items.

Angela would have wondered if it had really been worth the effort but for a conversation she had with the attendant on duty as she and Leanne searched through the ladies' belongings.

The woman looked to be in her early forties, roughly the same age as Angela. She had introduced herself as Megan and something about the way she hovered as they opened each door showed an eagerness to peek inside the lockers herself.

"Isn't it awful?" she said, her voice breathy. "I could hardly believe it when I first heard the news."

"Yes, it's very sad," agreed Angela.

"Of course, I know that you police deal with this sort of thing all the time so you're used to it, but I mean – Petar Belic! Who'd have thought it?"

Encouraged that Angela seemed to be at least half-listening, Megan warmed to her subject, confiding, "He had a lovely game in his day, I know, and he was a great champion, of course, but personally I always liked to watch Danny Moore playing. He's the one I had a soft spot for – well… soft spot?" She laughed. "Mad keen on him, I was."

Angela cast a brief appraising glance at Megan, wondering if she had ever come to Wimbledon sporting a T-shirt with a huge letter on the front. "Oh, really?" she said.

"Yes, it's funny," Megan continued with apparent irrelevance, "but I was wondering if Petar was going to come into the restaurant where I was on Sunday. My husband took me out for my birthday and, well, you could have knocked me down with a feather when who should come into the same restaurant for a meal but Danny Moore. I mean, all those years of following him and being a fan and never really getting close, and there he was with his wife. I've seen her picture in the papers. I recognized her at once. My husband said it was a nice little extra birthday present to see Danny there – my hero when I was a girl! Obviously I couldn't help hoping that Petar would be joining them too so I'd see them both. But he didn't and now I can't help wondering if it, you know, was happening while we were sitting there. Every time I think about it I go all funny."

The voluble Megan finally ground to a halt as if suddenly aware of the silence that had fallen upon the two policewomen.

"Where was this, Megan?"

A worried look appeared on Megan's face. "It was in the Village. That new Italian place, Cam something. *Da Camisa*, that's it. They do beautiful pasta. I couldn't see what Danny was eating. He wouldn't… oh dear! Oh, I know you have to ask about everything, but Danny and Petar… Weren't they in business together as well? I mean, they were good friends."

In business together? Alarm bells rang in Angela's mind as she now recalled having read something about the two men being joint owners of a sports promotion agency. Megan looked frightened now. Knowing, vaguely, the people involved in a murder was one thing; being a material witness was quite another and she clearly didn't like it. Angela smiled as kindly as she could, and spoke gently. "Don't worry, Megan. Danny's probably completely innocent, but I do have to get as complete a picture as I can of where everybody was in the hours leading up to Petar's death – the people close to him, I mean." Megan's mouth trembled and Angela injected a brighter tone into her voice. "I'm even going to have a chat with Una Belic later today," she said, trying to make it sound as though she was going for afternoon tea anyway and would be throwing in a couple of questions about the murder while she was there.

"Yes," replied Megan in a small voice.

"Er…" Angela was very conscious of the impediment to her investigation she would cause if she pushed too hard and actually made Megan cry. She kept her tone friendly, conversational. "What time did you leave the restaurant?"

Megan took a deep breath and made an effort to calm herself down. "We – we were there until about twelve. Well, it was also our anniversary."

"Your wedding anniversary? Oh, congratulations! How special to see Danny on that day. And he was still there when you left – or had he already gone?"

The merest nod of the head. "Yes, he was still there." Megan was extremely distressed.

Angela smiled kindly to reassure her. "Tell you what, Megan. I'll leave Leanne here with you. The pair of you can have a nice cup of tea together while she goes through things with you, OK?" This suggestion seemed to relax Megan somewhat and Angela took her leave, phoning Gary as she went and asking him to meet her at the car park.

It took a couple of calls but ten minutes later she had discovered the name of the agency, learned that Danny Moore was expected back from a meeting within the hour and that he would be able to see her as soon as he arrived.

When he joined her, Gary climbed into the car still chomping on the last of a barbecued chicken baguette. "Have I spoiled your lunch?" she asked.

He grinned. "Sorry, guv."

"Not at all," she said. "A growing detective constable needs his food. I think there are some toffees in the glove compartment if you're looking for dessert. Come to think of it, give me one, please."

He did so and they were happily munching on toffees as she pointed her car in the general direction of South Kensington, where Bel-Mor Sports was located. She hoped they wouldn't get snarled up in the midday traffic as they crossed the river.

Chapter Nine

The reception area of the agency jointly owned by Danny Moore and Petar Belic exuded success. From its luxurious carpet to the designer wallpaper, the whole place spoke of taste, discretion and money.

Angela and Gary approached the manicured, coiffed and flawlessly made-up receptionist poised behind a desk Angela could see at a glance had not come from Ikea.

"May I help you?" asked the receptionist. Angela judged her to be in her early twenties. She made no attempt to smile, but stood up to greet them. To her neat, dark jacket and demurely buttoned white blouse this added a view of a remarkably short skirt and the legs of a model. Her demeanour might be lacking warmth, considered Angela, but apparently she had been selected at least in part for delectation.

"Detective Inspector Angela Costello and Detective Constable Gary Houseman," said Angela briskly, as they flicked open their IDs. "I believe Mr Moore is expecting us."

The woman glanced down at a large leather-bound diary which lay open on the desk and nodded. "I am afraid Mr Moore's meeting has overrun," she enunciated. "He's sent his apologies. He expects to be here very soon. Would you like a drink?" Professor Higgins would have been proud of her, Angela smiled to herself. She spoke as one reciting a lesson diligently learned.

Angela and Gary expressed a preference for coffee and the girl inclined her head, disappearing through a door behind her desk. Angela and Gary crossed the expanse of virgin wool to a pair of leather sofas beside a heavy coffee table supplied with geometrically arranged stacks of magazines, including *Country Life, The Tatler, The Economist, National Geographic,* a discerning selection of neatly arrayed daily newspapers and, of course, some sporting magazines.

In due course the coffee emerged, freshly ground and steaming in snow white porcelain cups. They sipped, savouring the rich aroma, as they settled back into the expensive upholstery, and took in their surroundings.

Every so often a door at the side of the room opened and one of the staff made the journey across reception to disappear through another door on the further side. Each time either one of the doors opened there rose and died again the hum of a busy office. Fax machines pinged, telephones rang, keyboards clattered softly and lively conversation was punctuated here and there by laughter. Angela had the sense of sitting between the worlds – a carefully fabricated showcase of elegant perfection fronting an otherwise regular office.

"This seems a nice place," said Angela, addressing the receptionist, her curiosity piqued by the dichotomy between the woman's elegant appearance and the lack of polish in her manner. "Do you like working here?"

The young woman looked up from her computer, fingers arrested mid-sentence. She seemed surprised to be addressed. "It's OK," she replied after a moment, forgetting to assume her practised diction and sounding altogether more ordinary.

Silence.

Angela cocked her head at Gary. "Nice boss, is he, Danny Moore?"

She pursed her lips and a shadow crossed her face. Angela and Gary glanced briefly at each other and Angela gave an almost infinitesimal nod at Gary.

Once again he was quick to act on his cue. "You understand why we're here, don't you?" he asked.

"Something to do with Mr Belic, I suppose," she said. "Him dying, I mean."

Gary kept probing. "Big shock for you all, I expect," he said.

"Yes," came the reply, followed by more silence. Angela wondered briefly about how the human resources department was managed at Bel-Mor. If she owned a prestigious agency this unresponsive young woman was definitely not the type of person she would want meeting and greeting her clients, in spite of the impeccable grooming.

"Did you know Petar Belic very well?" pursued Gary.

"A bit. He didn't come into the office too often. Danny's the one who really works here." As she pronounced his name the same shadow as before flitted across her face. The two detectives were on full alert.

"Did they get on all right?" asked Angela.

"I think so."

Beside her, Angela heard Gary's small sigh of frustration. She kept her voice determinedly cheerful. "What's your name?"

"Tara."

"Tara, if anything occurs to you that you think might be relevant to our enquiries – you know – Petar Belic might have come in one day in a bad mood or something like that and you might have heard a comment which puzzled you…" She paused, rejecting the notion of asking specifically what relations were like between the two men. "You never know what might be important in an investigation of this sort." She took a card out of her bag. "Will you contact me on this number?"

Tara took Angela's card and studied it for a moment, a calculating expression on her face, but all she said was, "OK." She looked more alert than she had since they'd arrived.

Angela had no idea what Danny Moore looked like these days and doubted if she would recognize him. But she found that she knew him the minute he walked in. He had hardly changed at all; a little fuller in the face, maybe, but not in the figure. Like Petar, Danny had taken care of himself. Dressed for the street in a white raincoat over a pearl grey suit, he came towards her, holding out his hand.

"Ah, you must be the police. I'm so sorry to keep you waiting." His handshake was firm and Angela waved away his apology, saying they had been very well looked after. Danny's gaze took in the now empty coffee cups on the low table and nodded.

"That's good." He smiled. "Would you like to come through to my office?" He lifted his arm to usher them courteously through to his office. "Hi, Tara," Danny greeted her as he passed. He looked at Angela and Gary. "Would you care for another coffee? I'm going to have one."

Angela and Gary nodded. Danny seated them in front of a curved executive desk in pale beech before divesting himself of his raincoat and hanging it up. When he turned round Angela was surprised to see a black armband high up on the left arm of his suit jacket. He saw her looking at it.

"He was my best friend. I hope you're closing in on the bastard who did it."

"So do I, Mr Moore." There was a small hiatus. Angela's gaze wandered across to a glass cabinet full of tennis trophies in an alcove. "That's a very impressive display."

Danny allowed himself to be deflected. "I was in the top ten for a few years, and even the top five for a while. I suppose I shouldn't be such a show-off, but I'm rather proud of my former career."

"So you should be," replied Angela.

He looked at her with a flash of gratification in his eyes. "Not as many trophies to display as Petar had, though," he said. "He was the tops."

"He certainly raised the bar," agreed Angela. She considered Danny for a moment in silence, a scrutiny he was clearly aware of and bore with a good-natured half-smile on his face. Just at that moment the coffees were brought in and Angela was relieved to see a plate of biscuits on the tray. A rumbling stomach didn't add to the air of authority a D.I. was supposed to exude.

Tara bent over Danny's desk to place his cup down. Although her blouse had been fastened up nearly to her neck in the reception area, Angela saw that two buttons had been undone. She couldn't be sure but she had the impression that Tara's skirt had been hitched up even higher. She cast a quick, amused glance at Gary and saw his eyes travelling between blouse and skirt as though he couldn't decide which region to settle on.

Danny, however, kept his eyes fixed firmly on the coffee. "Thanks, Tara, that's lovely," he said. His smile remained pleasant and his tone amiable but at no time did his eyes glance sideways. Angela was pleased to see that Gary was able to take his eyes off Tara long enough to note this and she was very aware that she, Danny and Gary were making a point of not looking at each other.

"Were you never jealous of his success?" she asked once the door had closed behind Tara. "I seem to remember that he beat you in a few finals."

Danny raised his eyebrows. "A few? And the rest!" He grinned. "Yes, I was the green-eyed monster personified. I hated him. Not only did he win a lot but he was so *nice* with it. He never threw a tantrum – you remember those days when some tennis players were known for arguing about any call against them? 'What? No way. That's not fair. That's outrageous!' *Slam* – and the racquet hits the ground." Angela nodded, laughing.

"Yes, he was charm itself, old Pete; I don't know how he did it. The mums drooled over him as well as their daughters."

An ex-drooler herself, Angela smiled at the thought. "So how come…?"

"We were friends? That's easy. We announced our retirement within months of each other and then found ourselves on the seniors' tour where we joined up as a doubles partnership, and I decided that I was too old for kids' stuff like jealousy. As a matter of fact, we were due to play in a tournament next month."

Danny's voice broke on the last word. He took hold of his coffee and made a business of blowing on it while giving himself time to recover. Eventually he replaced the cup in its saucer and leaned back in his extremely comfortable-looking swivel chair.

"So," he said, managing a twinkle. "Let the grilling commence."

Angela laughed again. "Not a grilling – at least I hope not. It's just that your name has come up a few times in connection with Petar and I was told you were close, which you've just confirmed. And of course, you're in business together, so I'm trying to get a more complete picture of him. There may have been something bothering him, for instance, which has a bearing on the death."

Danny swivelled a little to left and right as he considered her words. Finally he steadied the chair in the centre and looked at her.

"Well, it depends what you mean by that. There was lots of stuff on his mind." Danny looked steadily at Angela. She sensed that here was a man who liked to get to a subject in his own way. Since this was a fishing expedition and not – yet – the interview of a suspect, she decided to relax and let him get on with it. She raised her eyebrows in a query. Danny put his elbows on the desk, clasped his hands and leaned his chin on his two thumbs.

"There were family matters. His son, Milan, will be going into the sixth form in September; Pete and Una weren't sure for a while whether they'd made the right choice of college. And then there's a decision to be made about a senior school for little Lucija. She's nervous about moving up."

"Oh yes, I heard about all this from Lavinia Bannister."

"Yes, you would have done; bone of contention, believe me. I shall come to her in a minute." Angela began to see why he was the company director of Bel-Mor Sports. Proud though he might be of his former career, she had the sense that he had nothing to be embarrassed about in his current role.

"And there was the business." Danny allowed himself another little swivel, his gaze seeming to take in the whole agency. "This place is doing OK, thanks to Petar."

"Yes, I gather that this agency is a joint venture. How much stake did Petar have?"

"We were partners, fifty-fifty, straight down the line."

"Was he very active in the business?"

"Hmm… ish. He put up half the money when we started and he kept abreast of what state the business was in and who our clients were. He wasn't a sleeping partner by a long way, not even only half-awake; it's just that all the day-to-day running of it was left to me, which is how I wanted things, really. The agency had been my idea in the first place; I just didn't have enough of the readies to get started."

"Did he ever show any signs of wanting more involvement?"

Danny shook his head. "No, he was happy with the way things were. He was glad of the income, of course, but he'd always wanted to maintain an active role in tennis."

"Which was why he continued to coach?"

"Yeah, he enjoyed it. He had a real commitment to nurturing promising talent. It gave him a buzz."

"That sounds like Petar, from what I know of him," remarked Angela. Danny smiled and nodded.

"Yep, that was Pete all right."

"If we think it's relevant to take a look at the books…?"

There was the merest of pauses before Danny spread out his hands, palms upwards. "Not a problem; just say the word." His eyes flicked from Angela to Gary and back again.

Just so that he wouldn't be in any doubt that she'd registered the pause, she allowed another one to pass while she made a note before continuing. "Right; what else was on his mind?"

Danny looked at her and sat up straighter in the manner of one getting back to business. "Ah yes, then there was the nice stuff. He was getting back together with Una and that was very good news. Not many people get a second chance like that, and Helmut and I were on at him not to blow it."

"Would this be Helmut Wolf?" asked Angela.

"The very same; another one who should have hated Petar but didn't. Not that Petar needed telling, really – not to blow it, that is. He was really happy about Una, and the kids were thrilled. Petar was always devoted to the kids and I could never figure out why they split up in the first place, but there you go. Who knows what really happens in someone else's marriage?"

"That's true," agreed Angela.

"Of course, getting shot of his 'partner'," he sketched quotation marks in the air, "was proving to be a lot more difficult than he'd anticipated."

"Ah," said Angela. "Tell me about that."

Chapter Ten

Danny fixed Angela with an ironic grin. "Don't tell me you haven't come across her yet, Inspector," he said. "She's no shrinking violet, our Vinni, and I've no doubt she's been very keen to get in quick with an accusation against Una."

Angela had a little difficulty keeping her face straight. "We have spoken to Lavinia," she answered. "She was absolutely insistent that she and Petar were a full-on couple, but the evidence I've received so far would suggest otherwise."

Danny gave a grin that was somehow mischievous. "Go with the evidence."

"Ah."

"Yep, I was surprised when Pete took up with her in the first place. And to be honest I didn't think it would last as long as it did, but there you go. Pete had told her it was over but she's not a lady who easily takes no for an answer and, of course, what with the French Open, then Queens all happening so close to Wimbledon, and Vinni representing Candy Trueman and a couple of the other players, their paths were still crossing a lot in the past few weeks. And she can turn on the tears and the poor-little-me act when it suits her. From what Pete told me she was running a 'we need to talk about this' scenario – and that can carry on for quite a while with someone like Vinni. I saw her with him at Queens the week before last and she was all over him like a rash. It would have taken a while for him to get himself fully out from her grasp."

"So how did Petar take to that – her being all over him, even though he'd finished the relationship?"

"Well, he didn't encourage her, if that's what you're wondering. I think it annoyed him but he knew it would tail off in the end. He didn't like to be nasty to anyone, so he just tried to avoid her as best he could. It was all made a bit more difficult because Vinni had another card to play. She didn't just associate with him for personal reasons. It was business as well, because she was angling to get Stewart's account for her agency."

Angela's eyebrows went up towards her hairline. "Oh, really? Now that's interesting."

Danny nodded. His eyes had taken on a masked quality.

"Who's handling Stewart at the moment?"

"Ah, that's just it; nobody right now. He's been looked after ever since he won the juniors a few years ago by an agent that his club found for him. But now that he's in the big league, so to speak, his parents have terminated that contract and let it be known that they're open to offers. I don't know why Vinni didn't just go through the family."

"Go through?"

"The family; Lavinia's parents have been friends with Stewart's mum and dad for years."

"Ah yes, Stewart told me that."

"On the other hand, the family connection may not work to her advantage. They're all aware of her history in the fashion industry and might think that she hasn't been doing sports representation long enough to have the sort of credibility they're looking for. Who knows? In any case, she didn't pass up any opportunity to hang around Petar, and this offered a good one." Danny reflected. "To be fair, in her heart of hearts Vinni was probably fully conscious that she and Petar were history, but she's also a businesswoman. If her association with him would have helped her agency to win the Bickerstaff account, she'd have stuck to him like glue until the ink was dry on the paperwork."

"Wouldn't Bel-Mor like a slice of the Bickerstaff cake?"

Danny shook his head, still smiling. "It's not a cake that will keep."

Angela's eyebrows shot up again. "He's the British number one."

"I think he's peaked."

"Surely not?"

Danny's expression didn't change. "I believe his best tennis is behind him. Unless somebody could do a transplant and give him a brain that would make him listen to what his coach is telling him."

"But he's on the brink of breaking into the top one hundred."

"Mmm. He'll probably make it, too, but I'd be surprised if he got much beyond that. He might get through another couple of rounds this week. He shouldn't have too difficult a time according to the draw, and if he gets through he meets Philip Turnbull in the quarters – if Philip gets through, that is."

It occurred to Angela that maybe Danny's animosity towards Stewart sprang from the fact that Bel-Mor had already attempted to win the Bickerstaff contract and failed. This was something she felt sure she wouldn't find out from Danny – not at this meeting anyway – so she clutched at the mention of Philip Turnbull as a welcome change of subject. "I hope he gets through," she said. "I like watching Philip and he seems to have come on a lot in the last year."

Danny nodded his head slowly, thinking his answer through as he spoke. "Philip Turnbull… you're right. Now that's a young man whose game has become very exciting. And I'll tell you something else," he continued, leaning on the desk between them. "You might have a fantastic serve but you can't necessarily rely on it when Philip's on the other side of the net. He's the one Bel-Mor would go for." He paused and beamed at Angela. "Of course, he needs to find a cure first." Angela inclined her head and looked questioningly at him. "He's got the British disease, Inspector. No self-confidence, doesn't play to win, pulls defeat out of victory every time. I don't know – it hasn't ever been properly diagnosed.

He's doing OK so far in this tournament but he's got to sustain his current standard and then build on it. Mind you, if he can get whatever's going on in his head sorted, I think he can do it."

Angela nodded. She was fully aware of the state of British tennis but she preferred to remain optimistic. "Surely things have got better over the past few years?" she countered.

"Yes. Things have improved, and they'll go on improving, but we've got a long way to go..." He tailed off and furrowed his brow as he thought. "It really is a puzzle," he said, more to himself than Angela.

"What is?"

Danny looked up at her. "I can't figure out why Philip can't seem to get past Stewart, but he doesn't seem able to do it. He should do, he has the game for it. Beats me."

"Well, obviously Petar didn't suffer from the British problem," continued Angela, suddenly aware that she needed to get back on track. "Do you know if he had any enemies?"

Danny shook his head in a manner which left no room for doubt. "Absolutely not. I would have said that he was the last person on earth to have any enemies."

"And he didn't seem worried about anything lately?"

There was another vehement headshake.

"How did he get on with Stewart's parents?" Angela asked, suddenly remembering Stewart speaking of their involvement in the choice of Petar as his coach, and wondering if their names should have been up on the board in the incident room.

Danny gave a short bark of laughter. "They're another reason I wouldn't go for the Bickerstaff account. I'd be dealing with them!"

"Really? Are they very proactive in his career – on the business side of it, I mean?"

"They've always held the purse strings. Even though he's a big boy now, earning his own money, they haven't let go. It doesn't seem to bother Stewart from what I can gather. Mum and Dad do all the business while he swans around the circuit looking athletic. I expect that's how he likes it."

"How did Petar get on with Stewart?"

Danny's face suddenly took on a very guarded look and then his expression lightened. "Ah yes. Of course you'd want the inside dirt. Hmm, yes, well, he was getting a bit fed up with the Boy Wonder."

Angela cocked her head to one side. "You don't like him much, do you?"

Danny grinned and feigned a surprised look. "Oh, does it show?" He sat up straighter. "To be fair, I suppose it's not his fault. If your parents bring you up to think the sun shines out of your shorts you end up believing it. They're used to calling the shots, Stewart's parents, and they were in for a big shock because Petar's time as Stewart's coach was about to come to an end, and it wasn't going to be because Ma and Pa Bickerstaff had sacked him."

"Petar was planning to terminate the arrangement?"

"Indeed he was. He felt he'd taken Stewart as far as he could go which, I have to admit, is further than I would have expected. As you pointed out, he's likely to break into the top one hundred before he's very much older, and he's the British number one. But it was an uphill task and Petar didn't need the hassle."

"Hassle?" invited Angela.

"He's not a listening animal, our Stewart. Thinks he already knows it all. And, at the end of the day, he believes he can always serve his way out of any trouble he might get into in a game."

"So far he has," Angela pointed out.

Danny looked at her with a grim expression. "Yes, frustrating isn't it?" he said. "But as he moves up the rankings, he's going to find that he's got to develop in other areas or he'll slip back again. I know I'm a bit prejudiced. I had to develop a good all-round game because I didn't have any big weapons." He flashed

GAME, SET AND MURDER

her a sudden disarming smile. "I didn't do too badly on it."

"Indeed you didn't," she agreed, smiling back. "So when was the last time you saw Petar?"

Danny didn't even pause to think about the answer to this question. "Sunday afternoon," he said.

"Oh, at the club."

"Yes. Late afternoon. Pete and I were thinking of going for a meal together. He was going to call Una to invite her, and I was going to go and collect my wife, Heather. We planned to meet at the restaurant. We thought it would be nice to have a foursome and it would have been the first time, since the split, that Una would be... er..."

"Reintegrated into your circle?" suggested Angela.

"That's it," said Danny. "I just popped into the loo and when I came out again it had become a party – with Stewart, Candy, Joanna *et al*. I'm sure you've got a list of who was there."

"Oh yes," replied Angela. "But I haven't yet managed to get a clear picture of the time before the meal."

Danny's expression was sardonic. "I don't think there is a clear picture," he said. "When I came out of the toilet, Stewart, Philip and Candy were standing around with Petar, and Stewart was saying, 'So what time is the table booked for?' Pete gave me this apologetic look."

"What happened then?"

"Er, I think Joanna was mentioned about then... yes. Stewart said, 'Shall we go, then?' and Philip said we should wait for Joanna, at which point Stewart said, 'Oh. Of course.' I saw him flash this sort of embarrassed look at Candy and she said, 'Don't worry, it's OK. We can handle this, we're grown-ups.'" Danny paused for explanation. "I don't know if you're aware that Joanna and Stewart have been together for a couple of years but recently things have changed and he's been seen around with Candy. There's been no official announcement, though."

"Yeah, I'd picked up on the inter-relationships," said Angela. Danny nodded. "Nice kid, Joanna, and an impressive little game of tennis when she's on form. She's another one who needs a shot of confidence, but she's got through the first round and that's more than anybody expected. I just hope she can keep it up. So, where was I? Yeah, while they were having that little glitch about both Candy and Joanna being invited I got on Pete's other side and he said, 'I'm sorry, Danny. I'm not quite sure how this happened. Stewart just assumed it was a general gathering of whoever was around to go out for a meal. Unfortunately I'd already said I was going before it turned into a party and it'll look very odd if I back out now; Vinni's even coming, so I'll telephone Una and explain.' I told him not to worry about it and that we'd arrange something for later in the week. And that…" a tremble appeared in his voice, "was the last time I saw him alive."

Angela waited while Danny composed himself. "What did you do for the rest of the evening?" she asked after a few moments.

"I waited for Heather to join me and we went to the restaurant I'd been planning on going to anyway." There was a pause. "Oh, God… you want the details. It was near the club – that puts me in the area on Sunday evening; oh, God." The colour had drained from Danny's face.

"I have to ask."

Danny took a deep breath. "I know you do. It was an Italian place: Camisa's; *Da Camisa* is the official name, I think. We were there until about midnight," he added, anticipating her next question. "And no, I didn't nip into the club and kill him before I went home." Danny's voice choked on these words and tears filled his eyes.

"I'm sorry to cause you distress," began Angela, but Danny waved away her words.

"It's all right," he said thickly. "You just find the bastard who did it and leave me alone with him – or her."

A few moments later, Angela and Gary were walking out past the now buttoned-up Tara sitting primly in reception.

"And I wonder what all that was about," said Gary as the front door closed behind them. "The boobs and the legs."

"Indeed," said Angela. "She put on quite a little show for him, didn't she? And he didn't even look up."

"No bloke's got a right to that much self-control."

Angela laughed and handed the car keys over to him. "You drive. That'll help you keep your eyes fixed in front."

Una Belic lived with her three children in a beautiful, tree-lined avenue just over the county border in the affluent Surrey suburbs. Gary drew the car to a halt on the gravelled area in front of a double garage and they took a narrow path across an immaculately manicured lawn to the porticoed front door.

A slim young girl, a feminine version of Petar, opened the door when they rang the bell. She had hair darker than her father's but the cheekbones marked her out. Angela judged her to be about fourteen, and realized she knew the names of only two of Petar's children, information culled from her interviews with Joanna Clarke and Lavinia Bannister. This girl looked a little too old to be on the point of finishing junior school.

"Miss Belic?" asked Angela.

"Yes. May I ask your name?" she responded in a well-modulated voice.

"I'm Detective Inspector Angela Costello and this is Detective Constable Gary Houseman. I believe your mother is expecting us."

The girl nodded. Her expression was solemn and Angela was just about to get out her ID when she spoke again.

"Excuse me one moment, I'll just check with Mummy," she said, and the door was gently closed. Within a few moments it opened again and she asked to see their ID. She obviously found this satisfactory because she asked them to come in. They followed her into a room towards the back of the house.

Angela took in the view approvingly. They were in a very much lived-in space. Books were packed onto shelves set into alcoves, DVDs spewed around and underneath a large television, and a good selection of board games and jigsaw puzzles could be seen piled in one corner. A comfortable looking settee and a few armchairs provided rest and French windows overlooked a large, lush garden.

"Mummy says will you please excuse her for a few minutes; she has to finish a telephone call."

"She's been well trained," remarked Gary as the girl disappeared from the room and closed the door behind her.

"She has," agreed Angela, tearing her gaze away from the very enviable flowerbeds and turning back into the room, taking in her surroundings.

"Nice gaff, guv," remarked Gary.

Angela nodded. "Yes, it looks very comfortable."

There was a small pause. "Are you going to mention what Lavinia Bannister said?"

"I don't think so. Not at the moment. We're still gathering information. You can see where Lavinia was coming from anyway, and you could drive a bus through the hole in her argument. I feel a bit sorry for her because she's trying desperately to hang on to her illusion about her relationship with Petar, but the more you examine it in reality, it seems that she was just his —"

"*Whore!*"

Angela and Gary jumped and turned to the source of this new voice.

Milan Belic was standing in the doorway with a face like thunder.

Chapter Eleven

You had to be sixteen or thereabouts to be as angry as Milan looked. *And of course*, thought Angela, *he has a focus for his anger*. Tall and ungainly, as he came into the room towards them he seemed angular and awkward in his movements. His polo shirt and jeans looked brand new. Angela would have been willing to lay odds that he'd only recently gone through a growth spurt, leaving a whole wardrobe behind, and wasn't really used to his new length yet. He had dark, wavy hair and his scowl couldn't quite remove the twinkle from his eyes. He was going to be a stunner.

He stopped in front of Angela and Gary. She could see the hesitation and uncertainty behind his outward defiance. Well, that was par for the course; if you were going to be certain of nothing and angry about everything, sixteen was the age to do it.

"Are you Milan?" asked Angela.

"Yes, Inspector; I'm Milan Belic, Petar's son. So I know what I'm talking about; that's all she was, it meant nothing."

Angela made it clear from her expression that she was considering his words carefully.

"I can see that that's how the situation might have looked to you," she replied.

A flash of gratification flared in his eyes and he relaxed visibly. "Well, it's what *I* say," he insisted. "And I know Daddy was getting fed up with her." There was a minuscule pause and he fleetingly looked at her. Angela had the impression he'd suddenly realized that using the word "Daddy" shortly after "Whore" didn't support the sophisticated impression he was trying to give.

"Did he tell you that in so many words?" she asked. "That he was getting fed up with her, I mean?"

He hesitated before replying. "Well, no. But I could tell, of course. They'd hardly been out together in weeks and he and Mum were getting back together again. They weren't divorced, you know."

Angela considered his words. Milan's perception of his father's relationship with Lavinia was that they were "dating", a totally different concept from "living together".

"They'd never stopped loving each other really; we all knew that," he said.

Angela supposed that the "we" referred to was Milan and his sisters. Suddenly she saw that his eyes had filled with tears and he was biting his lip with determination. Her heart went out to him but she realized that any show of comfort would simply be an open acknowledgment of his evident distress.

She raised a hand to her forehead and rubbed it as if pondering her next question, to give him time to recover. "Hmm…" she mused. "How often did you see your father, Milan?"

He considered the question. It gave him the opportunity to gather himself, and when Gary took out his notebook a pleased look appeared on his face.

"All the time," he said, watching Gary record his words.

"Twice a week, three times?" she asked.

Milan shrugged. "We didn't have a routine. He came here sometimes – well, he came here more often lately. Or sometimes he'd ring and say, 'Fancy a burger?' or 'What about a film?' Or I'd just turn up at his place with no plans and we'd watch TV or a DVD together."

"And he'd bring you back?"

"Mostly."

"When he brought you back, did he come in?"

"Oh yeah, sure, he'd come in and have a coffee or something."

"What about your sisters?" asked Angela. Milan narrowed his eyes as he thought about this.

"Hmm… Sophija's gone to Dad's on the bus or the train a few times but I think they're both a bit nervous about her using public transport. They prefer her to be with me. Not Lucija, though, not yet. She's only eleven. I mean, she'd come with Sophija and me but not on her own."

"Was Lavinia Bannister ever there when you turned up unannounced?"

A disdainful look came in to spread across Milan's face. "Once or twice."

"And how did you get on with her?" asked Angela, even though, from Milan's expression, she thought she probably already knew the answer.

"I tried to be polite. Mum said I had to. Well, Dad did too."

"So how did it go on those visits?"

"Dad would say, 'Oh look, Vinni, Milan's here. Get another burger out of the freezer, would you, and stick some more chips on?' or something like that. I mean, it depended on the circumstances but he was always pleased to see us when any of us turned up."

"Was Lavinia equally pleased, do you think?"

Milan's expression became openly derisive. "No way. We – my sisters and me – would laugh at the way her mouth went all kind of tight and her face would look like she was constipated or something and she'd say, 'Oh, right; how super.' But you knew she meant just the opposite." He was silent, then spoke again. "I don't say 'whore' in front of my sisters, by the way." He thought for a moment. "Though I expect Sophija knows the word." Angela smiled and thanked him for his help.

"That's OK," he said with a nonchalant air, as if he was constantly helping the police with their enquiries. "I'd better go and get on with my homework. Mum won't be long."

"It's no problem. We're happy to wait."

"He's a lot less angry than when he came in, isn't he?" remarked Gary, as the door closed behind him.

"He certainly is," agreed Angela. She was silent for a few moments and then said, "What a nightmare."

"Guv?"

"Lavinia Bannister. I think, fundamentally, she did actually care about Petar. However, by her own and Milan's account it seems to have been very difficult for her that he was open to his kids dropping round on an *ad hoc* basis, was always pleased to see them and determined to make time to be with them."

"Nice sort of dad to have, even if he was separated from their mum."

"Exactly." Angela allowed her thoughts to wander to her own situation. Admittedly she had no first wife to worry about, but she knew that his fatherly concern for Maddie had been one of the things that drew her to Patrick. "I would have thought that Petar being a caring father would have been an attractive quality."

"I reckon so," agreed Gary.

"Perhaps she's just not good with kids."

"That's possible, but, well, she did seem to be quite into herself."

"Oh, no doubt; she came across as very self-absorbed, but in that case, and if she did really want Petar, you'd have thought she would have made more of an effort with his children."

Gary raised his shoulders and let them drop again. "Maybe she tried but didn't get very far. Milan doesn't exactly seem open to being on friendly terms with her either, does he? Probably he didn't want to appear disloyal to his mum."

"Dealing with stepchildren can be a minefield at the best of times," replied Angela, sending up a silent prayer of thanks for her own good relationship with Maddie.

They were prevented from any further speculation on the subject by the arrival of Una Belic. She was a woman of average height, elegantly dressed in stone-coloured chinos and a moss green cashmere jumper. As Angela had supposed, Milan had inherited his dark wavy hair and twinkling eyes from her. She shut the door behind her, apologizing for keeping them waiting and asking if they had been looked after.

"Milan came in, probably out of curiosity, and we ended up having a chat," replied Angela, suddenly remembering that the boy was under eighteen and wondering if she should have allowed the conversation to continue without his mother present. "We were asking him how often he saw Petar and what sort of things they did together."

Una was obviously astute enough to recognize the motive behind Angela's explanation; she smiled and waved the matter away.

"I don't have a problem with that, Inspector. Apart from all the usual stuff that comes with his age, Milan is full of anger and anguish at his father's death and he simply doesn't know which way is up at the moment. I would have been very surprised if he hadn't come in and spoken to you. Please take a seat. I hope you haven't been standing all this time. It's really naughty that neither of them made you more comfortable." Angela shook her head to dismiss Una's protests as she and Gary sat down.

"Is there any more you can tell me about Petar's death, Inspector?"

"Unfortunately not at the moment, Mrs Belic; the cause of death will be known after the inquest has been opened tomorrow morning."

"I see." Una took a deep breath and straightened her back.

"Before I get on to the questions proper, I need to know if Petar left a will."

"Oh, certainly. I'll give you the name of his solicitor before you leave."

"Thank you. When was the last time you saw your husband, Mrs Belic?"

"Please call me Una. He was here on Sunday morning before going off to the club. He popped in to let the children know when he would be able to take them to the tournament during the week. They loved going there with him."

"I'm sure they did. Did you have any other contact with him after that?"

Una creased her brow as she considered her response. "Well, yes, I did; but it was just on the phone and it was a bit tricky."

"Oh, really?"

"Mmm. He'd met up with Danny at the club."

"That's Danny Moore, the ex-player, right?"

"That's the one. They go back a long way and they're business partners as well. When Petar was here that morning he said he would suggest to Danny that we all go for a meal together – that's Petar, myself, Danny and his wife, Heather. I was keen to go because I hadn't seen either Danny or Heather since Petar and I had split and we'd all got on so well in the old days." She paused and looked directly into Angela's eyes. "I don't know if you're aware, Inspector, that Petar and I had become increasingly close over the past few months and we were seriously discussing the possibility of a reconciliation."

"I had heard the rumour. I think it was wonderful."

"It *was* wonderful. We were both very pleased with the way things were going. I can comfort myself with the fact that we'd got as far as we had. We were on very good terms when Petar died. It's something I can hold on to." A spasm of pain crossed her face and it looked for a moment as though she might break down, but she composed herself and flashed a brittle smile at them. "We were even talking about taking a holiday together in a month or so."

"That's a very real indication of good progress. So you had a phone call. When was that?"

"Oh, Sunday evening about 7:15, 7:30. He was apologizing because it had somehow become quite a party with a few of the other players, and someone had even invited Lavinia – though, to be honest, she wasn't above inviting herself along. Anyway, he said Danny thought it would be better to have our foursome on another occasion and I agreed, so that was that."

"Were there any other texts or calls?"

"A little later on. He must have been in the restaurant by that time. I texted him to say that he was very welcome to come round later for a nightcap if he wished."

"And did he respond to that text?"

Tears started in Una's eyes and she took a moment to collect herself. "Yes, yes, he did."

"Not – I'm sorry I have to ask. Not a negative response?"

Una's eyes softened at the memory. "Oh no, Inspector, quite the opposite; he made it abundantly clear that he would rather be with me at that moment."

Angela realized that this must be the text Lavinia had read when she took Petar's mobile phone out of his pocket. It would have been difficult to remain in denial about the state of her relationship with Petar after that. Angela couldn't help feeling a bit sorry for her.

It occurred to her that the distance from Wimbledon to Una's house wasn't very far. "And did he come round for a nightcap later?" she asked.

"No. Sunday morning was the last time I saw him."

"Ah. Were you disappointed?"

"Oh, not at all. He'd come round once or twice for a nightcap but there had been a couple of occasions when he felt a bit too tired. I didn't take it as a slight in any way."

There was an aspect of this story that Angela needed to

clear up but she didn't want to be indelicate. She furrowed her brow and looked towards Gary as he wrote in his notebook. "Nightcap," she whispered, as if considering the phrase.

Una was indeed an astute woman. "He hadn't yet stayed the night with me, Inspector. I didn't want the children seeing their father at breakfast until it had been decided that it would be a permanent arrangement."

Angela nodded but dug a little further. "So you weren't concerned that he might have gone to spend the night with Lavinia after all?"

Una gave a spontaneous burst of laughter. "I was completely up to speed on Petar's relationship with Lavinia, I can assure you. It was a good few weeks since he'd taken any pleasure between her sheets."

Angela put on a puzzled expression. "Yet I believe she called herself his partner."

"Oh, she's tenacious to a fault is Lavinia, and full of illusion. I think she imagines she has all the charm and allure of an attractive twenty-year-old." Angela's eyes opened wide as she listened, this description being so close to her own impression. But Una was continuing. "The trouble is that she's completely self-absorbed and more or less unaware of anything outside of her own sphere of interest. She didn't even begin to get to grips with Petar's devotion to the children." Una paused and looked at the two police officers. "I shall be eternally grateful to her."

Angela and Gary must have had an identical expression of surprise on their faces because she looked from one to the other and gave a mischievous grin before explaining.

"The thing is, Inspector, after Petar and I split up he dated a few women and they were fairly respectable, sensible ladies, not too different from myself. In theory any one of them could have become a permanent fixture in his life. Happily nothing came of any of those relationships. I suspect he was still too raw from our break-up. It hadn't been pretty and we were both very traumatized. But then he met Lavinia and she went all out to get him. I think he was flattered enough to be taken in at first. But he began to find her lifestyle draining. She's come to her current job of publicist to the stars through the world of modelling, and I don't know if you know but she lives at the centre of a social whirl. She likes to be seen as one of, and amongst, all the glitterati. I don't know if she does a good job for her clients but she's certainly her own best publicist – parties here, launches and openings there. Have you heard what one journalist said of her?"

"That she'd even attend the opening of an artery?" Angela smiled. "Yes, I read that somewhere."

"Well, that description isn't too far out."

There was a silence in the room. Eventually Angela spoke. "Er... I'm still puzzled by why you're eternally grateful to her."

"Oh – it's the contrast, you see. Petar began to realize that the life she represented didn't suit him at all, and that what he wanted was something he'd left several years before. Who knows, maybe he wouldn't have seen the truth otherwise. I always knew we were meant to be together and I knew that deep down he'd taken those vows as seriously as I did. No, Inspector, I shall always be grateful to Lavinia Bannister."

"Yes, of course," said Angela. "Sometimes going down the wrong path can be the best way of discovering where the right one lies. It's a shame Lavinia hasn't been able to take that on board even though, by all accounts, Petar really laid it on the line for her."

Una nodded and let her gaze settle on Angela for a few moments as if considering something. Then she spoke. "It's funny you using that word 'line'."

"Really?" Angela was suddenly alert. She felt her skin tingle.

"Yes, because there's that as well... line... or rather, lines. I think Lavinia has done a few too many of them and quite frankly it's beginning to show."

"Oh?" queried Angela, making an effort to keep her voice neutral as the tingling sensation intensified. "You're talking about...?"

"Coke, Inspector."

"Not the fizzy drink."

"No."

Chapter Twelve

"I just knew there was something about that continual sniff during the interview with Lavinia," said Angela to Patrick later that evening. "But I was so intent on getting the basic questions answered that I put it to the back of my mind." They were sipping coffee, watching the tennis and talking over the day's events.

"That certainly ties up with the image she presented when she came to the mortuary," he agreed.

"Mmm," she mused. "From what I can gather, Una picked up on this before Petar. Petar always kept himself well clear of anything to do with drugs and wasn't really aware of the signs. She said he wasn't particularly naïve – just not interested. But I got the impression Una's a lot more aware of the underbelly of the world of glamour than Petar. She still works as a journalist – freelance mostly, these days."

"A working single mum, effectively at least. That can be tricky."

"It sounds like she's got a good arrangement. I didn't see her there today, but as we were leaving, one of the girls came in and said something about Granny being at a whist drive. It seems Una's mother lives with her and looks after the kids when she's out working."

"That's handy."

"Yes, so anyway she – Una, that is – has been at a couple of functions in the last six months where Lavinia was present, and there was clearly something going on in a back room somewhere."

"Did she tell Petar?" he queried.

"No, she didn't. I asked her that question but she said until recently she didn't really know how enamoured Petar was of Lavinia, and was aware that dishing the dirt on his girlfriend could make him cling to her even more tightly."

"Hmm, so she was playing the whole situation very cagily; shrewd of her."

"Yes, I'm inclined to agree," said Angela. "Hey, it looks like Stewart's in a bit of trouble." Angela's attention was distracted by the activity on the screen where Stewart, having battled through four sets in his second-round match, was into a tiebreak to decide the fifth. He was two points down.

"He'll serve his way into the lead again," remarked Patrick, and they watched as he did just that and took the match. "So that's both Stewart Bickerstaff and Philip Turnbull through to the third round," he said as they watched the players leave the court. "I saw Philip's match earlier, before you arrived home. I must say, I prefer his style of play to Stewart's. He has imagination, and some of his returns are scintillating. I wonder why he isn't higher up the rankings."

"I've wondered that myself," replied Angela. "I think there's a confidence or self-belief problem there. If he could get over it he'd be even better than Stewart."

"Well, nobody can deny what a fantastic weapon Stewart's serve is, but when you take that away, his groundstrokes are OK, but…"

"Exactly," agreed Angela. "That's all they are. He relies far too much on his serve. Una said the same thing as Danny, that Petar was finding working with him increasingly frustrating."

Patrick raised his eyebrows and looked at her with a speculative expression.

"Ah… have we been getting inside information on the tennis scene?" he asked.

"Unfortunately not." Angela gave a rueful grin. "I shall have to find someone else to pump." Patrick laughed and Angela continued: "She had no problem talking about Lavinia. She thinks there must have been some event or whatever at which Petar either realized or even witnessed Lavinia doing what she would no doubt call 'recreational drugs'. Maybe he even saw Lavinia snorting a line in her own home. She's sure, though, whatever the occasion, it finally clicked with Petar. As far as Una could tell from the timing, it was about three weeks ago, and Petar hasn't officially dated Lavinia since. From then he's been much more full-on about getting back with her. But she does insist they were edging back together before this."

"Ah. And when did she give away that little morsel about Petar being frustrated with Stewart?" asked Patrick.

Angela frowned at the effort to remember. "It followed on from the mention of the drugs, I think. Yes, she said, 'So that's a change he'd made in his personal life.' And then she went on to say, more to herself, I think, that he had also hoped Stewart was going to come to his senses because he had been wondering how much further he could go with him. Danny said much the same thing."

"Oh, did she think Petar would be leaving Stewart's employ? I've got that right, haven't I? The coach is employed by the player?"

"Yes, you have, Paddy. Though I suspect in Petar's case he was employed by Stewart's parents. And I suppose, generally, the coach needs to work. That's where it was a bit different for Petar. He made pots of money from his time as a player, all of it soundly invested, and he had the agency with Danny. He continued to coach because he loved the game and wanted to nurture talent, pure and simple."

"I see. So did she say anything more about the possibility of Petar no longer being Stewart's coach?"

"No, I think she realized very quickly that even though Petar's dead, there might be client confidentiality issues if she discusses what she knows of his relationship with Stewart. I got the impression that she felt OK talking about Lavinia, based on what she herself had seen or heard. But after that little slip she didn't refer to Stewart again. It all became very non-controversial and we ended up talking about her children and their interest in tennis, which is quite lively, apparently. Both Milan and the elder girl, Sophija, are county standard."

"Hmm; still, you struck gold with the drugs connection."

"I'll say. It might have no bearing on the murder, of course, but I shall have to follow it through." She looked at him. "I need to figure out the best way of doing that."

"It really is a curse, isn't it? You can't go very far in any direction in today's society without coming up against a narcotics association of some sort."

"Tell me about it!" answered Angela, with feeling.

"Mind you, I suppose glamorous circles will be more prone to it and the world Lavinia Bannister inhabits definitely fits that profile. Who does she represent?"

"Well, Candy Trueman for one," replied Angela.

"Ah," he responded. Angela allowed herself to be distracted from her thought processes.

"Why do you say 'ah' like that?" she asked.

"It tightens up the circle, that's all. You've told me about this meal, and it makes sense, but at the back of my mind I was also wondering why they were all so pally. I mean, I know it's a small world and all that, and they see each other all the time on the tour, but that doesn't mean they live in each other's pockets or that they necessarily wish to socialize with each other. But of course, if Candy is Lavinia's client as well as being Stewart's new girlfriend it all gets a bit more entwined, doesn't it?" Angela laughed. "Especially," he continued, "when you consider that Stewart's sort-of-but-not-officially-confirmed ex, Joanna, was also there."

"You've got that right," agreed Angela. "But just as long as I find the murderer they can all stay as entwined as they like."

Patrick laughed. "And are you ready for tomorrow?" he asked.

"What, the inquest? It'll just be a formality, won't it? They'll open and adjourn it, pending police enquiries." She stopped, taking in his quizzical expression. "Ah, you mean afterwards. My fifteen minutes of fame."

"That's exactly what I mean; facing the media. Has Stanway phoned you and given you the benefit of his fatherly advice about dealing with the press?"

Angela giggled. "He phoned for an update as I was leaving Una Belic's place. Once I'd brought him up to speed he realized I would have to make some sort of statement after the coroner's court tomorrow. So he asked if I was OK about talking to the ladies and gentlemen of the press. When I said I was fine with it, he said to keep it short and sweet and to not let myself be drawn into unnecessary explanations or speculation because journalists can be very wily.'"

"Well, he's not wrong there, is he?" said Patrick. He was silent for a moment and then spoke again. "He's not exactly breathing down your neck on your first case as a D.I., is he?"

Angela looked at him. "Don't you believe it," she replied. "For every call he makes to me, he makes two to various other members of the team. I reckon he's got some radar that tells him when there's only a single D.C. or D.S. in the incident room and then he homes in. And we're having to fax copies of everything to him."

"Ha, that sounds more like it. I would be worried if he wasn't keeping a close eye. This is a very high-profile case, after all…" Patrick's voice tailed off.

Angela looked quizzically at him. "Do you mean you're wondering why they've put a newly promoted D.I. on such a case?"

"Well, it did cross my mind."

"Hmm, you've got a point. But remember, it started off only as an unexplained death progressing through 'suspicious' to 'murder'. The PM could have discovered natural causes, wrapping up the whole thing in a couple of days, for all anybody knew. Now it's murder it would be most unfair to pull me off after I've already done so much groundwork. And if you're thinking of PR, I don't suppose it would look too good in the club's eyes, either, to have the investigating officer chopped and changed about."

"Fair enough," Patrick conceded the point. "And how do you feel about facing the press?"

Angela smiled. "I feel fine. I've sat in on enough of these things to know the form. I'm sure I'll be OK."

"Good. Well, I'm sure you'll be fine too. Are you going to wear your best suit?"

Angela shook her head. "Nah, let's not go mad. The jacket and trousers I wear for work are quite smart enough." She grinned. "All a girl needs when dealing with wily journalists is a bright smile and a healthy glow."

"I know something that will give you a bright smile and healthy glow," said Patrick, moving towards her.

Angela smiled and reached out to him.

The inquest into the death of Petar Belic was opened the following morning and immediately adjourned pending police enquiries. The whole process took less than forty-five minutes and by 10:30 Angela, complete with bright smile and healthy glow, was reading out a carefully prepared statement to a gathering of journalists.

Although, as she had assured Patrick, she had attended several such gatherings, she hadn't grasped quite how much difference it would make that the case was sensationally high profile in nature, coming as it did right in the middle of the Wimbledon season, when the eyes of the world were already on this same group of protagonists.

She found out very quickly.

The press conference took place in the press centre at Wimbledon, and heavy traffic delayed Angela's journey across from the inquest. By the time she arrived, the place was noisy and heaving with bodies. At first she could only see the rear view of people and her request of "Excuse me, let me pass, please" went unheard. After a couple more tries she gave up and tapped fairly hard on the nearest back.

Its owner wheeled round, looking ready to do battle. His expression turned to one of bemusement when he saw Angela.

"Did you hit me?"

"Yes, I'm sorry. I was just trying to get someone's attention. I need to get into this room."

He laughed outright at this. "Don't we all, sweetheart? But I don't think you stand much chance. You should have got here earlier. Petar Belic's death is mega news. We're just waiting for the police."

Angela smiled sweetly at him. "I am the police. If I don't get into the room the conference won't start." She held up her ID card.

"Ah," he said and turned back to the room. "*Gangway!*" he boomed across all the noise. "*The police have arrived!* We can get this show on the road." As if by magic a channel appeared, and Angela pushed her way in, followed by Rick and Jim. Once inside, they saw a table and chairs set ready in one corner.

A very large selection of nations and each of the five continents were represented. They were seated on the chairs, perched on the tables and standing cheek by jowl all round the edges of the room. If there had been rafters, Angela thought, no doubt they would have been hanging from them. It was a very impressive turnout and Angela was only sorry they were going to get so little information for their effort.

"Good morning, ladies and gentlemen," she began. "I'm sorry for the delay but I was held up in traffic. I thank you for your patience. Well, we all know why we're here and I won't waste any more of your valuable time."

So far, so clichéd, she thought, taking a moment to look around at them all and feel her way into things.

"The simple fact is this," she continued. "The post-mortem examination on the body of Petar Belic has shown that he died as a result of a massive injection of insulin, and the investigation into his death has now become a murder enquiry."

Her statement was greeted with a brief, stunned silence. Some of the journalists looked at each other, eyebrows raised, astonishment visible. Then the texting and the scribbling began in earnest. *Isn't anybody going to ask me a question?* she wondered, not realizing that she was experiencing only the briefest of calms before the tempest let rip.

"Do you know when this would have been administered?" began a voice from the back of the room.

"This matter is still under investigation."

"Do you have any ideas as to who did this?" called someone close to Angela.

"A police investigation is underway," she said. *Weren't you listening?* she thought.

"Can you tell us anything about how the investigation is progressing?" asked an unidentifiable accent somewhere on the left hand side of the room.

She took in the speaker's face and wondered if he was a fellow countryman of Petar's. "It's too early to say anything at this time."

"Are you saying that you have no suspects as yet?" asked someone else.

"I'm sorry, but I have no more information at the present moment."

"Is it true that Petar Belic was involved in a love tussle between his wife and Lavinia Bannister and that this has a bearing on the murder? Is it, in fact, a crime of passion?"

Angela turned her eyes to the last speaker. *I bet you're from a tabloid,* she thought. "I don't know," she answered. "But if you know anything about the case you will be required to make a statement." There was a ripple of laughter.

"Can you tell us exactly in what position the body was lying?"

"Supine," she said. There was a very slight pause and she wondered if they were all trying to remember what the word *supine* meant, or merely amazed that a cop would be familiar with it.

"I believe the body was found in the centre of Court 19," came another voice. "Can you tell us anything more about that?"

Oh, you have been ferreting around, haven't you? she thought. "I'm afraid I'm not at liberty to discuss the murder scene at this juncture," she replied. *Ooh, that sounds pompous; very "Somebody of the Yard".*

She knew that they'd realized they weren't going to get any juicy revelations once they went on to peripheral questions. She went on to field enquiries about how long the insulin would take to work after the injection, and how close the police were to apprehending the perpetrator. One person even wanted to know about the degree of rigor mortis when the body had been discovered, just before another slipped in a query about whether the police were closing in on any suspects. There were some questions as to Petar's whereabouts on the evening before his death, and was it true that Una Belic and Lavinia Bannister were fighting over him and both of them had given him an ultimatum? Oh, and did the police have anybody in the frame for the killing?

"I'm sorry, I can say no more at this time," she repeated for what seemed like the hundredth time. They were phrasing the same question in a variety of different ways but she had no time to be creative with her answers. She glanced at Rick and Jim and then at her watch, wondering when on earth this press conference was going to end.

She had done this twice when she realized that as the senior investigating officer and the person chairing this meeting it wouldn't stop until she drew it to a halt. Feeling rather sheepish she rose from her chair.

"Ladies and gentlemen, I thank you all for your time but I'm afraid that's all the information I'm able to give you today." She nodded at Rick and Jim and they stood up and started to push their way back through the crowd, making a pathway for her. Questions were still fired at her every step of the way but she didn't attempt to answer and didn't look back.

She felt such relief when they got away. Outside, she turned to Rick and Jim.

"It was very stuffy in there," she said, pleased with the understatement. "I'm going to take a turn round the grounds to clear my head. Danny Moore dined at *Da Camisa* in Wimbledon high street on Sunday evening. Can you get along there and check out the time? He says he was there until about midnight."

"But does the waiter say the same thing?" queried Jim.

"Yeah, you know the drill. I'll catch up with you later."

"Sure thing, Angie," said Rick, as they headed off in the other direction.

Angela loved the club at this time of day. The impatient throng still milled about outside, champing at the bit to be let in, and although plenty of people were around, there was still an air of calm over the whole place, a sense of waiting for the day to begin.

Angela's route took her alongside the practice courts again and as she passed by she saw Joanna Clarke heading away from them and back, she presumed, to the changing rooms. Joanna, biting her lip, appeared deep in thought. Angela raised a hand in greeting and said, "Hi, Joanna." The young woman looked up, attempted a smile and nod in return but didn't stop.

Five minutes later, cup of coffee in hand, Angela paused by a secluded table in one of the eating areas at which, staring abstractly into space, sat Philip Turnbull. She watched him for a moment. He seemed to be deeply preoccupied, his brow furrowed, his hands engaged in the destruction of a polystyrene cup as he gazed into the middle distance. He jumped and looked up at her with a startled expression as she spoke his name. He immediately registered who she was and his good manners kicked in.

"Ah, Inspector," he smiled. Angela indicated one of the empty chairs at the table. "Please do," he responded. She sat down and he sat up slightly straighter.

"Congratulations on winning your second-round match," she said. "I watched it and I must say I was very impressed. Your game is coming on in leaps and bounds."

Philip shrugged in what was probably meant to be a self-deprecating manner but he couldn't hide the pleasure that spread across his face.

"Thank you. I've had a new coach for about six months now, and so far it seems to be working out well."

"It shows," agreed Angela. "Your return is something I've noticed particularly. I should think you're a good match for even the most powerful of servers." Philip turned his head away for a second and it was suddenly as though the sun had disappeared. Angela sipped her coffee and watched him out of the corner of her eye. "I've seen from the lists that if you both get through, you and Stewart will be meeting in the quarter-finals," she added. "That'll be a game to watch."

Philip stared down at the table. "If I get through, that is. I'm not looking that far ahead. In any case, Stewart... I can't – I don't normally manage to beat him."

Angela had a sudden urge to grab Philip by the shoulders and give him a good shaking. She knew it was entirely possible to get into the habit of failure and wondered if that was his problem. He just didn't seem to have the confidence to go for his shots when playing Stewart and she wanted to encourage him. She sensed a certain distress in him, however, and thought it wise to say nothing. When he met her eyes again his smile was back in place, so she moved the conversation on.

"I've just passed Joanna," she said. "She was looking very worried but I suppose she was deep in concentration. She's got her second-round match later, hasn't she?"

Philip nodded animatedly and she had the impression that he was eager to grasp the opportunity to talk about a game other than his.

"Well yes, she's a bit tense at the moment. It's all rather scary."

"What's she frightened of?"

"Losing her second-round match."

"Nothing else?"

"Winning her second-round match."

"Ah, yes, success, failure; a rock and a hard place."

Philip nodded. "Something like that."

There was a pause. Angela looked past Philip and found her mind going back over the course of the investigation so far. She didn't think Philip, like Joanna, was frightened of losing matches. She thought he was keen to get onto the court and do the best he could. But she did think he was frightened of something. She remembered a recent conversation she'd had with Patrick. He said that she'd been promoted because it was perceived that she had the necessary imagination to do the job. In her anxiety to make sure she followed correct procedure she hadn't really given rein to that quality so far.

Bidding Philip goodbye, she left him to his thoughts.

She went back to the police room, sat down and stared at the wall. *OK, Angie,* she told herself. *Let your mind roam free.*

She let the minutes tick away. Two young tennis players, Joanna and Philip should have been full of bounce and cheer at advancing in their games in just about the most prestigious tournament in the world. Instead they both seemed worried, distracted.

The germ of an idea about the reason for Joanna's preoccupation had first occurred to her by the practice courts yesterday. And it hadn't gone away. She knew she would be speaking to Joanna again soon, to get it out of her head if for no other purpose.

As for Philip, he seemed to be a troubled young man and Angela didn't really like the notion, forming at the back of her mind, as to why.

Chapter Thirteen

Angela sat in the security office watching the grainy, black-and-white images of nothing much happening on the screen and felt grateful that Rick and Jim had already done the donkey work, saving her the fate of sitting through hour after hour of this mind-numbingly tedious footage.

"It's just coming up now, Angie," said Rick from behind her. Angela leaned forward a little. The time on the screen read 1:03 a.m.

Petar Belic had been caught on camera coming in through the Church Road entrance. His cream suit stood out almost fluorescent on the film. He hurried by on what were clearly unsteady legs. Just before he passed out of view he seemed to stagger, half-turn a little and raise his right arm slightly.

Then he was gone.

"May I see it again, please?" Angela asked the security official running the tape for them, and they all sat through it again. Once she felt satisfied with what she saw, Angela nodded at the security man and he switched off the screen. Angela turned to Rick and Jim.

"What do you reckon?" she asked.

"It's definitely him," said Jim, stating the obvious. "We've watched the tape for at least an hour on each side of this but we didn't clock anyone else, apart from night staff, who are all accounted for."

"He didn't look too steady on his feet," said Rick. "We noticed that the first time round."

"Hmm. He didn't, did he?" mused Angela. "What do you make of him putting his arm out when he staggered?"

"Putting it out to steady himself, like you do," answered Jim. Angela looked from one to the other of the two detective sergeants. Angela could see a watchful yet somehow sheepish look in Rick's eyes.

"I think there may be another explanation," she said, very conscious that Rick and Jim weren't meeting each other's gaze. "Someone might have called his name. I think the slight turn and raising of his hand might have been to acknowledge that."

"Yes, that's possible – somebody just out of shot," said Rick. He and Jim still didn't look at each other.

"It's important to make sure that nobody's fallen through the net. Not amongst Petar's friends or the staff here. We need to know if he was acknowledging someone or just putting out his hand to stop himself falling."

"Yes, Angie," said Rick.

"Check it out and let me know."

"Will do," said Jim.

Angela got up and made for the door. "I'll leave you to it, then," she said. "We'll revisit this matter when you've got some information for me."

They were muttering their acquiescence as she left the room. *You've let a witness among the security staff fall off your radar*, she thought, as if speaking to them. *I've given you a chance to get it sorted, so don't blow it.*

Angela spent what little remained of the morning going over her notes, marking any points requiring clarification. She contented herself with a sandwich for lunch, finding herself a quiet, shady spot to enjoy it while she pondered on the ideas that had taken hold of her. The moment she came back into the police room, Leanne brought her a note from Rick – Mr and Mrs Bickerstaff wished to see the senior officer in charge.

Angela studied the note for a few minutes, thinking about the coded message it contained. She smiled and wondered if the subtext was: *They weren't going to be fobbed off with a D.S. like Jim or me.*

"Is the whole team here at the club?" she asked Leanne.

"Yes, guv; I'm not sure where D.S. Wainwright and D.S. Driver are at the moment but Derek and I are collecting fingerprints. Petar's car has been found and we've got to get the prints for elimination purposes. Stewart was known to have driven it on occasions as well as Petar's girlfriend, and quite a few of the other players have been in it at one time or another."

"Oh, really? I hadn't heard that – about the car, I mean. Where was it found?"

Leanne gave a small grin. "The news has only just this minute come through. It's in the pound. The police found it parked somewhere it shouldn't have been and towed it away."

"Ah. Do we know if it tells us anything yet?"

"We've got no information so far."

"Any personal effects?"

"I do know that his mobile phone and his car keys weren't in it, but it's still being gone over, of course."

"Of course. OK," she tapped the note in her hand. "I'd better sort this out; get it over with."

Gary arrived in time to usher Stewart's parents into the room a short while later. Stephen and Julia Bickerstaff, a well-groomed, sleek couple in their early fifties, entered with assurance, proffering hands to be shaken, smiles in evidence.

"What can I do for you?" Angela asked them after a brief pause in which it became clear that they expected her to open the proceedings.

Stephen Bickerstaff looked at his wife before replying.

"Well, the thing is, Julia and I are a little concerned about the fact that this has become a murder enquiry. We're worried about the effect this will have on Stewart's game."

Angela opened her mouth and shut it again very quickly,

knowing that anything that came out of it at that moment would be offensive. However, Julia Bickerstaff spared her the necessity of formulating any sort of reply.

"It's all been very upsetting for him," she broke in.

"Poor old chap," added her husband.

"He's coping very well, of course," continued Julia. *Of course,* thought Angela. "But this year is particularly important for him in terms of ranking points. He's hoping to break into the top one hundred, you see."

Angela gave the Bickerstaff parents her full attention. "I'm not quite sure...." she began.

"Oh, we understand you have a job to do, absolutely. Poor Petar, such a nice man," said Julia, hurrying on. "It's a question of solidarity, you understand."

Angela didn't and made no pretence that she did. "Solidarity?" she queried.

"Yes, we want to show that we're with Stewart in this," Julia explained. "It's how we are, as a family. He's had a bit of a rough ride recently; a favourite great-aunt of his died. I mean, she was very elderly but Stewart was close to her nonetheless, visited her a great deal and so forth, and the death hit him hard. And now this nasty business, of course, so we just thought we'd come along and have a word. Naturally we want to assure you of our full cooperation. And we know that at such an important time for them all you don't want to upset any of the players more than you have to."

There was something about the way Julia Bickerstaff had spoken this last sentence that gave it the quality of a cue being fed to her husband, and Angela suddenly got an angle on where they were planning to go with this conversation. She put on her most helpful smile and waited. They had come here with an agenda and were going to stick to it.

Stephen Bickerstaff relaxed a little in his chair and crossed one leg over the other, the quintessential urbane man-of-the-world. He reminded Angela of Stewart. When it came to style, at least, the apple hadn't fallen very far from the tree.

He picked up on his wife's cue. "Oh, I'm sure the inspector understands that, Julia," he said with a smile. He turned back to Angela. "By the way, Inspector, I believe we have an acquaintance in common." *Oh, I'm sure we do,* thought Angela. *I'm sure it'll turn out to be a policeman, and what's more I bet it's not somebody from one of the lower ranks.*

She wasn't disappointed.

"Yes, Superintendent Stanway and I go back quite a way, what with the Rotary Club and the occasional round of golf." Stephen Bickerstaff smiled as if in reminiscence at some pleasant social occasion passed in the company of Angela's boss. Angela nodded to acknowledge Stanway's name and immediately decided that two could play at this.

She bestowed a benign smile upon Mr Bickerstaff. "If you're speaking to the superintendent in the near future," she said, injecting enthusiasm into her voice, "you'll be very impressed by the close eye he's keeping on us here at the club." Bickerstaff opened his mouth to speak but Angela continued smoothly on as if she hadn't noticed. "And he's very happy with the way that we're following procedure."

"Oh, of course, of course," Bickerstaff smiled and managed to avoid bluster. "I know what a tight ship Stanners runs."

Stanners, thought Angela. *Lord, have mercy.*

Just at that moment there came a knock on the door. Gary put aside his notepad and, after a quick glance to verify he had Angela's permission, opened the door to reveal Mr Burrows accompanied by an elderly lady dressed in a cream jacket and beige skirt. She stared anxiously into the room, smiling nervously when Stephen Bickerstaff swivelled round in his chair, indignant at the interruption.

"Ah, Gracie!" he said, turning back to Angela to explain. "This is a cousin of ours. She lived with Aunt Margaret – that's the aunt who died recently – cared for her. Did you wonder where we'd got to, Gracie?"

"Er, I wasn't sure... I'm sorry to be a nuisance," she replied timidly.

"Not to worry," said Bickerstaff. "Did you get yourself something to eat?"

After a moment's thought, Gracie recollected that she'd had lunch, nodded and said, "Yes, thank you." She stood, somewhat irresolutely, just inside the room.

"All right, then. We're just finishing here," said Bickerstaff. He stood up, closely followed by his wife. "Well," he turned to Angela. "It's very kind of you to take the time to reassure us, Inspector." He held out his hand. "We're very grateful."

Angela watched the trio disappear and said nothing until they were out of earshot, at which point she let out a long breath.

"Guv?"

She turned. "Yes, Gary?"

"What was all that about?"

"That, Gary, was the comic turn in this drama. They came here specifically to make sure that I don't lean so heavily on their baby boy that he's put off his game, and to let me know that if they have a cause for complaint they don't need to use the established procedure that's reserved for the plebs."

"They'll just buy 'Stanners' a drink in the bar at the Rotary and tell him all about it, right?"

"Got it in one, Gaz; you're a sharp lad. Now, would you mind getting me a cup of coffee? All of a sudden I have a nasty taste in my mouth."

"No probs," Gary smiled and went off to fulfil the errand as Angela slipped into the corridor, where she nearly bumped into

Jim and Rick. Rick cast a glance at the retreating Bickerstaffs, correctly interpreted the look on her face, and grinned.

"Hey, don't shoot the messenger, Angie," he said.

Angela made a gun with her hand and pointed it at him. "Bang," she said and blew on her fingers. Rick slumped against the wall.

"Were they that bad?" asked Jim.

"Not really. Usual sort of thing – be gentle with our boy, and if you're not, we've got friends in high places."

"They got up my nose all right: 'We would like to speak to the officer in charge please, Sergeant,'" mimicked Jim with irritation.

"Ah, diddums," grinned Angela absently, knowing how easy it was to get up Jim's nose. "I was just letting them know, ever so politely, that they were going to get nowhere, when the poor relation turned up and they found it necessary to terminate the conversation. Now then, have you discovered if we've missed anybody out in our interviews so far?"

"A couple of names came up, Angela," said Rick. "One or two ex-players he was particularly friendly with." Rick consulted his notebook. "Helmut Wolf, who lives in Germany. Danny Moore. He's already on our radar." She nodded. A brief silence followed and she became aware of a certain veiled tension.

"Anyone else?" she asked, aware that they were again avoiding each other's eyes.

"Yeah… well, one of the security guards, a chap called Doug Travers; we haven't managed to talk to him so far. He put his back out at the beginning of the week so he's at home on sick leave at the moment." Angela noted the blanket phrase "the beginning of the week" and suspected this man should have already been spoken to, or at least been part of the first interview with the security guards. She wasn't going to let the matter drop but would choose her own time to ask when, exactly, he'd gone sick; she'd got the name now and would deal with it.

"OK, Danny Moore I've seen. I'd like to have a word with Doug Travers, though. Would you set that up for me, please? Right now I want to check on something. Get me on my mobile if you need me," she added over her shoulder.

She had just emerged into the sunshine when she became aware of a certain buzz. She hurried to the main bulletin board. Contrary to expectation, Joanna Clarke had won her second-round match. What's more, she had beaten an opponent ranked fifty places above her. Angela punched the air in delight. As she did so, she caught the flash of a PR badge, saw Janina Duncan hurrying past and moved quickly to catch up.

"Janina!" she called. The other woman stopped, turned round and smiled when she saw Angela.

"Oh, hi, Inspector. How's it going?"

"We're making progress," answered Angela. "Great news about Joanna, eh?"

"Oh yes, absolutely. I was watching. She just seemed to grow in confidence throughout the game and you could tell she was on the most fantastic roll. Mind you, she still managed to look worried again by the time she left the court."

Angela nodded. She had her own ideas about that. "Has she finished her post-match interview, do you know?"

"Yes, as a matter of fact I'm off to see her now. I've got a couple of things to talk to her about."

"Would you ask her to come along to our room once she's finished with you, please? Nothing to worry about, just something I need to go over with her."

"Yes, of course," smiled Janina, and hurried away.

Angela doubled back to the police room, glad of an opportunity for reflection before Joanna arrived. Ten minutes later, Wimbledon's most recent British victor sat across the desk waiting for her to speak.

"Great going into the third round, eh?" beamed Angela. Joanna flushed with pleasure but it was obvious that her joy was muted. *At least she can't put her preoccupation down to poor form,* thought Angela. "You're really on a roll at the moment, aren't you?" she said with a smile.

"I'll say. I just feel amazing," agreed Joanna. "I don't know what's come over me, but I wake feeling so full of beans at the moment. If I lived in a hilly country I'm sure I'd be running up and down them right after breakfast. And I'm so alert. I've never hit the ball so cleanly."

"I know it can be like that sometimes," said Angela, carefully. A flicker of acknowledgment came and went in Joanna's eyes, followed immediately by a look of alarm.

"I'm not taking anything," she said.

"No, I didn't think you were."

Joanna gazed down at her knees without speaking and Angela let the silence lengthen. Eventually Joanna brought her eyes up to meet Angela's. There was an instant when one sought permission to continue and the other gave it. It was nothing as obvious as a nod, even a small one, but Angela could tell that Joanna had suddenly realized that she would find it a relief to confide in her. She thought again of the delicate knitting wool they had found in her locker.

"You're pregnant, aren't you?"

Chapter Fourteen

Huge tears welled up in Joanna's eyes and poured down her cheeks but she said nothing as she gazed into Angela's face.

"Would you like a cup of tea?" asked Angela. Joanna nodded silently. The tears rolled unabated. Angela telephoned the instruction to Gary and looked at Joanna with what she hoped was a reassuring smile.

"I've been absolutely frantic."

"I'm sure you must have. Most people, as far as I'm aware, have been thinking you're anxious about your form and the… the situation with Stewart."

Joanna managed a grim smile through her tears. "I've let people think that; it's been convenient. Actually, I got over Stewart very quickly. I was devastated at first but about a week after I knew he'd had his first date with Candy I realized I felt relieved. Does that sound strange?"

"Not at all," responded Angela. She thought back briefly to a time in her late teens when a boyfriend had dumped her. Instead of the sorrow she might have imagined, she had felt only as though a burden had fallen from her shoulders.

"Mmm… I mean, I loved Stewart, or thought I did, at least, but it took me a long time to realize that I could never quite relax with him. I always felt I had to look good, dress to impress and stuff like that, and kind of behave in a particular way. It's his parents as much as him. You can't slob out with the Bickerstaffs."

Angela thought back over her meeting with Stewart's parents and knew exactly what Joanna meant. "I can understand that," she said. "I'm assuming, though…" Her voice tailed off and she dipped her head in the general direction of Joanna's abdomen.

"Oh yes, it's Stewart's baby." Joanna's tears were drying up now.

"Does he know?"

"Oh yes. To be fair to him, he said he'd do the necessary."

"What does he consider 'the necessary' to be?"

"I think he means he'll pay for an abortion. When I spoke to him he just said that when I've sorted out the operation to let him know and he'll do the necessary." Joanna shuddered and tears started up in her eyes again. "I've been beside myself," she said again, "wondering what to do, how to handle it. And it's really odd to have this tremendous sense of well-being at the same time – physically, I mean."

There was a brief pause as the door opened and Gary came in with a cup of tea, and the coffee that Angela had ordered earlier. He glanced at the two women, realised that his presence wasn't required and left the room. Angela was impressed with his sensitivity.

Once the door had closed behind him, Joanna spoke again. "How did you know?"

"Well, when you're conducting an investigation you get pretty well attuned to when people have things on their mind and when they're not telling you everything. It was obvious that you've been preoccupied and though, believe me, I've got nothing but sympathy for your predicament, my concern has got to be whether or not what's troubling you is related to the investigation." Angela smiled. "In your case, a couple of things came together. When I saw you on the practice courts the other day you overran and nearly bashed into the net post. If you'd gone into it you would have been hit right in the abdomen. There was a look of sheer terror on your face just before you managed to avoid the post."

Joanna opened her eyes wide at the memory. "Yes, that was a scary moment."

"And then I remembered that knitting wool we found in your locker when we did the searches, and couldn't help wondering."

A dreamy look came into Joanna's eyes. "Yeah, I haven't knitted in years but I started a little coat after I had my scan. I could hardly believe it when they first gave the picture to me. I was just blown away. I was, like, that's my baby… my baby. I've got a whole other person inside me. I couldn't stop looking at it. I keep it with me all the time."

There was a pause.

"I don't want to have an abortion."

"I'm sure you don't. I don't blame you."

Joanna's eyes widened in surprise. "You don't?" she asked.

Angela looked at her, thinking again of the knitting wool. This was a woman who wanted to give life to her child. She decided on the direct approach.

"Why should you have an abortion?" she replied.

Joanna's look of puzzlement would have been comical if the matter hadn't been so grave.

"Well, there's my career. I'm a sportswoman. People will expect… Stewart seemed to think it automatic that I get rid… My parents have invested so much in me, to help me get into tennis." The tears were starting in her eyes again.

"I'm sure your parents have been glad to help, Joanna. That's normal; most parents would do all they could. But I don't for one moment suppose that they would want you to get rid of your child. In any case, being pregnant is obviously helping your game."

Angela watched Joanna considering the implications of this for a moment.

"They'll think I'm throwing my whole career away."

"Why so? How far gone are you?"

"Twelve weeks."

Angela looked at her. She was already twelve weeks pregnant so she'd probably had the first inklings of her condition about two months ago or more and she'd done nothing about getting an abortion. She had, however, done something about getting antenatal care, and had had a scan. Angela strongly suspected that her plan had been to go on saying nothing until her bulging belly had begun to cause comment, by which time she would present her pregnancy to all concerned as a done deal.

This woman wanted her baby.

"So, the baby's due in... January?" asked Angela. Joanna nodded. "OK, so you'll have to miss the American and the Australian Opens and whatever other tournaments you would otherwise enter, but after January there's a whole five months to get back into training for next year's Wimbledon. Really, when you come to think of it, tennis players can spend that amount of time out of the game just because of injury anyway."

"Oh my goodness, I hadn't thought of it like that." Joanna laughed, the first time Angela had seen her do so, and her face was transformed. Then her expression became serious again and she was silent for a few moments. "Actually," she said, "I think my mum's guessed already."

"I wouldn't be at all surprised; mums are like that," replied Angela.

A silence descended in the room, during which it became obvious to Angela that the woman sitting opposite her was entirely different from the scared girl who had walked in.

"I'm going to go and tell her," said Joanna, after a few moments. "I can do it now. I'm not frightened any more." She turned a radiant smile upon Angela. "Thank you so much, Inspector. I can't tell you how much you've helped me. I'm only sorry that I can't help you with the investigation. What was bothering me had nothing to do with it, obviously."

Angela waved away her regrets. "It's a question of elimination. It all helps in the long run," she assured her as she watched her depart. This situation was turning Joanna into a strong, confident young woman. Angela thought it quite possible that she would advance through a few more rounds in this tournament and she had no doubt that she would come back next year determined to do even better.

"So that's sorted, then," she said aloud to herself. She yawned and stretched, suddenly very tired. Winding things up for the day looked like a very attractive option. She called all the team and they set about gathering their things together. Jim and Rick began to debate which pub they could reach most easily and Leanne freshened up her lipstick. Gary was having a good-natured argument with Derek about football when Angela's mobile rang.

"Hello, Inspector Costello speaking."

Silence.

"Hello?"

"It's Tara."

"Tara?" Angela racked her brains.

"Tara Simpkins, from Bel-Mor Sports Agency."

Light dawned. "Oh, right – Tara! I remember."

Across the room she saw Gary register the name, and from his expression and gestures it was clear that his memory featured the amount of cleavage and leg on display in Danny Moore's office. He turned to his male colleagues, saying, "Hey, you should have seen this girl…"

Thankful that he had the good sense to keep his voice very low, Angela grinned and turned away. "How may I help you, Tara?" she asked.

"I've got some information, to do with the case. Well, *I* reckon it's to do with the case; you know, about Petar Belic."

"Yes." Angela turned back towards Gary and raised her eyebrows in his direction. "Where can we meet you?"

"Er, dunno," she said finally. There was a pause. Clearly Tara had expected to be asked to come to a police station.

"Where do you live, Tara?"

"Balham."

"That's not too far from Wimbledon. Shall we come to you?"

"All right," she said, and gave her address. Angela wrote it down, finished the call and turned to Gary. "We've not quite finished for the day after all, Gaz."

"Are we going to see the luscious – ?"

"Yes we are," she smiled, "and I expect you to keep custody of the eyes, as the nuns used to teach me at school."

"Yeah, right," grinned Gary, following her out through the door. Within moments they were settling themselves into Angela's car and heading out through the gates of Wimbledon. "You've got to admit, that was quite a display she put on yesterday."

"It certainly was," agreed Angela. "I think she failed to reach her target audience, though."

"Yeah, what was that all about? Oh, is that what you mean by 'custody of the eyes', the way Danny Moore made such a point of not looking at her... her...?"

"Charms?"

"Yeah, right, her charms."

Angela laughed. "Exactly so. Let's find out what she's got to say."

Tara Simpkins lived in a terraced house not far from the underground station. If Gary had been hoping for the same display of flesh as he'd had the previous day, he was disappointed. The smart working suit had been replaced by jeans, a loose T-shirt and trainers. Chewing gum, Tara showed them into a cosy sitting room. Family photographs adorned the walls, in which Angela and Gary could recognize younger versions of Tara with her parents and children too similar to be anything other than her brother and two little sisters.

"D'you want to sit down?" she asked.

They took a seat on a floral patterned sofa set into a bay window. Silence settled on the room. Tara looked nervous and slightly pale.

Angela smiled in encouragement. "There's nothing to worry about, Tara. If the information doesn't seem relevant to the case after all, we won't talk about it to anyone."

Tara nodded and gave a small smile of her own in return. "I could tell you a lot about that place," she said suddenly, then lapsed back into silence.

Angela looked at Gary and raised her eyebrows. A bit of softening up seemed to be required.

"Is it a good place to work, Bel-Mor?" she asked.

"Yeah, it's quite nice."

"Have you been there long?"

"Nearly three months."

"And Mr Moore – he's a good boss?"

This seemed to do the trick. "Goody two-shoes if you ask me, *him!*" snapped Tara with venom. She shot a look at Angela as if wondering how this would be taken.

Gary got busy with his pen and Angela nodded, carefully digesting what she had just heard. "In what way, Tara?" she asked.

Tara shrugged. "It started off all right. Danny was friendly and at first he'd stop by the reception and ask me how I was getting on, you know, with the job – and he sort of spent time chatting to me. So I took it that he was interested."

"You thought he was giving you the come-on?"

"Well, yeah."

"Did you fancy him?"

Tara looked blankly at Angela for a moment as if the question hadn't crossed her mind. "Well, yeah. I mean, he's the boss, isn't he? He owns half the company. I thought I could be on to a good thing," she said, frankly.

Angela managed not to raise her eyebrows.

"Anyway," continued Tara, "he said I could take my problems to him if I needed to talk about anything. 'We're all one big happy family at Bel-Mor' – that's what he said." Tara lifted her eyes to the older woman's face. "It's my first job as a receptionist, and I was lucky to get it."

I'll say, thought Angela.

"So, of course I thought: this is good. I could do all right here." She looked at the pair of them and moved the gum round in her mouth. "I've really done my best, right? I've stayed late, 'cos that was when there was the best chance to talk to him alone. And I showed I was keen. I talked to him as much as I could. I've even invented a few problems to get him interested. See, my mate Lauren, she's got the same sort of job as me and she's really cracked it. Her boss buys her stuff, takes her out. She was taken to a champagne bar last week in a stretch limo and it didn't cost her a thing."

Angela hid a smile. *Oh, I'm sure some sort of payment was extracted from your friend Lauren,* she thought, *but that's part of the arrangement, as you very well know.*

"Anyway," continued Tara, "I really thought I was on to something last week. Lauren said to talk to him about the boys round here, say they're not sophisticated and that I need a mature man. So I did that."

There was a strangled kind of cough from Gary. Angela forced herself to keep her eyes fixed on Tara. "And what happened?"

"Cor, you should have seen him! Big eyes, mouth drops open. 'Tara, you're not seriously suggesting... I had no idea that this is what you meant! You're young enough to be my daughter, sweetheart. I was just trying to be nice.' I mean, was I humiliated or what?"

Tara's eyes moistened with tears of frustration as she seemed to contemplate the champagne bars and stretch limousines that other women had, and Danny Moore could have if he wanted them, but she knew she would never attain, not if she saved for a lifetime.

Angela thought back to the display of the previous day. "You haven't given up, though, have you?"

Tara wiped away a tear and threw Angela a calculating glance. "Well, I thought about what he said, and it occurred to me that if he thought of me like a daughter then he needs to see that I'm, you know, a woman with, like... needs." Tara blew a huge bubble with the gum and expertly gathered it back into her mouth as it burst.

Angela couldn't help feeling sorry for the girl. *You're chasing an illusion, Tara*, she thought, *and I've no doubt you're courting heartbreak.* "Made any progress?" she asked after a moment.

Tara shook her head reluctantly. "I can't seem to catch his eye. I'm a bit worried now, as well, because they've extended my period of probation."

"I see," said Angela. *I'm not surprised*, she thought.

"Anyway," continued Tara, "for the last week or so his wife's been popping in around home time, so I've just had to leave the office without any chance to talk to him."

Angela couldn't be quite sure whether or not Tara had drawn the connection between her – no doubt very clumsy – attempt at seduction, the extended probation and Heather Moore "popping in". Tara seemed to combine a mix of amazing naïveté and animal cunning, and Angela was reminded a little of Lavinia Bannister. In any case, all this was getting her nowhere; she wanted to get home and had no doubt that a pint was waiting in a pub somewhere for Gary.

"Well, I'm sorry things are difficult for you at work at the moment, Tara." *Did I keep a straight face as I said that?* "But I need to get to the information that you said you had for us."

"Yeah." Tara shifted animatedly in her seat, a not very pleasant smile playing around her mouth. A bombshell was about to be dropped. Unless Angela had guessed wrongly, Danny Moore was about to become very sorry that he'd resisted Tara's blandishments.

"Would you like to tell me what it is?"

"Yes," she said, in the manner of one pulling an ace from her sleeve. "Petar was about to pull the plug on the company. Danny was going to be ruined."

Chapter Fifteen

Angela and Gary exchanged glances.

"If this is true it's a very serious matter, Tara."

"I know," replied Tara, pleased with the effect of her words and clearly basking in the attention.

"OK. What makes you think Petar was going to ruin Danny?"

"I heard Danny say so. He was very frightened."

"Tell us exactly what you heard."

Tara settled herself more comfortably into her seat. "It was a few weeks ago. I'd stayed late because I wanted to – you know – talk to Danny. But he'd already said goodnight, so I think he must have thought I'd gone home, which was all right as far as I was concerned because I wanted to surprise him. I'd gone into the loo to check my make-up and that; then when I came out I saw his wife going into his office, so I stepped back out of sight. I didn't want her to turn round and see me."

"So she's always been in the habit of popping in?"

"No, this was unusual. I mean she's been coming most nights since – you know – but at that point I'd hardly seen her in the office."

"I see. And what happened?"

"Well, she hadn't shut the door properly, probably didn't think there was any need to; so I heard them. They seemed to be, like, arguing and that made me think that if they were having marriage problems I was in with a chance."

Angela nodded. *You certainly push the envelope when it comes to being upfront, don't you*, she thought. "Go on," she said.

"Anyway, after I'd listened for a bit I realized it wasn't a proper argument. She was trying to get something out of him and he was upset. I think he might have been crying at one point." Tara's eyes widened at the memory. "I'd never heard a bloke cry before; not a grown-up one, that is."

You just carry on the way you're going and you'll come across plenty of it, thought Angela. "What were they saying?"

"She was saying, 'Come on, darling, it can't be that bad,' and he was going, 'Oh yes it is, Hev. I've really screwed up, *screeeewed* up like you wouldn't believe. What am I going to do? Pete will never forgive me. He'll ruin me and he'll be right to do it. I deserve nothing less, but I honestly thought it would be all right, Hev. I was so sure it would come good.' Then it went quiet for a bit and then she said in this, like, really stern sort of voice, 'I've got to know, Danny,' and then it was quiet again and finally he spoke. It was a whisper, really, but I heard it OK. He said, 'I've used Bel-Mor money to finance a private project and it's gone pear-shaped.'"

They were with Tara for another hour, taking her carefully over everything she'd seen and heard. They finally drove away having made arrangements for her to come in to the station and sign her statement.

"This puts Danny Moore slap bang in the centre of the frame, doesn't it, guv?" said Gary, as they made their way from the quiet side street to the main road.

"If what Tara says is true, it would definitely give him a very strong motive," agreed Angela.

"You think she could be lying, trying to stir things up because she couldn't get inside his pants?"

"It's a possibility but somehow I don't think so. She seems to be an amoral gold-digger but that doesn't make her a liar. It's curious, though, because according to her, she overheard this conversation a few weeks ago. Well, we were there just yesterday and it looked like prosperous-business-as-usual, didn't it?"

"That's true; plus the fact that they've extended Tara's probation period means that the powers-that-be at the company aren't expecting to go bust anytime soon."

"Hmm… it'll be interesting, taking a look into Bel-Mor's books. We'll get started on that in the morning. Ah, here we are," she said, as Tooting Broadway station loomed into view. "Will this do you?"

"Yeah, this is perfect. Thanks for the lift."

He got out of the car and gave her a thumbs-up as he walked towards the entrance. Angela pulled out into the traffic again, this time for Richmond and home. She wondered what Patrick would say when she told him the news about Joanna.

"Nice one," said Jim the next morning, after Angela had recounted the gist of Tara's story. "We might have known there would be a money motive somewhere. Stick him at the top of the suspects list, Leanne."

"Just put a question mark over his name, Leanne," countered Angela. "You and Derek get on to the Financial Investigation Team and ask them to have a look-see at the Bel-Mor Sports Agency finances. We're looking for the movement of a large amount of money – no, make that *any* unusual movement within, say, the past six months. If you don't find anything there, extend the search."

"It all sounds very likely, though," persisted Jim.

"Anything's possible at the moment," replied Angela. She had a sudden flashback to the press conference, and the journalists nosing around Petar's intimate relationships. "It could even turn out to be a love tussle between Lavinia Bannister and Una Belic. And we still haven't looked at the *cui bono* motive."

"Kwee what?" asked Jim.

"Who benefits from the death. Will you check out his will, Jim? You'll find his solicitor's details in the system."

Jim dipped his head but couldn't completely hide a mulish expression. He fancied himself as a man of action rather than a pencil-pusher. "OK, Angie," he said.

Angela kept her face straight. She knew Jim's working preferences and wouldn't choose him for any paperwork that required finesse and diligence. But he couldn't go far wrong in finding out the terms of Petar's will. "OK, I'll be at Wimbledon if you need me," she said, picking up her bag.

"Oh, Angie, Rick and I got hold of that security guard, Doug Travers. He's still off sick and has a hospital appointment today but can see us at home tomorrow."

"Thanks, Jim, but I'll cover this one," said Angela, keeping her voice level. Out of the corner of her eye she saw Rick's head jerk up.

"It won't be any problem to do, Angie," said Rick.

"I know, but I'll deal with it," she replied. There was a procedural and maybe a discipline issue here, and Jim and Rick needed to know she ran a tight ship. "Text me the details," she added, as she headed out through the door.

It was another warm, sunny day, perfect weather for tennis. Back at the club she found herself a patch of grass amidst all the hubbub of people taking time out from the games to eat their packed lunches and relax in the sunshine. The atmosphere brimmed with festivity. She sat cross-legged on the luxuriant green and tried to put herself mentally into that crucial Sunday evening, just before Petar and the others left for the restaurant. Later on she would go into the office and write it all down, but for the moment she wanted – needed – to let it ferment in her mind. She sat there at a comfortable remove from all the laughter and chatter going on around her.

Fragments of conversations and impressions joined up, separated and reformed as if an invisible hand inside her head was putting together a jigsaw puzzle. After what seemed a long time she tuned into the world around her again.

She found her mind returning to her interview with Danny Moore. She couldn't rid herself of the notion that something had been said of greater significance than appeared on the surface, tying up two questions that had been bothering her. One of her questions had been answered; that was Joanna's pregnancy. Now she had to seek an answer to the other. But it would take very delicate handling.

Angela put off her return to the police room by searching out a bite to eat. She found herself standing in a queue for a sandwich behind a woman's figure that seemed familiar. When the woman turned in her direction to point out the item of her choice to the assistant she caught sight of Angela and a smile of recognition lit up her eyes.

"Oh, hello! You're the police officer investigating Petar's death, aren't you?"

Angela smiled, nodded and was thankful that a name suddenly popped into her head. "Hi, it's Gracie, isn't it – a relative of Stewart's?"

Gracie beamed as she paid for her purchase. She seemed delighted that Angela had remembered her name. "Yes – his great-aunt Margaret was my cousin." She picked up her food-laden tray. "Are you looking for a seat? Shall I save one for you?" she asked. Angela hadn't been planning to sit in the cafeteria and would have politely demurred but Gracie had already launched herself among the crowded tables with her tray held steadily aloft, the din of conversation from all the diners rendering any attempt at remonstration useless. When Gracie turned back and waved in triumph as she secured a just-vacated table for two by a pillar, it seemed churlish not to follow.

By the time she reached the table, Angela had revisited the previous day's encounter and made up her mind to be friendly. She remembered Stephen Bickerstaff asking Gracie if she'd got herself some lunch, and here she was again, eating in one of the cafeterias while Stephen and Julia must be lunching in the considerably more opulent surroundings of a restaurant somewhere. Clearly the Bickerstaffs were prepared to own Gracie as a relative but didn't wish to sit at the same table as her.

"I like eating here," began Gracie, smoothing her paper napkin on her lap. "It's so lively."

Angela smiled at her. "It certainly is that, all right," she agreed, thinking longingly of the peace and quiet of the police room. "Do you come to watch the matches every day?"

"Oh yes, I've always liked the tennis, long before Stewart developed an interest."

"Do you have to queue up?" asked Angela, thinking that it couldn't be the sort of thing that an elderly lady would want to do.

"Well, I used to do that a lot, it was all part of the fun, but nowadays, fortunately, Stewart sometimes lets me have a ticket from his guest allocation. If not, I've got to know a few people over the years and can sometimes find another guest ticket going begging. I don't often have to queue these days, which is a blessing as I'm not as young as I was. You know how it is," she smiled. "And how about you? Are you making progress in your investigation?"

"I think so."

"Of course I know you can't discuss it," continued Gracie, biting into her prawn and avocado baguette. "It's such an awful thing to have happened. I couldn't believe it when I first heard. Poor Petar, he was such a nice man."

"Did you know him?"

"Oh yes, he came to the house on several occasions. Stewart often popped in from his coaching sessions and Petar was usually with him. Most of Stewart's tennis friends have been to the house, you know. Joanna, of course, though I think that's all over now." Gracie blushed a little and cast a surreptitious glance at Angela. "And Lavinia, of course," she hurried on. "Well, she's a family connection anyway. I even came back from shopping the other day and passed Philip Turnbull in the hallway. Stewart was very close to his great-aunt Margaret, and she doted on him; so he popped in frequently and very often had someone with him. She didn't have any children of her own. Stephen Bickerstaff is her brother's son. Stewart was very upset when she died."

"Did she die suddenly?" asked Angela. It seemed only polite to ask.

"No – at least, nothing new or alarming. She was very elderly and had a few things wrong with her. It would be difficult to get to your eighties without at least one chronic condition, but Margaret always took good care of herself and obeyed her doctor's orders to the letter. It was just that... well, the time had come."

Angela considered Gracie carefully as she brought her own sandwich to her mouth. She must be into her seventies herself, from the look of her. She wondered what the future held for her. Almost immediately her unasked question was answered.

"Of course the house will have to be sold," continued Gracie. "It's far too large for me to live in by myself." She beamed a broad smile at Angela. "I shall be looking for a little flat. I'm hoping to get one in West Ealing near my best friend, Edith. We've been friends since we were girls. Can you imagine? Over sixty years!" Angela raised her eyebrows and looked suitably impressed. "She's away at the moment, otherwise she would probably be here with me; she's just as keen on the tennis as I am but she's in Australia, visiting relatives." Gracie paused and took another bite from her baguette but kept her eyes fixed on Angela.

"Australia, eh?" remarked Angela, having the impression that some sort of comment was required.

"Yes, I helped her to plan the trip and we had a very exciting time getting everything together. You just didn't do that when we were young; if somebody emigrated to Australia you waved them goodbye and expected never to see them again. That was another way in which Margaret was very good to me," she continued. "She was very accommodating about dear Edith visiting me, which she did every week. She – Margaret, that is – took me in many years ago when my dear father died. I'd been looking after him, you see, but couldn't stay in that house because it was a rented property and the owner wanted it back for his own use. Of course, I helped Margaret as much as I could, especially once she got older and started to become frail. It worked very well; we were used to each other's ways. And she always insisted that there would be enough for me to have my own little flat and a reasonable pension once she was gone. A reward, as she put it, for my faithfulness."

Angela could see that if she wasn't careful she would get caught up in the tangle of Bickerstaff family history. Sometimes a woman in Gracie's position ended up with no other source of conversation. She moved in quickly to head her off at the pass. "So, how did you find Petar when he came to the house?" she asked.

"A gentleman. Absolutely a gentleman," said Gracie without hesitation. "He was such a dear man. He always paid me attention, asked how I was and... He was so sweet – so attentive always."

Angela caught the wistful note to her voice, and watched the look of sadness pass across her features. From what she'd seen of the younger Bickerstaffs, she wouldn't be surprised if attention didn't very often come Gracie's way. She smiled at the elderly woman. "I haven't found anyone with a bad word to say about him so far," she remarked.

"Nor will you. Oh, Stewart had been out of sorts with him sometimes lately, but that happens between a coach and a player, doesn't it? And Stewart can be a determined young man. He's been somewhat spoi…" She stopped and a sudden look of alarm flashed across her mild countenance.

Her distress at what, Angela was sure, was about to be a comment of disloyalty to her family and her embarrassment about the continuing silence was so evident that Angela quickly moved in to her rescue.

"A little indulged, maybe?" she essayed with a smile. "It happens sometimes, doesn't it, especially if a child is particularly charming?"

Gracie's brow cleared immediately and she reached for the lifeline thrown her. "Yes indeed," she replied in gratitude. "He was a lovely little boy, but it was always the same. If Stewart thinks something should be done a certain way, he will *not* be deflected."

Angela nodded, looking at her and thinking back over her conversation with Danny Moore, recalling his much less inhibited comments about Stewart. Even here, from this faithful family member, she was getting the message that relations between Petar and Stewart had not always been harmonious. She started to be rather glad that her lunchtime had been hijacked by this old lady. She settled herself down to enjoy her sandwich and, like Petar, pay Cousin Gracie some attention.

Chapter Sixteen

Philip Turnbull still found it hard to keep his face from breaking into huge involuntary smiles as he sat in Angela's office an hour after winning his third-round match in four sets. She congratulated him on the victory, leading into the interview by way of a discussion about a couple of tricky points which could have turned the match against him. She watched him finally manage to subdue the huge beam into serious concentration.

"You haven't got me here for a point-by-point analysis of today's match," he said. "I suppose you've got some more questions relating to Petar's death." He paused, thinking. "It's a sad irony, really, that Petar helped me to win today."

"Oh, really?" Angela raised her eyebrows invitingly.

"Hmm, he gave me some hints about my game; a couple of tactical things that I don't normally do. On reflection, I think my own coach had also been trying to get me to understand the same things, but somehow it wasn't clear, or…" He grinned. "Maybe I'm just too thick to take it in. But when Petar spoke to me he made sense of it so that I felt confident enough to have a go. It was a bit of a risk today, but it paid off – as you see." The big grin was once again in evidence. "Mind you," he added, a slightly puzzled expression creasing his brow, "I really do think I've told you all I know."

Angela hastened to explain. "Yes, I'm sure. But you know how it is. As we learn more, we find ourselves having to go back over what we've already heard and get clarification."

"Yeah, that makes sense."

"By the way, when did Petar give you these *hints* about your game?" she asked, as if it was an aside.

"On Sunday afternoon, when I was here practising," he replied.

"Was Stewart there at that moment?"

"Well, no; I don't know where he was just then. Petar wouldn't have…" He stopped, a mild look of embarrassment in his eyes.

"Petar wouldn't have advised you about your game in Stewart's presence," said Angela.

Philip's brow cleared and he gave a sheepish grin. "No. I think Stewart would have taken a dim view of his coach giving advice to another player, especially one that's going to be his rival quite often." He attempted an insouciant grin but there was a cloud behind his eyes now. As with the first time she had interviewed him, he found something fascinating to study on the back of his hand. When he looked at Angela again his expression had become what she could only describe as stoic, all joy extinguished.

"But you're also his teammate in the British squad."

"Ah yes, but, you know, he who pays the piper and all that. Stewart was the one paying, and Petar was the piper in this particular case."

Angela nodded as she thought about this for a moment. She couldn't imagine anybody who remembered Petar at the top of his game recognizing him from this description. She found it easy to believe, however, that this is how the Bickerstaffs would view the situation.

"Yes, I suppose so," she said slowly. "That might have put Petar in an awkward position. But from what I hear, he really was very keen on nurturing talent where he recognized exceptional ability. So I expect he just couldn't resist coming out with things here and there that would point someone in the right direction."

"That was Petar all right!"

"You do have exceptional ability, you know, Philip."

"Thank you." Philip couldn't hide the look of gratification on his face but Angela sensed an underlying fear. In the brief silence that followed, Angela realized Philip had no intention of picking up the cue she'd offered him. This hesitancy only served to strengthen her conviction.

"Why aren't you ranked higher, Philip?" she asked, as if the question had just occurred to her and it was an aside to the main thrust of the interview.

She experienced a momentary elation as he flashed her the wide-eyed, frightened look of a rabbit caught in headlights before lowering his head to study his hand again. She was sure she had found the right track. "Oh, I'm a bit of a late developer," he said, with an attempt at casualness. "My game's only been really coming on in the last year or so."

"This is true," agreed Angela, in the manner of a tennis expert. She let another pause elapse between them. "But I find it quite amazing that with your game, and your ability to return, you haven't beaten Stewart since goodness knows when."

Philip again tried to find something interesting about the back of his hand but Angela fixed her eyes on him and waited. Eventually, as if against his will, he brought his face up to hers, pale with fear.

"He's a better player than me?" The proposition came out in a subdued voice quite devoid of conviction.

Angela smiled kindly at him and gently shook her head. "No, he's not," she said. Philip stared wildly around as if looking for some means of escape. Angela sat forward slowly and leaned on the desk.

"What's he got on you, Philip?" she asked.

If Angela had stripped Philip naked in a roomful of people he couldn't have looked more exposed. In the moments after she had spoken, he stared wide-eyed at her and in those eyes she read a strange mixture of panic, despair, fear and, somehow, relief. Then his face began to crumble; he aged visibly about fifteen years and buried his head in his hands with a deep, anguished groan.

Angela allowed a few minutes to pass. Although she was sure Philip was innocent, she was acutely conscious of her primary function at this club and realized that the best way forward was to proceed along official lines. "Did you kill Petar Belic?" she asked.

His head jerked up at once. On his haggard, strained face there was a look that managed to be astonished and horrified at the same time. "No!" he protested.

Angela had guessed what his answer would be. "I have to ask the question," she said. He nodded and slumped back in the chair. She could already sense an easing of the tension in him because he now had a forum where his secret could come out.

"What are you going to do?" he asked.

Inwardly Angela smiled. Philip was speaking as if he had just made a full and frank confession of whatever the issue was between him and Stewart, whereas he'd said nothing and had simply responded to what was, in fact, a shot in the semi-dark on her part.

"I need to hear what you've got to say first," she replied, deliberately vague. In spite of the relief that her shot had gone home, she still didn't know what she was encountering, aware that although she'd caught him off guard he might get his head together any moment, start getting cagey and demand a solicitor be present.

"Oh, it's all so stupid!" he said. But she could see him relaxing. He had the opportunity to let out something that had been bottled up for a long time and wanted to take it.

"Philip," she said, "before you begin, I would like to remind you that I'm investigating a murder and I'm only interested in what might have a bearing on that." She caught and held his eyes. "I work for the Metropolitan Police, not the International Tennis Federation." A responding gleam in his eyes showed that he understood her meaning. He leaned forward onto the desk between them and prepared to unburden himself.

"It all began a couple of years ago. I just can't believe how crass and stupid I was. I'd just been accepted onto the British squad and I was full of it. Full of myself I suppose, as well," he added with a rueful grin. "Anyway, I wasn't meant to be playing, that's why I took the risk. Stewart invited me to this party. It wasn't a party that had anything to do with the tennis world. Vinni had invited Stewart and he asked me if I wanted to come. Really, looking back, I think he just wanted to have someone drive him home, because when he asked me if I wanted to go with him the question of going in my car got mixed in with the invitation. I looked up to him a bit because… well… he was the main man, I suppose; the star with a glittering future and me just the new boy on the team. I think I felt flattered that he'd asked me. I thought, 'Hey, I'm going partying with Stewart Bickerstaff, tennis star!'"

Angela nodded.

"Anyway," continued Philip, "you can guess what happened. There were drugs going round at this do. I didn't notice at first, but as the evening progressed I saw certain people disappear into a room down the hall and when I heard a couple of whispers about 'lines' I guessed they must be doing coke."

"So what did you do?"

"I didn't know what to do at first. I went up to Stewart and got his attention, because he was in the middle of some group, chatting and laughing. Anyway, I managed to whisper my concern and said, 'Should we be here?'"

"How did he react?"

Philip shrugged at the memory. "He didn't seem bothered. He said what 'some' people might be up to in a room down the hall was their business. Then he smiled at me and said, 'Why don't you try some?'"

Philip paused and Angela raised her eyebrows. "What did you say to that?" she asked.

"I said, 'No way, man, that's the pits,' or something like that. I felt outraged, to be honest. I forgot all about my gratitude at being invited in the first place. And I was embarrassed because I didn't know anybody else there. I didn't even know Vinni then; I only knew her as somebody in the fashion industry and a connection of Stewart's. She became a sports promoter later. But Stewart just smiled and told me not to get my knickers in a twist. He said he didn't mean it. He meant if I fancied a little lift, just to give me a buzz, not the hard stuff. All he had to do was ask Vinni. Why not give it a go? That's how he put it. It wouldn't do any harm."

"Oh dear," said Angela. "The slippery slope appears."

"Yeah, got it in one," agreed Philip. I hedged and said what about our tournament? We had one on the go at the time but I'd already played my matches. Of course, Stewart knew this and said it would be perfectly safe as I wouldn't be playing again. Well, I didn't want to appear naïve, or too innocent, and having started off getting outraged about coke I felt it would be a bit silly to get on my high horse about a lesser drug."

"The softening-up process."

"Spot on, and didn't I just fall for it so easily? Well, long story short, I took some speed."

"What happened then?"

"I felt bad about it but told myself that I'd been stupid and should put it out of my mind. But wouldn't you know it? One of the other blokes on the team got some sort of a bug and I had to take his place in a doubles match the next day. I was sitting in the locker room before the match. Stewart came up to me and asked if I'd enjoyed the party last night, and I just said how good it was, thanks again for inviting me. And it started as simply as that. He sat down beside me and said, 'Don't worry about the speed you took last night; I'm not going to say anything.'"

"What did you say?"

"I just said, 'Thanks. Cheers, mate,' but something about the way he said it gave me a really hollow feeling."

I'm sure it did, thought Angela. "Has he ever mentioned it again since?"

Philip looked at her with a very bleak expression on his face.

"Only every time we play," he said.

Chapter Seventeen

"What a piece of work," said Patrick, a couple of hours later, his eyes widening as he listened to Angela recount her conversation with Philip. "Of course, I shouldn't be surprised. I was a policeman myself for far too long to be surprised at anything, but you've got to feel for young Philip, haven't you? Mind you, he does sound a bit innocent, from what you say."

"He's honest," said Angela. "Honest people don't generally think in devious, underhand ways. And they assume the rest of the world doesn't, either. The trouble is that even though a urine sample wouldn't be any good after this amount of time, he was seen to take the drug. So if the incident came to light and an investigation was launched, he couldn't deny it."

"Hmm… bang to rights, poor chap," said Patrick, as he ladled a generous helping of beef stew onto a small pile of new potatoes, and placed her plate on a tray. "Would they still slap a ban on him this long after the event, do you think?"

"Well, Philip seemed to think they would. He's too scared to take the risk and tell them. Look at all that fuss when Andre Agassi confessed to drugs."

"You're right, there was quite a hoo-ha about it, and that was several years after he'd retired."

"It's unfortunate for the innocent, of course, but they do have to be hot on drugs in sport."

"Well, yes, of course they must. He's paying a high price for a moment's weakness." Patrick dished up his own dinner. "Does it have a bearing on the murder, do you think?"

"Well, that's the big question as far as I'm concerned," replied Angela. "But I think I'm beginning to join up the dots."

"Always an absorbing part of any investigation."

They carried their dinners into the living room and settled down in front of the television.

"Oh, look who it isn't," remarked Patrick, gazing at the screen on which could be seen Stewart Bickerstaff and a South African player just coming onto court.

"Hmm," said Angela, acerbically. "If he gets through this, he plays Philip in the quarter-finals." She sighed. "In the car on the way home, I was listening to some commentators having a round table discussion on the tournament and they took it as a foregone conclusion that a quarter-final between Stewart and Philip means we'll have Stewart in the semis. It just makes my blood boil."

"Don't let it get to you, sweetheart."

"It's very difficult not to, sometimes. In any case, it wasn't getting to me as a policewoman. I was getting emotional as a tennis fan with inside knowledge."

Patrick laughed and picked up a bottle of wine. "Here, this will calm you down," he said, pouring her a glass.

They turned their attention to the screen as the unseeded South African player put up a very spirited fight against Stewart. He even managed to win a set, but in the end Stewart's powerful serve knocked the life out of his game, and two hours later Stewart was smilingly talking his way through the highs and lows of the crucial moments in the post-match interview.

"Have you shut up shop for the weekend?" enquired Patrick.

"Well, the incident room will be manned but I don't expect to see the players again before Monday. Things should be easier for me tomorrow, though."

"Oh?"

"I'm finally going to see the security guard who should have been interviewed by Rick and Jim days ago. He's been off sick for most of this week."

"And you don't want to send Jim and Rick?"

"No; I don't really trust them. They skimped on their security guard interviews at the beginning and although they've pulled their socks up now, I'd better take this one on." She looked thoughtfully at Patrick. "Petar staggered into that club at one o'clock in the morning and I think he slightly turned and began a hand wave to this man. I want to check it out myself."

"Very wise," said Patrick.

"And then I really am shutting down for the weekend," she said, "and going to the supermarket."

"Really?" Patrick raised his eyebrows.

"Yup. It's about time I produced a meal around here."

Patrick smiled. The next tennis match grabbed their attention.

Doug Travers lived in a terraced house in Wandsworth. Snowy white net curtains at the front windows and a highly polished brass letter box indicated an assiduous attention to domestic duties on the part of somebody, an impression confirmed by the small, slightly built woman who opened the door to Angela's knock. She wore a spotless white jogging suit and carried a dustpan and brush in one hand. She regarded Angela with profound suspicion.

"Mrs Travers?"

"Yes," said the woman without moving from the spot, utilizing only the muscles in her mouth necessary for the uttering of that one syllable.

"I'm sorry to disturb you, Mrs Travers," continued Angela, "but I wonder if I might have a word with your husband."

"Who wants him?"

"I'm from the police." Angela got her ID out of her bag and held it out to the woman. "I'm leading the investigation into the death of Petar Belic at Wimbledon on Monday last and was hoping that your husband might be able to help me. One of my junior officers called yesterday, I believe."

Mrs Travers sniffed but made no other movement. Angela had met women like Mrs Travers before. In her experience they had always been the wives of habitual criminals, which immediately raised the question in her mind as to how Mr Travers had come by his present job. Behind Mrs Travers, Angela could see ample evidence of her industry. The telephone set square on a highly polished table, pictures behind gleaming glass hung spirit-level straight on the walls, and no dark patches could be seen on the light beige carpet. It was impressive. Mrs Travers clearly had a passion for cleanliness and order, and Angela wondered when she would realize that keeping her out in the street made the place look untidy.

It didn't take long. She stepped back. "You'd better come in."

Determined to rise above the hostility bristling out of Mrs Travers, Angela dispensed one of her most cheerful smiles and crossed the threshold.

Mrs Travers pushed open a door on the right, motioning Angela to enter. "You've got a visitor, Dougie," she called.

In the living room, Angela found herself looking into the bright brown eyes and lively, somehow simian, face of Doug Travers. "Right-oh, Connie," he responded as the door gently closed.

Doug was a small, wiry man, not much bigger than his diminutive wife, and even though obviously incapacitated by his back condition, Angela had the impression that his movements would normally be quick and decisive. This room also bore witness to Connie's relentless cleaning skills but the effects here were overlaid and softened by the things Doug had gathered about himself. A small table at his side contained an ashtray, a pouch of tobacco, cigarette papers, a lighter, the daily paper open at the racing page and a half-full glass of beer. Angela saw that he was watching her as she took in the surroundings, an amused smiled hovering about his mouth.

"I suppose you're the Old Bill," he said. "You took long enough to get here." He grinned in a relaxed manner which only served to emphasize the attractive, monkey-like quality of his features.

"Detective Inspector Angela Costello," she said. "May I sit down?"

"Be my guest, Inspector," he said. Angela sat in an armchair positioned so that she could easily see him. She couldn't help wondering if he had a criminal record. The demeanour of his wife certainly indicated that she had spent a good portion of her marriage either fearful of, or dealing with, visits from the police. Somehow, though, Doug's manner and attitude didn't quite match up to such a history and she was intrigued.

"Yes, I'm sorry it's taken a while," admitted Angela. She looked at him and smiled. She could tell he was enjoying this occasion so she decided that she might as well enjoy it with him. "The thing is," she said, "we like to save the good stuff for later."

He chortled with appreciation, his eyes crinkling in a way that reminded her a little of Patrick when he laughed. "You trying to wind me up, Inspector?" he asked.

"Not at all," replied Angela, taking her notebook out of her bag. She was a little thirsty and wouldn't have minded a cup of tea but was sure that Connie's hospitality didn't stretch to giving refreshment to officers of the law. "So," she began, "I just need to get a few details from you."

"Fire away."

"Right. You're a security guard at Wimbledon," Angela dragged on the words "security guard" a little, and Doug picked up on her cue with a grin.

"You think I've got form, don't you? And you're wondering how come, if that's the case, I've managed to get a job as a security guard. It's always the same. Your lot always assume I've got a criminal record."

Angela suspected that it gave Doug a great deal of pleasure to be saying this to her, so she humoured him a little more. "And have you?" she asked.

He treated her to a wide-open direct gaze. "Nope," he replied, unable to keep a trace of smugness from his voice.

"Actually," said Angela, "I don't know that I would have thought about it at all, but the way your wife greeted me at the door got me thinking. So she's protecting someone who doesn't need protecting?"

Doug gave another grin and shrugged. "She's naturally suspicious, is my Con; door-to-door salesmen, evangelists, the Old Bill… She treats 'em all the same."

Angela nodded and made a business of opening her notebook on the next blank page and taking her pen out of her bag. She wondered idly if Connie had form. She would have wagered the only reason Doug didn't was because he hadn't been caught, and she wouldn't have been at all surprised to learn that he'd at one time done a thriving business selling merchandise of questionable provenance from a lock-up garage somewhere. She shook her head to rid herself of this speculation. She wasn't interested in Doug's past – not beyond the previous Sunday evening, anyway.

"OK, Doug," she said. "We'd better get on." Doug raised himself in his chair but he did so with a careful movement and a slight wince. The bad back seemed genuine enough.

"Did you know Petar Belic?"

"Only in passing; I've been working at the club for a few years now so I've seen him coming and going quite a bit. He'd say, 'Hello, Doug' and I'd say, 'Hello, Mr Belic' and that about wrapped it up."

"How did you get on with him, generally?"

"Always seemed very pleasant."

"Right; you know where they found him, don't you?"

"Yeah, I read it in the papers. On one of the courts – 19; am I right?"

"Yes, at about seven o'clock in the morning. What time did your duty end?"

"Well, they'd managed to get someone to come and relieve me before my shift finished. My back gave me such gyp that night, I just needed to go home. I left the club about four-ish."

"So you did your normal shift until about four in the morning?"

"That's right," confirmed Doug.

"We know that Petar went out for a meal with some companions during Sunday evening. Think back. What time – as accurately as possible – did you last see him?"

Doug smiled as one who had saved his most powerful card until last and knew that it was going to change the course of the game. He gazed around the room as though ruminating on his answer and finally gave Angela another direct stare. "I think it was just about one o'clock on Monday morning," he said.

Angela didn't begrudge him the effect of his words. She opened her eyes wide and stared at him with an amazed expression.

"One o'clock Monday morning?" she repeated. "Where did you see him?"

"Coming through the gate of the club."

"Anybody with him?"

"No."

This tied up exactly with the CCTV footage. Angela gazed at him, trying to keep her expression steady. She took a deep breath.

"Didn't it strike you as odd that he should be coming into the club at that time of night?"

Doug gave a semi-nonchalant shrug. "He had a pass and I knew him well enough. I mean, anybody could forget something and come back for it later."

But at one o'clock? thought Angela. *It would have to be something very important for a person to come back to get it at that time.* "Did anybody come into the club before or after him? It doesn't matter how long before or after."

"No; well, only the normal people you'd expect, of course. Ground staff going home, caterers clearing up and clearing off. Everybody signed in and out as they should, though."

Angela knew those books would be examined minutely on Monday. Furthermore, Rick and Jim would be given the job. Through their negligence, Doug was being interviewed on Saturday morning and not the previous Tuesday.

"I don't suppose you remember who signed in on either side of Petar?" she asked, knowing the question to be a very long shot. To her surprise, for the first time since she had arrived, Doug looked somewhat uncomfortable.

"No. Well… it'll be in the book, won't it?" he said, but his eyes didn't meet hers and he squirmed as much as his bad back would allow. Angela knew the value of silence. After a few moments it paid off and he spoke.

"He didn't sign in," he said, making a great study of his beer. Angela got to it straight away. "Did anybody else not sign in?"

"No." The direct, open gaze was back.

"OK," she said. "Why did you let Petar in without signing?"

Doug paused for a moment as though he knew his answer would surprise her. "I didn't think he could write his name," he answered.

"What?"

"He was as drunk as a skunk," he said.

Chapter Eighteen

"Drunk?" repeated Angela, although she'd heard perfectly clearly.

"Reeling," Doug asserted, nodding his head. "I marked him in the book to show that he was there, like, for Health and Safety. Then I got worried when he didn't come back, but by then my back was playing up something awful and I didn't have any painkillers with me; I'd left them at home."

"Did you tell the person who came to cover you that Petar was in the club somewhere?"

Once again Doug found something absorbing to study in his beer, the level of which, Angela noticed, hadn't moved since she'd arrived. "Well, no, they'd see it from the book, wouldn't they?" After a moment, Doug's slightly defiant eyes met Angela's. "One or two of those blokes over at the club – well, they're always on the lookout for a bit of news or scandal. They can be a bit star-struck; the bigger the name the more they're interested. Gets on my nerves, it does. If I'd said that Petar Belic was sleeping off a bender somewhere about the premises, we'd have had him all over the front pages of the tabloids before you could blink."

Angela stared, speechless, at him before finding her tongue. "You didn't want to tarnish his reputation?" she said eventually.

Doug's expression became distinctly sheepish. "Well... He never did me no harm, old Pete. And the club doesn't need that kind of publicity, does it? Specially not on the first day of the tournament. I've had a decent living out of them for a good few years now."

Angela didn't know whether to go over and give the man a hug for his loyalty or a tongue-lashing for withholding vital information.

Doug grinned. "There are security guards and there are security guards."

Angela chuckled at the momentary rapport between them. She stayed with him for another ten minutes, double-checking people coming into the club before, after or with Petar, but she got nothing new. However, Doug's information meant that the time of death could now be narrowed down.

Petar had still been alive at one o'clock in the morning. Nobody had mentioned him drinking too much in the restaurant and Angela felt pretty certain it wouldn't have gone unremarked. They would check it out, of course, but in all probability he'd left *Le Grand Accueil* sober.

Doug's testimony had him reeling drunkenly through the gates of Wimbledon two hours later. So where had he gone to drink? And, more importantly, had he been alone?

Angela tapped her ballpoint against her teeth. Danny Moore had admitted to dining in a nearby restaurant until about midnight and this had been verified by the waiter who had served him. What if he didn't go straight home? Jim and Rick had spoken to the waiter but maybe another trip was indicated.

She put away her notebook and took her leave, smiling pleasantly in the face of Connie Travers' obvious relief at her departure. Now that she'd spoken with Doug, she understood. Connie's hostility was specific to the events of last Sunday. The tiny, fierce protector must have feared for Doug's job once the details of his oversight came out. Worse, he could have become an accessory to the crime. Angela felt nothing but sympathy for the woman. She hoped the cordial visit had set her mind at rest. She was sure that when she sent Leanne and Derek round on Monday to take an official statement they wouldn't experience the same frosty reception.

The question of Petar Belic's drunkenness occupied her mind all the way back to the club. She wanted a quick peek at the signing-in book for the night of the murder. She was also hoping to find out which guard had replaced Doug.

Deciding first to get a sandwich, she went to the cafeteria. Amazingly, in almost a replay of her previous visit here, she found herself standing near Gracie in the queue.

"Hi, Gracie, how are things?" began Angela, but even as she spoke she could see that all was not well with the other woman. Gracie's previous jauntiness had disappeared and, when she turned towards her, Angela was shocked by the change in her expression. Where there had been ebullience there was only now a downturned mouth in a pale face and sorrowful, lacklustre eyes. However, Gracie came from the generation that tried to put a good face on things, and attempted a smile.

"Oh, hello, Inspector," she said and paused.

"Gracie?" asked Angela in a concerned voice. "Are you all right?"

Gracie nodded and had another brave stab at a smile. "Yes, I'm fine, thank you, Inspect..." She stopped, looked Angela firmly in the face and apparently decided to junk nearly seventy years of social training. "No, I'm not. I'm not all right at all, Inspector," she said, her eyes filling up with tears.

Mentally, Angela postponed her plans. She couldn't leave this woman in distress. "Do you want to talk about it?" she asked. She looked around the crowded cafeteria. Gracie would be mortified to be the centre of attention. "The police have a private room here; we can use that, if you like."

Gracie looked like a drowning woman who'd just been thrown a lifebelt. "Oh, please, Inspector. Edith's still away," she explained through tears that were now rolling down her cheeks, "and I haven't been able to talk about it to anybody."

Angela remembered that Edith was Gracie's lifelong friend and that she was hoping to buy a flat near her, to enjoy her long-awaited retirement.

"Okey-dokey," said Angela, falsely cheerful. "Let's just pay for our food and get out of this crush."

Once in the room, Angela allowed a little time for Gracie to wipe her eyes and compose herself.

"You're very kind, Inspector."

Angela smiled encouragingly at her. "Please call me Angela."

"Angela – what a lovely name. I suppose you'll think me a silly old woman."

"I'm sure I won't," replied Angela in a robust tone. "I don't think for one moment you'd get upset for no reason."

Thus encouraged, Gracie continued. "It's the will, you see."

"The will?"

"Yes, my cousin Margaret's will. Margaret, Stewart's great-aunt."

"Oh, that will!" said Angela. "Yes, you were telling me the other day that she had made provision for you, hadn't she?"

"Yes, well, she had. She had it drawn up a couple of years ago and showed it to me. 'Just to reassure you, Gracie,' she said. 'You see, I've made it clear that you're to have enough for your own place and a pension.' Well…" Tears began to roll down Gracie's face once more. "It seems she made another will about six months ago."

"Oh dear," responded Angela, anticipating what was to come. "And is there no provision for you this time?"

"Oh, Margaret has made provision for me – she would never forget me – but it's not specific. Stewart is instructed to make sure that I'm 'looked after' but the whole estate goes to him."

"Ah… but surely he'll honour your cousin's wishes? I expect he knows about the previous will and about your hopes for your own place, doesn't he?" Even as she spoke Angela realized that things weren't going to be as simple as they seemed.

"Oh, he knows, you can be sure of that, but he's been discussing it with his parents and they're interpreting the provision for me according to their own convenience."

"What does that mean?"

Gracie looked bleakly into Angela's eyes. "Stephen and Julia live in a large house. They're going to make a couple of rooms into a self-contained granny flat for me."

"Ah," replied Angela, trying to keep a note of puzzlement out of her voice. "That won't be so bad, will it?"

"You don't know them like I do, Inspector. I'm going to end up as the unpaid help. It'll start off nice and gently – 'Oh, I'm a bit busy this morning, Gracie, would you be a sweetie and run the vacuum over the living room carpet for me?'" she mimicked.

"Ah," said Angela.

"Before I know where I am, I'll have a set list of jobs to do and they'll tell their friends at their dinner parties, to which I shall never be invited, that they're giving me a sense that I'm still useful and wanted, because old people can become very depressed at the thought that they no longer have a useful function in life."

"It sounds a bit grim," admitted Angela.

Gracie's face was pale. "I'm trapped, Inspector," she said.

"Surely, though," added Angela, trying to find a silver lining in this cloud, "you'll still be able to get out and visit your friend Edith, won't you?"

"Oh, it's not going to be nearly so easy to get over to see her. And I'm certain she won't be able to stay with me. Julia will always have some excuse as to why it's not convenient. Edith was a frequent and very welcome visitor to Margaret's house, and the three of us had such jolly times together. I don't know what Edith's going to say when I tell her."

Gracie's tears were rolling freely down her cheeks again. Angela felt very sorry for her but, apart from showing sympathy, knew there was nothing she could do. A will was a legal document, after all, and she had no doubt that this one was watertight. Gracie's story cast a not very flattering light on the Bickerstaffs, however. Given what she already knew of Stewart, Angela was fast coming to the conclusion that they were a very unpleasant bunch of people, and anyone facing the prospect of living under the same roof as them deserved a great deal of sympathy.

She had no doubt that the late cousin Margaret had indeed doted on Stewart. It was also quite possible that Stewart's frequent visits and the assiduous attention he paid his great-aunt had some influence in the drawing up of the latest will. But unfortunately, it didn't sound as though anybody could do anything about it.

Angela made them both a cup of coffee and listened to more stories of happier times with Edith and Margaret. After about an hour, seeming much more composed than when she had arrived, Gracie left, thanking Angela profusely for her kindness.

Discovering that Doug's replacement on his night shift wasn't on duty that day, Angela decided she shouldn't be either, and went out to where her car was parked.

Three hours later she was gazing with unconcealed affection across the dining room table at Patrick, as he tucked appreciatively into a *sole bonne femme* she had just prepared.

"Drunk?" he said, unconsciously repeating the words she used that very morning to Doug Travers.

"Yes, which ties up with the staggering on the CCTV shot. It's very odd because at no point in the investigation so far has anybody said anything about him drinking a great deal in the restaurant. That's the trouble; we've got a black hole here. We've still got that gap between him leaving the restaurant and being found. In theory he could have gone somewhere, or even gone home, and got legless." Angela frowned in frustration. "That doesn't seem to fit in with the picture I have of him, though." She looked up to find Patrick grinning at her. "What?" she asked.

"You're right. It doesn't tie up with what you know of him. I think the chances are that he was stone cold sober."

Angela's eyebrows shot up into her forehead. "What? But he was staggering, drunk as a skunk. Why would Doug lie?"

"I don't suppose he did," replied Patrick, smiling.

Angela narrowed her eyes at him. "What are you playing at, Paddy? There'll be no dessert until you tell me."

"Oo-er," he laughed. "It's very simple. I don't know from which case I picked up this snippet, but the fact is that if somebody receives an overdose of insulin they'll reel about and get woozy, exactly as if they were drunk."

"Oh wow! Doctor Costello, you're a star."

"I do my best."

Angela narrowed her eyes as she thought through the implications. "I wonder if it's possible to speak to a doctor today."

Patrick feigned a hurt look. "You don't trust my medical expertise?"

"Idiot," she smiled back at him. "OK then, how long after the injection would this woozy state last?"

"Ah, there you have me." He grinned. "OK, I give up. You need to talk to a proper doctor to get the full information. As it happens…"

"Yes?"

"The pathologist on the case and I have played our share of squash together and I've got his mobile number. I might just reveal it to you, if you're nice to me."

Angela bunched her fists. "I'll throw you to the ground and wrestle your phone off you."

"Oh, result! I didn't realize you'd be that nice. I tell you what. I'll give you the number if you promise to throw me to the ground and wrestle with me anyway."

"You're on," laughed Angela. "Of course, this means…"

"That the insulin was administered outside the club and he then staggered in. You're absolutely right. This dessert – is it that chocolate mousse I saw you putting in the fridge earlier?"

"Yes." She beamed at him. "Take a double helping, darling."

Chapter Nineteen

"OK, everybody, may I have your attention please?"

Angela planted herself in front of her team the following Monday morning. Every eye immediately turned towards her.

"Right," she said, looking round at them all with a big smile on her face. "What's one of the most puzzling things about this case?"

The team hesitated, looking at each other.

"Come on," she said, enjoying the suspense. "It's not a trick question."

"How on earth the murderer put the body on the court, guv?" ventured Leanne.

"Well done, that woman!" exclaimed Angela. "Well, I had a bit of a breakthrough over the weekend and I'm now 99 per cent certain I know who put Petar's body on the court."

She gazed round at them for dramatic effect, relishing the moment as her team shifted in their seats, straightening up and looking expectant.

"Hey, that's good news," said Rick, speaking for them all. "So who *did* put his body there?"

"He did."

This was greeted by a stunned silence.

"Er…" began Jim, after a pause. "I don't quite get it. Are you saying…"

"That's exactly what I'm saying, Jim," replied Angela. "Petar had been shot full of insulin and he knew that he was dying."

"How did he know?"

Angela felt slightly irritated. "Because…" She stopped. Jim had made a good point. She thought for a moment. "He would have known that he'd received an injection and I presume he'd guess the perp wasn't trying to pump him full of vitamins."

"The murderer could even have told him," suggested Rick. "You know how some people like to taunt others."

"That's true," said Angela. "We've got no way of knowing what happened between the murderer and Petar leading up to the death. If someone sticks a needle in you, though, you can be pretty sure they mean to harm you. It looks as if the perpetrator cut off any means of getting help, which is why we still haven't found his mobile phone." Angela waited a moment while her team digested this.

"So he staggered drunkenly, because that would be the effect of the insulin, into the club and got himself to Court 19, where it all began for him at Wimbledon. He must just have had enough strength and awareness left to stagger to the centre and collapse." She looked around at the team and waited through another silence.

Rick spoke first this time. "But why would he do that? It seems a theatrical sort of gesture."

"Oh, I know why," Gary cut in. "If you find a bloke who's slumped in his car or whatever you just think he's injected himself."

"Yeah, under those circumstances you'd just think, 'Oh, what an awful shame,'" added Leanne, "but he wanted the death investigated as a murder, which is exactly what's happened."

"You've hit the nail on the head," agreed Angela with enthusiasm, but at the same time quelling a sense of frustration that it was two of the most junior officers on the team who were joining up the dots in this picture. "All right," she continued, "what we really need to know is what happened before he staggered into the club. For all we know, he was sitting in the car with the perp. Maybe the murderer planned to drive him away somewhere and bury the body. We've now got to look much more closely at what was happening outside the front entrance. It can't have happened too far away, and one of those tennis fans camping overnight might have seen something. Yes, I *know!*" she said as an involuntary groan broke out from all of them. "Questioning them all is a bit of a slog but it's essential, so get to it, everyone. Derek, would you pop out and get me a coffee, please?"

"OK, guv," said Derek, rising and moving across the room. Angela watched Rick and Jim heading in the same direction.

"Just a minute, you two," she called as they reached the door. "I want a word with you."

Rick, she noticed, looked somewhat abashed, but Jim was feigning a bewildered air as if he had no idea why Angela would want a word in private. She waited until the others had left and the door had closed behind them before she spoke.

"Do you know where I got this information?" she asked them. It disappointed her that a frown of feigned puzzlement appeared on Jim's brow. She realized that he was going to try to bluff it out. Rick redeemed himself somewhat by not trying to be obtuse.

"You've been doing some more digging over the weekend, Angela," he said.

"Yes," she said, keeping her tone serious. "I was digging in a field I originally told you two to turn over at the beginning of the week. I went and saw Doug Travers, who was sent home sick in the wee small hours of Sunday." She fixed her eyes on both of them in turn. "I've known about your corner-cutting all week, which is why I took this on myself. I hope you take this as a lesson learned because I promise you, if you ever let a vital witness fall off your radar again, you'll be back directing traffic. Do I make myself clear?"

"Ah, Angela, we – " began Jim, but Rick interrupted him.

"Yes, we get it, Angela. We're sorry. It won't happen again."

"See that it doesn't," she said, noting that Jim could only bring himself to mutter something incomprehensible, looking mutinous. She had hopes for Rick, but was beginning to wonder how Jim had got promoted to detective sergeant. Once the door had closed behind them, she sat down. She needed to think for a while.

Back to basics, she said to herself. She opened her pad and wrote two words: *Cui bono?*

As instructed, Jim had got a copy of the will and it had been waiting on Angela's desk when she came in that morning. Petar's children, Milan, Lucija and Sofija were his main beneficiaries, with legacies to his siblings, a Croatian Catholic relief organization and a couple of sporting charities. As things stood, Una didn't benefit at all from Petar's death.

She wrote Danny Moore's name down next. He was Petar's business partner and claimed Petar as his best friend. Well, actually, thought Angela, Tara's evidence didn't contradict that fact. They *were* good friends and Danny *had* been very upset about the failure of some scheme in which he'd invested. From the sound of things he had only wanted the use of the money in the short term. She wrote the phrase *financial gain/ruin* on her pad, circled it, then covered it with a large *X*.

Underneath that doodle she wrote the name "Lavinia Bannister", sat back and stared into space. She wrote another word, *cocaine*, beside Lavinia's name, then attached a question mark. Maybe Petar had threatened to go public on her predilection for the drug. She crossed that out with an impatient gesture. To whom would he have revealed the details? So many people seemed to know of her habit that the prospect of exposure hardly constituted a threat.

A memory pulled at the corners of her consciousness. Her ballpoint paused in its mid-air circular motion. Who had been talking about Lavinia recently? Suddenly she sat bolt upright and stared, mesmerized, at the wall opposite.

Philip Turnbull. Just three days previously he had sat in this very room and confessed that a couple of years ago he had received his first (and last) upper from Lavinia. They were at a party to which he had been invited by Stewart.

Galvanized, Angela wrote Philip Turnbull's name on the page and Stewart Bickerstaff's next to it. Then she wrote Petar Belic. She stared at the names for a long while as if willing something to spring out from the ink and paper.

Lavinia Bannister – not the most likely of suspects. The *modus operandi* suggested careful, calculated planning and she didn't seem to fit that profile. But Angela stopped and thought. She kept letting the jerky, distraught woman-with-a-habit image prejudice her. Lavinia Bannister was also a successful businesswoman and Angela knew that she had to keep the whole picture in mind. If she had killed Petar, she wouldn't be the first person to kill somebody she loved because the relationship had ended, even allowing for the public display of grief to be genuine. Angela thought that in spite of the woman's posturing and histrionics, it probably was.

Her claim to be at home alone meant that she had no verifiable alibi. Angela frowned. She didn't like the notion of Lavinia as the perpetrator but she couldn't be ruled out of the list of suspects.

After a long moment during which she barely noticed Derek coming back into the room, placing a cup of coffee on the desk and leaving again, she carefully brought down the ballpoint with the intention of scoring through the name "Philip Turnbull" on the grounds that there was no point in wasting public money chasing rank outsiders. But she paused.

No, Angela, she thought. *You leave everybody in the frame, even if you think they're cute. And talking of "cute"...* She looked at Danny Moore's name again.

She looked at the page. The names Stewart Bickerstaff, Lavinia Bannister, Philip Turnbull and Danny Moore danced around Petar Belic. Angela sat back and stared at what she'd written until the ink started floating before her eyes. OK, checking up on Lavinia was tricky because even if they couldn't place her going home on the underground, they had no evidence of her being back at the club around one in the morning. They still had to wait for the information on Bel-Mor's finances, and Philip didn't look a likely contender at the moment but that could change. The only person she could go to work on right now was Stewart, and he had an alibi.

She blinked and became aware of a faint tingling sensation pulsing through her. *What if?* she thought to herself. *What if Petar had somehow found out about Stewart's hold over Philip? What if he had discovered more?*

Stewart's presence at that party and his relaxed attitude to what was going on there revealed a connection between him and drug-taking circles at least.

Angela paused for a moment as a childhood memory stirred. What did her dad used to say? "Show me the company you keep and I'll tell you who you are."

It was Stewart who, by Philip's account, had first made the suggestion that Philip try some. The fact that tennis authorities had a whole raft of rules, regulations and procedures for dealing with drug misuse showed them to be only too aware that in tennis, as elsewhere, there was a ready market for such substances. And here, while unburdening himself of his tale of woe, Philip had shone a light on the fact that Stewart had access to this market. Perhaps it went further. He had had no qualms about suggesting a "little lift" to Philip. Perhaps he had progressed since then. Market forces were the same in the drugs world as in the high street. Wholesalers need retailers and the retailers have to be close to their customers.

Had Stewart become a retailer? And if so, did Petar know about it?

She sat motionless, her coffee forgotten as her mind raced away. Petar cared about tennis. He cared about the integrity of the game and the welfare of the young players coming into it. His desire, passion even, to nurture young talent had been established beyond doubt for many years. Would such a person sit idly by if he'd discovered Stewart's involvement in drugs? She was certain that the answer would be a very resounding *no*.

And what about Stewart blackmailing Philip? If Petar had known about it, Angela was certain he wouldn't have let the matter rest. To have a gifted young player held back by such means went against everything Petar had stood for in the sport.

And how would Stewart react to the possibility not only of the curtailment of his activities but the exposure of them? Stewart was a supremely arrogant young man. He liked a rich, lavish lifestyle and he liked being associated with success; hence the out-of-form Joanna Clarke put aside for the highly ranked and much more glamorous Candy Trueman. The newspapers promoted him as the darling of British tennis and he enjoyed playing up to the image. He thought very well of himself and liked everybody to share that opinion. What was the expression Danny had used when she went to see him? "He swans around the circuit looking athletic." It was very apt.

But in reality Stewart was ruthless, as his treatment of Philip proved. He didn't care how he won, as long as he won. Angela's mind went to Petar. He wouldn't have been able to turn a blind eye to what lay behind Stewart's public persona. He would have had to act on it. She recalled her interview with Danny Moore. He'd made it clear that Petar had plans to terminate his contract with Stewart. Una Belic had later hinted at the same thing. In both cases the explanation given was that

Petar had felt he'd taken Stewart as far as he could, but what if he had another reason?

There was one objection to Stewart as a suspect, though. As the fatal dose of insulin entered Petar's system, Stewart was tucked up in bed with Candy Trueman.

Hmm, thought Angela and laughed to herself. *Come on, you can't want to eliminate Philip because you think he's cute yet finger Stewart because he's not craggy enough for you. Think like an investigating officer, woman.*

In spite of the whimsy in her thoughts, Angela discovered that her breath was coming in short, shallow gasps. She could feel the trail narrowing now and that was always an exciting moment in any investigation. She looked back at the top of the page where she had written her first question.

Cui bono?

OK, Angela, don't get carried away, she said to herself. *We've got the slightly unstable Lavinia Bannister anguished at the loss of her prestigious lover, Danny Moore facing financial ruin, Stewart Bickerstaff looking at professional disgrace and Philip, who's in the frame for opportunity, at least, but I haven't found a motive for him. Besides all of which we haven't yet discovered the means for any of them. There are some very important "ifs" in those propositions at the moment. We've got to concentrate our efforts and see which one turns into a certainty.*

Chapter Twenty

Right, she said to herself. *There's not a lot I can do about Danny Moore until Leanne comes back to me but I'm in a very good place to get a closer look at Stewart Bickerstaff.* She thought back to the beginning of the previous week, remembering her strong sense of something left unspoken when Stewart Bickerstaff's name came under discussion. She'd sensed it with Joanna, with Philip and, to a lesser extent, with Tessa Riordan. Tessa was a very recent addition to the circle but she seemed to be an astute woman. Perhaps she had observed elements in the relationship between Philip and Stewart that puzzled her.

Philip and Tessa had been seen openly around the place holding hands in the past few days and the gossip columnists had already caught on to the budding relationship.

Angela knew one thing for sure: nobody would prise information out of these people easily. They all valued their careers very highly and not one of them would be willing to do anything to damage someone else's; with the possible exception of Stewart, of course.

Angela dialled Gary and asked him to track down Una Belic. Within a few minutes he called her back.

"Mrs Belic is at the tournament today, guv. Do you want me to find her?"

"Here? Really? I find that quite surprising." Angela looked at her watch. Play had already started on the outside courts, so Una might well be watching a game with her mobile switched off. "Yes, please, Gaz. Would you ask her if she could spare me a few minutes?"

"No probs," came the cheerful reply.

Twenty minutes later, Una Belic took the chair opposite Angela, and Gary was heading for the side of the room.

As before, Una looked very elegant and cool, today in a cream seersucker shirt and bottle green trousers. A slide held back her thick, chestnut hair from her face. "Thank you for coming in to see me, Una. How are things?"

"Pretty ghastly most of the time, but I can't bear being stuck in the house."

"Ah, I did wonder. But I didn't expect you to be at the club, especially not so soon."

"I'm here on business, in fact – a job I was asked to do several weeks ago. I have a commission from a women's magazine for a behind the scenes look at the tournament. I know I'm reminded of Petar round every corner here but somehow, surprisingly, it helps."

"Right, I see. I'll try not to take up too much of your time."

Una smiled and made a small inconsequential motion with her hand. "Not at all, Inspector; I hope the investigation is going well."

"We're making progress," said Angela, "which is why I wanted to speak to you again. You must know what it's like; questions and answers just produce more questions that need answers."

"I can imagine that, yes."

"I'll get straight to it. You dropped a hint last time I spoke to you about Petar planning to terminate his professional relationship with Stewart. I wonder if you'd care to be more specific." She looked very pointedly at the open notebook on Gary's knees. "I do understand there might be client confidentiality issues here *vis-à-vis* the Bickerstaffs and, for the moment, I'm willing to make this off the record if you wish. Though I have to warn you, you could tell me something that I might need to use later in evidence."

Amusement glinted in Una's eyes. "My goodness, you have been busy, haven't you?" she said. "No, that's all right, Inspector. I'm happy to have this conversation recorded."

"OK then. For the record, did Petar plan to finish with his job of coach to Stewart Bickerstaff?"

"Yes."

"Why?"

Una relaxed a little more in her chair before speaking. "There were a couple of reasons. It's as I hinted before: they got on well enough but Petar was increasingly frustrated with Stewart's attitude. It's going to sound catty, Inspector, but Stewart's full of himself; as far as tennis goes, a bit of a superannuated teenager in that he thought he knew it all, thought he'd already arrived, if you see what I mean. He didn't listen to Petar and I think that fundamentally Stewart and his parents wanted the prestige of having the great Petar Belic as coach more than they thought Stewart needed coaching." She looked at Angela with a wry grin. "They'd fallen for their own publicity, I'm afraid."

"Ah."

"Yes. You know the expression 'trophy girlfriend'?"

"Yes."

"Well, Petar told me once that he felt the Bickerstaffs regarded him as their trophy servant."

"What?" Angela was shocked, but then an image of Cousin Gracie floated into her mind and on reflection she found herself able to go along with Una's view of the Bickerstaffs easily enough.

"Yes. Petar had no arrogance but he knew his own worth and I think he'd become fed up with them."

Angela allowed a small pause before speaking. "And the other reason?" she asked eventually.

"Ah, yes. I knew I'd be asked this eventually," said Una. Her voice took on a sombre note. "This is much more serious."

Angela leaned forward a little and rested her chin on her hands. "Oh?" she queried invitingly.

On the other side of the desk, Una's brow creased as she gathered her thoughts before meeting Angela's eyes with a clear, steady gaze. "Stewart has been doing a nice little sideline, peddling uppers and cocaine."

Angela raised her eyebrows and exhaled slowly. Partly this was to acknowledge the seriousness of the allegation but also it was partly relief that her guesswork had been correct. "Would you like to enlarge on that statement?" she asked.

"I'll gladly tell you all I know, Inspector," Una replied, "and everything I think. But, as you can imagine, it's all hearsay. How you're ever going to get any evidence is beyond me."

"Maybe, but I still need to hear it."

"OK, well, Petar wasn't a naïve man, but drugs weren't on his radar. He didn't touch them, wouldn't have touched them and couldn't have told you the signs of their use." She gave another wry grin. "Anybody else in a relationship with someone like Lavinia Bannister would already have been asking themselves months ago what she did in her spare time, but it's entirely typical that it didn't occur to Petar. He only asked her outright after a conversation with Danny made him suspicious."

"He always struck me as someone who favoured a direct approach."

"Oh yes, straight to the heart of the matter – that was Petar. As I say, he asked her if she did coke – that's what Danny had told him – and she, not reading him nearly as well as she should have done, given the amount of time she'd known him by then, thought he was trying to score and offered to get him some."

An involuntary laugh burst from Angela and Una smiled. "Yes, I know," she said. "You just couldn't make it up, could you?"

"What was Petar's reaction?"

"Well, horror, frankly, which is exactly what I would have expected. Petar and I had started meeting again by this time, but we'd kept it very quiet and were taking it mega-slowly. Up until then, Lavinia probably had every reason to suppose everything in their love life was just fine. From that moment, though, he pursued our reconciliation with more vigour. And of course, the one thing she never did get to grips with..."

"Yes?"

"Petar didn't want any sniff of drugs within a million miles of the children."

"Ah, of course."

"So really, on reflection, I think the final nail went into the coffin of their relationship there and then."

"When did this happen?"

Una narrowed her eyes and stared at the ceiling as she thought about this. "Within the last four weeks," she said eventually.

"Right, so where does Stewart's little sideline come in?" asked Angela. All she was hearing about Lavinia, though interesting, didn't add anything new to what seemed to be common knowledge anyway.

"Yes, I'm sorry; it must seem that I'm taking the circuitous route to the point but Lavinia is the connecting link, really."

Thinking back over Philip's account of the party and wondering if Una knew about Stewart blackmailing Philip, Angela waited.

"Stewart introduced Petar to Lavinia; that's how they met, at a party – I think the Bickerstaffs and the Bannisters have known each other for years. I believe that party would have been a couple of years ago. Anyway, cut to the present day, Petar was already tiring of Lavinia when he learned of her habit, so he told her the relationship was over. To be fair to her, I think she genuinely cared for him; she didn't see him as a trophy boyfriend, but her lifestyle is so fast and superficial that she wouldn't have been able to hold on to him even without the drugs issue. Unfortunately she took it badly when he finished with her, and she's not someone to take no for an answer easily, so she was clinging on and on and on. She'd got into this thing of 'we need to talk', 'we can work this out'."

Angela nodded, remembering how Danny Moore had said more or less the same thing.

"Petar came round to me a few weeks ago because he wanted to talk things over with me. In fact, he came to me from Lavinia's after she'd offered to score for him. Part of him was disgusted, part of him wanted to laugh out loud, but for the most part he felt very angry – and uncertain how to act for the best."

"What had happened?"

"Well, he'd tried to make it clear that their relationship was finally over, but since he also told her that he'd realized about her habit, she got the idea that he wanted to finish with her because of that – or at least, she kidded herself that was the reason. So she immediately went into an 'I'll stop the coke' speech. She insisted that she only did a bit now and then and that it wouldn't be a problem to stop. Reckoned she'd had enough of it anyway, if you can believe that."

"Did Petar believe it?"

"No, he didn't. He knew as well as anybody else that you can't kick a well-established habit just like that. In any case, she showed no disposition to change her lifestyle. She just wanted to keep Petar and carry on as before. He said that she should seek help for her own good and she, probably trying to impress him with her sincerity, said that she was determined, and to prove it she was going to ring her connection right away and tell him. So that's what she did, apparently. She rang someone and told them she wanted to cut the habit and that she was going to get herself clean."

Angela looked at Una with a quizzical expression.

"Yes," agreed Una, "it might seem a bit melodramatic but I have to keep reminding myself that she actually did love him. Petar wasn't very impressed by the pantomime, believing it to be just that. But something else troubled him. While she was making the call he could hear a bit of the voice on the other end of the phone. He didn't recognize it, as such, but there was something tantalizingly familiar about it. He suddenly realized that he would surely have met Lavinia's connection at a party somewhere. So she ended the call and they talked a bit more, and Petar again tried to get it through to her that they were finished anyway. To cut to the chase, she had to go to the loo and, so he told me later, he was just waiting for her to come back into the room. After a moment he suddenly found himself really curious about the voice he'd heard and he thought: well, why not?"

"Ah."

"Yes. She hadn't made any other calls since then, so it was just a case of checking the last number dialled. He got the shock of his life when he saw Stewart's number on the screen."

Chapter Twenty-one

Angela went back to the incident room, fed Una's latest statement into the computer and clicked on "save". Leanne and Derek were on the other side of the room, Leanne tapping away in front of a computer, Derek leaning over her. The information on the screen was taking up all their attention but something about their posture – he bending over her in a very relaxed manner, she leaning back slightly towards him – made Angela wonder if an office romance was brewing. She went over to them.

"How are things going with the Bel-Mor questions, Leanne?"

"I've set up the enquiry, guv, but the Financial Investigation Unit hasn't got back to me yet."

"OK, we've got no choice but to sit it out. There's no need to panic. I don't think any of our suspects are going anywhere."

"Who have we got in the frame?" asked Derek.

"The front runners are Lavinia Bannister, Danny Moore, Philip Turnbull and Stewart Bickerstaff... What?" she asked as she saw Leanne's mouth turn down at the corners.

"Oh, I wouldn't like to think it's Stewart. He's cute."

"Cute? No way!" exclaimed Derek with alacrity, making Angela wonder even more about them.

She grinned. "Yes, and I believe Dr Crippen was a charming man, but it didn't stop him killing his wife."

Leanne laughed. "Yeah, I know; I'm not thinking like a police officer, am I?"

"Not to worry," said Angela, moving away. "Just let me know when the FI unit has been in touch."

"Will do."

Angela had a sudden thought and turned back to them. "Oh, Derek, I've got a little job for you."

Derek straightened up. "Yes?"

"I need the calls to and from Lavinia Bannister's mobile checked, going back over the last, say, five weeks. Her number's in the system."

"No probs. I'll get on to it."

Angela went and sat in her office feeling rather pleased with the junior members of her team. It was only when she considered the two sergeants that she found herself sighing. But she hadn't been there for more than five minutes when she had cause to revise her opinion.

She was just debating whether to go to the coffee machine when Rick and Jim appeared in the doorway of Angela's office looking pleased with themselves.

"Hello, you two," she said, beckoning them into the room. "Had a result, have you?" They found perches for themselves, one on the edge of the desk and one in the chair.

"It's Gary's mate in uniform, guv," said Jim.

"Martin Pearse, yeah."

"Oh right, is that his name? Well, anyway, he's kept his ears open, specially near that bunch of girls who spell out Stewart's name by the letters on their T-shirts. He's got the hots for one of them if you ask me, but the upshot is that we've got a sighting on Belic's car round about half-past midnight, Sunday last, in Church Road, very close to the club."

"Ah! Great stuff! Tell me more."

Jim and Rick looked from one to the other. "We can do better than that. We've spoken to the girl who wears the 'W'."

"And what does Miss W say?"

"She can tell you herself, Angie, she's downstairs. Her name's Michelle Davies."

"Oh, that's terrific. Show her into the interview room. Oh, and ask Leanne to stop what she's doing for now and sit in with me. I'll be down in a jiff."

Michelle Davies, a large green "W" emblazoned across her frontage, was chatting with Leanne when Angela arrived. She displayed no qualms at the turn of events and even seemed pleasurably excited to be in a police interview room. Angela introduced herself and sat down at the table opposite Michelle.

"Thank you for coming in to see us. Did you want a cup of tea or coffee?"

"No, I'm all right, thanks," said the young woman, pulling a bottle of water out of her bag, which was on the floor.

"OK. I know you've told your story to the two detectives who brought you here, but I'd like you to go through it again, if you don't mind, Michelle."

"Sure, anything to help you; well, to help Stewart as well, really," said Michelle.

"Help Stewart?"

Michelle smiled and looked a little embarrassed. "Yeah, well, I know you have to suspect everyone but Petar got out of the car and went into the club and Stewart drove off, so he can't be a suspect. I mean, we all know he couldn't possibly have done it anyway, it's nonsense. But the police have to have a different attitude, don't they?"

Angela breathed in and out carefully a couple of times and kept her voice neutral. "Yes, indeed, Michelle; you're right. We have to check all the facts very carefully. Why don't you tell me the whole story from the beginning?"

Michelle settled herself more comfortably in her seat and took a gulp of water. "Yeah, well, Chloe and I had a bit of a row. I'm sharing a tent with Chloe."

"This is round in Wimbledon Park, right?"

"Yeah. So I'd gone off… well, in a huff, to be honest, and I ended up in Church Road. It was a bit scary 'cos it was so quiet. There's nobody around at that time of the night – well, morning, really."

"What time was this, Michelle?"

Michelle screwed up her face in the effort to remember. "Gone midnight," she said eventually. "Maybe nearer one o'clock; I was just beginning to regret flouncing off when I saw Petar's car parked a little way from the entrance to the club, so I went towards it. I mean, if I could have spoken to Petar it would be something to tell the others about when I got back."

"You're sure it was Petar's car?"

"Oh yes, no question. We've watched Petar and Stewart coming and going at a lot of tournaments. We know their cars very well. We know their numbers backwards, and the numbers of their previous cars."

"Right, so what happened then?"

"Just as I set off towards them, the driver's door opened and Petar got out and went off into the club." Michelle paused and her brow furrowed. "It was odd."

"Why, what was odd about it? I mean, I understand you weren't expecting to see him there at all at that time in the morning, but did something else strike you?"

Michelle thought some more about what she had seen. "Hmm… he didn't look well," she said finally. "He kind of staggered a bit as he got out of the car."

Angela nodded, thinking of the image she had seen from the CCTV footage. To this young woman he hadn't looked well; by the time Doug Travers saw him, he'd seemed reeling drunk. She took comfort from the fact that it was probably too late to do anything by then anyway. "What did you do then?" she asked.

"I went up to the car, but before I could get really close Stewart had shifted across into the driver's seat and he drove off. The car shot away from the kerb really quickly. I was really disappointed because I'm sure Stewart would remember me from other tournaments, and to have been able to say 'hello', well, that really would have been something to take back to the others."

Angela nodded. Hadn't she once felt exactly the same about Petar? "How did Stewart seem to you? Were you able to get any idea?"

"It's difficult to say, really. I didn't get a good look at his face." Michelle was frowning down at the table in the effort of concentration and didn't see the sudden anguished glances of frustration that Angela and Leanne threw at each other.

Angela, her heart sinking, kept her voice level. "What exactly did you see?" she asked.

"Well, just the back of his head, really, but I knew it was him. I could tell, you know. I just knew it was him, even with the hood."

"The hood? He was wearing a hoodie?" Angela wondered if it was possible for this interview to get any worse.

"Yeah," beamed Michelle. "He's got a couple and he looks really good in them. He wore this one a couple of times when he came to Queens the other week."

"And he had this hood up?"

"Yeah." Michelle had a big smile on her face. She was clearly enjoying the sense of importance she was getting from being brought into this interview room, and even happier that she could establish Petar was alive and in the club somewhere before his car had been driven away.

"Michelle, do you think there's any chance that it might have been someone other than Stewart?"

Michelle's mouth dropped open. "Someone else? Who else would it have been in Petar's car?"

"I'm not sure but a lot of the players wear similar hoodies. Could you say for certain that it was Stewart?"

"Well... well, now that you put it like that... I suppose you might be right. I mean, I've seen him arrive for matches or practice so often with Petar – in Petar's car, I mean. But, well, I didn't actually get a good look at his face." Michelle spoke reluctantly, disappointment etched clearly onto her features. *Poor Michelle*, thought Angela, *your dreams of being a key witness are sinking fast.* She supposed that was one of the problems with celebrity. The public built up a picture of somebody's private life based on just the little bit they were able to observe. Angela pasted a smile onto her face, thanked Michelle for her help and told Leanne to arrange for her to be taken back to her friends once she had signed her statement. As soon as she had gone, Rick and Jim appeared in the room

"Well?" asked Rick.

"No-go, unfortunately."

"Oh?"

"It was a good try, chaps. It looked promising for a moment, but she's a fan who imagines herself in love with Stewart, and when you strip away the 'yes, of course it was him, I'd know him anywhere, even from the back of his head', you won't have much left."

"The back of his head?" queried Jim.

Angela nodded. "With his hood up."

"What a bummer," added Rick.

Angela sighed. "Yeah, she imagines it was Stewart because she wants to have seen Stewart so that she can boast to her friends about it. But what she actually saw is someone from behind wearing the same sort of warm-ups that she's seen on Stewart. In fact," she continued, "she's just the sort of witness that defence barristers practise their demolition techniques on."

"In any case, doesn't Stewart Bickerstaff have an alibi?" said Rick.

"Yep – at home, or rather at Candy's place, tucked up in bed with her."

"I wouldn't say no to an alibi like that," said Jim.

"Hello, been watching the tennis, have we, Jim? Seen the gorgeous Candy playing? I thought you were a sharp-pointy-object-and-a-cork-board type of man."

"Yeah, but those little dresses they wear... I mean, her legs; have you seen her legs?"

"It beats a pub with a load of beery blokes, doesn't it?" Angela laughed. "Anyway, what Michelle told us helps us a bit. We've now got a sighting outside the club to tie up with the CCTV footage from inside, and we know that Petar was there in his own car."

"Yeah, and not alone," said Rick. "If Stewart was at home in bed, who else do we have that's likely?"

"Well, there isn't a wide field. Danny Moore was possibly in the area, and we'd have to include Lavinia Bannister, whom nobody saw after she left the restaurant... What?" she asked as she saw Jim goggling at her.

"Lavinia Bannister? But she's... she's..."

"Yes?" *I think I'm behaving with commendable patience,* thought Angela.

"Well, she's a woman."

Angela fought down a wave of irritation. "Think about it, Jim. Lavinia isn't so very short; OK, she's a lot shorter than Danny and Stewart, but the person in the car was sitting down and that can sometimes make it difficult to judge."

"Oh, yeah, yeah, of course; I get you."

"Hood up, not a good view of the face; we can't rule out that it was a woman in the car with Petar."

"It could also have been that other bloke – Philip Turnbull."

"You're absolutely right," said Angela, her heart sinking as she said it.

"Nah," said Jim. "He was tucked up in bed as well, wasn't he, with that other American player, Tessa whatsername?"

"No. Think back over his initial interview," said Angela. *Read and digest, Jim,* she thought. "He wasn't in bed with Tessa." Angela almost laughed out loud at the bemusement on his face. "Tessa tries to live her life as an obedient daughter of the Church. She's not into jumping into bed with her boyfriends. He left to go back to his place after a snog – well, after coffee and a chat. That's how he put it, anyway. Philip has no alibi, either."

"What motive would he have, though, Angie?"

"Ah, there's the rub. I haven't found one yet; keep digging."

"Will do," they muttered as they edged back through the door.

Angela sat in her office for a long time after they had left. She thought very deeply about Philip as a suspect. She had kept to herself so far Philip's off-the-record confession to taking speed. It had not seemed germane to the investigation at the time. Things looked different now. That information might have to enter the arena.

Both Stewart and Lavinia had been at that party and, now that Angela came to think of it, it must have been close to the time when Petar and Lavinia had first got together.

Look at it from Philip's point of view, she said to herself, and concentrated on doing just that.

Stewart and Lavinia were party to Philip's fall from grace. Almost immediately the blackmail started, and at virtually the same time Petar and Lavinia become an item.

Angela paused as the idea took hold, then allowed her mind to run on to the next logical thought.

Supposing Philip came to the conclusion that they were all in on it together, all laughing at him behind his back as he struggled up the rankings, not getting very far. The helpful snippets of advice that he claimed to have received from Petar would then become derisive scraps thrown to a pathetic dog. It could gnaw at a man, that kind of situation. It could build up inside him, smouldering away for months and years until it became too much to bear.

If that was the case though, why just kill Petar?

Suddenly Angela broke into a cold sweat.

If the murderer was Philip, perhaps he would be going after Lavinia and Stewart next.

Chapter Twenty-two

OK, let's not panic, thought Angela to herself. *It could have happened that way; it's a possible scenario. We'll need to check his alibi. Proceed with caution, D.I. Costello. Let's see what else we've got.*

She sat for a while, allowing a whole collage of images from the last week to float through her memory She ran snatches of remembered conversation like a video tape before her mind's eye.

Automatically, even as she reconstructed everything she had noticed, every detail she could unearth, she found herself writing down and drawing rings around three words: *Restaurant, Sunday* and *Evening*. In thinking about where everybody had gone after the meal, she realized that she hadn't thought too much about what had happened before it. It had seemed the usual sort of occasion. Friends and colleagues, on the eve of an event of major importance to them all, for a variety of reasons, had decided to go for a meal together. So far so normal – that's how it had seemed at first.

But now Angela thought about it in the light of various interviews she had conducted since then.

Petar hadn't intended to join the others for a meal at all. Both Una and Danny had spoken of the plan for a foursome. The intention was for the meal to be a private affair to reintroduce Una back into Petar's circle.

It had been Stewart, Angela now realized, who had turned it into a come-one-come-all event, and not so very subtly either. Before Petar had known where he was, he had been put into the position of cancelling Danny, Heather and Una and facing the prospect of an evening in the company of Stewart *et al*. Not the evening he'd planned at all.

In fact… Angela stopped doodling and looked down at the words on the pad. It didn't take a big leap of the imagination to come to the conclusion that the gathering in the restaurant had been engineered by Stewart.

Angela scratched her chin as she thought. She couldn't really believe even Stewart could want to spend an evening in the company of his ex and his current girlfriend, much less Philip and Tessa. But if he wanted to stay close to Petar then he had to try to gather a party which hung naturally enough together to cause no comment.

And it had worked. The meal had passed leaving Petar still in the area around midnight. But not Stewart. He was in bed with Candy. So if he engineered the meal – why? *Perhaps you're making too much of this business, Angela*, she said to herself. *Maybe all Stewart wanted was for them to all eat together like one big happy family*. She thought a bit more, and dismissed her own objection. *That doesn't compute with what I know of Stewart.*

OK then, Angela, she said to herself, *there's definitely a question mark hanging over this meal. And given what Michelle Davies said about a person wearing a hoodie sitting in Petar's car, it wouldn't hurt to have another go at Lavinia Bannister.*

Ten minutes later she was behind the wheel of her car heading in the direction of Church Road.

It was another beautiful day, hardly a cloud in the sky, and although she had no doubt they had raincoats and umbrellas tucked away close to hand, everybody was dressed for summer.

People were all over the place, ambling, hurrying and standing still in front of the huge scoreboard. A waving arm caught her attention and she turned to see Gracie with another woman, white-haired with a very deep suntan and wearing a summer print frock. *Ah*, she thought, as she cheerily returned the wave, *that must be her friend, Edith, back from the visit to Australia.* Gracie made her way towards her and, realizing that it would seem rude to hurry on, Angela slowed her step until the two women had drawn alongside.

"Oh, I'm so glad I caught you," beamed Gracie. "I want to introduce you to my friend Edith. Why don't you join us for a sandwich? We've brought our own picnic lunches today and we've got plenty."

Angela's first inclination was to decline politely, but she hadn't realized how time had marched on. In fact it was nearly past lunchtime, so why not? After the episode on Saturday, Gracie obviously felt a bond between them and was already cheerfully leading the way to a vacant bench, where she sat and spread her bag to one side and her raincoat to the other to lay claim to both spaces.

"There, that's jolly handy," she said. "I used always to eat my picnic lunches on the grass. I've still no objection to doing that, but these days I have trouble getting up again." She laughed. Angela and Edith joined her on the bench. "Inspector, this is Edith Charlton; Edith, this is Angela Costello. She's the officer leading the investigation."

Angela and Edith nodded at each other while Gracie dived into the bag of food.

"I must say you've got a job on," remarked Edith. "I don't envy you at all."

"I'm not, strictly speaking, in charge," explained Angela. "There's a detective chief inspector heading up the case."

"Yes, but I expect it's you that's doing all the legwork," interjected Gracie with a perspicacity that surprised Angela, as she pulled a couple of packets out of the bag. "Still, it must be good exercise for your little grey cells," she finished, demonstrating her familiarity with at least one fictional detective.

Angela laughed. "Not just *my* grey cells, thankfully," she replied. "There's a whole team of us on the job."

"Of course there is," said Edith. After sandwiches of choice had been distributed and each woman had a drink, there was silence as they started their lunch.

"It's very kind of you to share your lunch with me," said Angela.

"Oh, nonsense." Gracie was dismissive. "It was very kind of you to spend time with me on Saturday when I was so distressed."

"You seem to be in better spirits now," commented Angela.

"Well, I'm very pleased that Edith is back and that helps. I'm still upset at the way things have turned out, but I don't see what I can do."

"The bastards," muttered Edith on Gracie's other side.

"Edith!" exclaimed Gracie, scandalized.

"It's no use, Gracie. I call a spade a spade, always have done; you know that," replied an unrepentant Edith. She leaned round Gracie and addressed Angela. "She's been shafted, Angela. That's the beginning and end of it."

"Edith!" repeated Gracie, turning a delicate shade of pink.

Edith cast an affectionate glance at her friend and clicked her tongue indulgently. "Too loyal for your own good, that's your trouble, Gracie," she said. Edith turned again to Angela. "You know, even after Saturday she was worried that although you were so sympathetic she'd discussed family business with a stranger and you might think badly of the Bickerstaffs because of it."

"Well, I also want to protect Margaret's memory, Edith," protested Gracie. "She was a Bickerstaff as well."

"As are you," Edith reminded her. "Though you wouldn't think it from the way they behave."

"Oh, don't worry," Angela reassured Gracie. "I don't form snap judgments about people."

"I'm very glad to hear it," said Gracie, and they munched in companionable silence for a few moments until Edith spoke again.

"Shafted, that's what," she reaffirmed. "I was very shocked when Gracie told me about the new will. Mind you, I should have seen it coming, the way Stewart was always coming round toadying up to his aunt. I watched him as he set about charming Margaret – such a nice old lady but a bit innocent, really, just like this one." Edith cocked her head towards Gracie. "She's led a sheltered life. But I haven't, and I really should have guessed what he was up to with his 'Can I get you anything, Aunt Margaret?' and 'Are you comfortable, Aunt Margaret?'. Oh yes, I watched him, all right! He didn't realize it, of course – so full of himself – ah well, there's nothing like twenty-twenty hindsight, is there?"

"Still," said Angela, not wanting to get caught up in Bickerstaff probate considerations, "it *was* Margaret's money."

"Yes, indeed," said Edith. "No use crying over spilt milk." She gazed without blinking into Angela's eyes. "And then to come back to this news about Petar. What a shock. Giving you plenty to think about, I've no doubt. I've been reading up on it. I'm following the case as closely as I can. It seems pretty tricky." Angela smiled at her and made no comment. "Hmm… yes, I understand. You can't talk about it; only right, really, but I'm fascinated by the whole process."

They finished their sandwiches. Angela thanked them for their hospitality and remained with them long enough afterwards not to appear rude.

A short while later, she found Lavinia sitting at a bar sipping champagne in the company of a man she didn't recognize. Approaching them, Angela asked if she could have a word, at which point the man stood up and excused himself, telling Lavinia he would catch her later.

Angela sat down and apologized. "I'm sorry," she began. "I was about to ask you to come to our room later when you'd finished your drink."

Lavinia made a small hand-waving motion. "It doesn't matter," she said. "We were having an informal business meeting."

"Oh, I see. Is he one of your colleagues?"

"Yes, he's responsible for bringing the Candy Trueman account into our company."

"Oh," said Angela. "Isn't she playing today? I didn't take note of the score as I passed the board."

"She's just won. She's through to the quarter-finals," replied Lavinia. "Have you found out who killed Petar yet?"

If you're thinking you're going to pressurize me, don't bother, thought Angela. "We're getting there," she said. "That's why I came looking for you."

A look of self-importance passed across Lavinia's face and she shifted her chair forward. "Yup, fire away," she said.

"I need to ask you a bit more about Sunday evening. You know, when you all went to the restaurant."

Guardedness instantly replaced all preening. "Yes?"

"How did it come about – you joining the others for a meal, I mean?"

Angela had interviewed many suspects over the years, and was instantly attuned to when someone tried to manipulate her opinion of them. She could see it happening again now. Lavinia settled on imperiousness. She raised her eyebrows in the manner of one who thinks she's been asked a silly question. "Petar was my partner, Inspector. Why wouldn't I go for a meal with him? Who else would he ask to go with him?"

Angela kept her expression neutral and continued. "Yes," she said, "but that's not how it happened, is it?" She deliberately left it there.

After a moment, Lavinia gulped down the rest of her

drink in an angry gesture. "Stewart said they were going to a restaurant," she said, looking crossly at Angela.

"Did he suggest you join them?"

Another pause. "Yes."

Having gained a foothold, Angela ploughed on. "Lavinia, I've been told that you and Petar had actually – or…" she added, seeing Lavinia twist agitatedly in her seat and shake her head, "at least, that there were some problems in your relationship," she finished. *Let her save face*, she thought, *as long as I get the answers I need.*

Lavinia's glance took in all four corners of the bar and her empty glass before she finally met Angela's eyes. "What couple doesn't have problems from time to time?" she asked eventually.

"Indeed; I couldn't agree with you more."

"We were talking it through."

"Yes, I've heard that as well," replied Angela, cutting her a bit of slack. "Er, I gather that Petar had become aware of the fact, and wasn't too happy to know, that you like to do a line here and there." *That's about as diplomatic as I can get it*, thought Angela as she saw a look of fear come into Lavinia's eyes. "I'm not part of the drugs squad," she hastened to add. "I'm trying to solve Petar's murder."

Lavinia relaxed. "He wasn't very reasonable about it," she said after a long moment. "I've stopped now, of course."

"Of course." Angela didn't allow her expression to change by so much as a twitch.

"It's just how I wind down – used to – now and again. But he just didn't get it."

Angela tried not to raise her eyebrows at this. She took a deep breath. Now was no time for pussyfooting. She had a jugular ripe for puncturing in her sights.

"How did he react when he discovered that Stewart is your connection?" she asked casually.

Alarm flared instantly in Lavinia's eyes and Angela was reminded of her interview with Philip just a few days previously. She gazed wildly all around as if seeking a means of escape. Eventually she brought her gaze back to Angela.

"I don't know why you think he's my connection. What on earth makes you think that?"

"Lavinia," said Angela carefully, "I know that Petar confronted you about your habit and you thought he wanted to try some, so you offered to score for him."

"What were you, a fly on the wall?" Lavinia's expression was a mixture of horror and anger. Angela kept her gaze fixed on the woman. Eventually Lavinia dropped her eyes. "He was furious. He said he was going to talk to Stewart about it," she muttered at last.

Angela exhaled silently. *Bingo.*

"Did you tell Stewart that Petar knew?"

"You are joking, of course!"

"Not at all; you might have wanted to warn Stewart that Petar was aware of his drug dealing."

"Well, I didn't!" snapped Lavinia. "It's just... I want a line now and again and Petar didn't understand. I thought maybe he'd realize that it wasn't worth bothering Stewart about, especially not before the tournament."

Angela couldn't decide if Lavinia was completely naïve or merely disingenuous. "I understand that you think doing a line here and there is a bit of fun; maybe you think it's harmless, Lavinia. But for many people, most people, it's serious – very serious. And it's scary." Lavinia met Angela's gaze without blinking. "Let's come back to last Sunday evening. How did you get to the restaurant?"

There was a long pause. "I went in Stewart's car."

"I see. Did Petar take his own car?"

"Inspector, I really don't see what all this has to do with

Petar's murder," said Lavinia, with another attempt at imperiousness that didn't even begin to work.

Angela smiled, completely unruffled, and could tell that this annoyed Lavinia even further. "Ms Bannister, I'm trying to find out who killed a man. All sorts of questions have to be asked. Some of them might seem irrelevant and some, I admit, do turn out to be just that. But they all have to be asked, unfortunately."

"Apart from me, everybody took their own cars."

"Why did you leave before the meal was over?" Angela asked, and earned herself another angry glare.

"I had a headache," snapped Lavinia.

Yeah, right, thought Angela. "The thing is, you see," she said, "we've got a bit of a problem with your alibi."

Lavinia blinked. "My alibi? What alibi? Why on earth would I need an alibi?"

"A person was seen sitting, with Petar, in his car in Church Road just prior to the probable murder time. This person could have been a woman," Angela said, hoping that Lavinia wouldn't ask too many precise details about the description. She needn't have worried.

"There, I told you she did it! She must have been brooding on us being in the restaurant together." Her face lit up in triumph. "Ha! I bet the thought of us getting back togeth… the fact that we were still together drove her frantic. She probably spent all evening going over and over it in her mind until she couldn't stand it any more and then she drove to Wimbledon to confront him. That's what must have happened. His relationship with me was eating her up, Inspector!"

Angela felt she now knew what it was like to have wandered into the twilight zone. She also thought it would be unproductive to point out that if Lavinia was still in a relationship with Petar, she would hardly have travelled to the restaurant in Stewart's car, much less be present only because Stewart had invited her. In any case, she had no time for this. Jumping through the hoop would be the quickest way to progress. "You're talking about...?"

"Una, of course! Isn't it obvious?"

"I'll check Mrs Belic's alibi, naturally, but I'd like to go over yours if I may."

"That's a bit rich, isn't it? I left the restaurant while they were all still eating."

Come on, Vinni, you're not that stupid, thought Angela. "Yes, I know that, but all the same – did you speak to anyone?"

"I don't speak to strangers on trains."

"Did any of your neighbours see you going into your flat?"

"I don't know; you'll have to ask them."

"Do you have a hoodie?"

"A hoodie?" She could have been Lady Bracknell doing the famous handbag line.

"Yes, you know; a sweatshirt with a hood. Do you own one of any kind?"

"I know what they are. No; I don't do hoodies, Inspector."

I can't think why not, thought Angela. *I'm sure Gucci or Versace have a nice selection of them.* She decided to leave it there. "OK, thanks for your help," she said. "I'll let you get back to your business." She was reasonably certain that Lavinia's fit of pique in the restaurant had stemmed from the fact that she had discovered what Petar had originally planned to do that evening.

Chapter Twenty-three

"Philip Turnbull?" said D.C.I. Stanway, as he wrote the name down. He lifted his pen from the paper, looked at Angela and raised an eyebrow. "Your reason for keeping him in the frame?"

"He could think Petar was in with Stewart on the blackmail that prevents Philip ever beating him. It may have been gnawing away at him for a couple of years. He could even think that Lavinia is part of the conspiracy."

Stanway made a note. "And are you thinking that if Philip has killed Petar he might now set his sights on Stewart and Lavinia?"

"It had crossed my mind, sir."

He looked at her for a long moment. "You mustn't allow yourself to become too scrupulous, Angela. We are mostly in the business of detecting crimes after they've been committed. If we get the chance to prevent a crime we do so, that's only right. But if we don't manage to prevent a crime, the blame for it rests fairly and squarely where it has always been: with the perpetrator."

"Yes. Thank you, sir."

Stanway allowed a small, avuncular smile to pass across his features before continuing. "Danny Moore?"

"He was Petar's business partner and he's been up to no good with the company funds. According to our informant, Petar was about to pull the plug on the company and ruin him."

"What does the Financial Investigation Unit say?"

"We're still waiting for them to get back to us."

"OK. Stewart Bickerstaff?"

"Petar had discovered that he dealt in drugs and might have been about to blow the whistle on him. His career would have disappeared down the toilet overnight and he really likes the limelight."

"Hmm, there's a crossover here between option one and option three, but the investigation is a work in progress, so we'll live with it for the time being. Lavinia Bannister?"

"He was my man and he done me wrong, sir."

Stanway gave a bark of laughter. "That old favourite! I see." He finished writing and leaned on the desk, steepling his fingers.

"How normal would it have been for any of these people to be sitting in Petar Belic's car between half-past midnight and one o'clock last Monday morning?"

"Probably not very normal, but then probably not so very strange either. Danny Moore, by his own admission, was in a nearby restaurant until at least midnight. He knew that Petar had gone for a meal, and could have texted or phoned on the off chance that Petar was still up and around. Philip has already indicated to me that Petar helped him with his game, but discreetly so Stewart's feathers wouldn't be ruffled. He could even have spoken quietly to him during the meal and they might have arranged to meet later after he'd seen Tessa home." She went on, "With Stewart it could have been the same sort of thing, on some pretext or other; pre-tournament nerves – 'I'm feeling very nervous, coach; please come and stroke my ego' would probably do. It would be arranged that Petar comes to meet whoever near the club."

Stanway nodded as she continued.

"They sit and chat in Petar's car. It's the same with Lavinia Bannister. She'd been clinging on to Petar for several weeks, from what I can gather, running a 'we've got to talk' scenario that she was spinning out."

"OK," said Stanway, writing again.

"You know, sir, I wouldn't be surprised if the venue was Petar's choice. Say one of them asked to meet up with him.

He'd just spent an evening in their company and although he'd want to help with whatever problem they said they had, he probably wouldn't want anyone calling at his flat because it could all go on a lot longer than he would like. It can be hard to get rid of a guest from your own home sometimes."

"Indeed it can. He lived in Wimbledon Village, didn't he?"

"Yes, sir. So, whoever, feigning a desire to talk, asks if they can meet up. Petar, wanting somewhere neutral and away from his own place, might think that Church Road is convenient and discreet. He would assume a need for discretion."

"Of course. Otherwise the conversation could have been had openly earlier in the evening, either at the club or the restaurant. That's a good point. There are no houses on the other side of the street there. So he or she parks near the club and walks into Church Road and gets in beside Petar in his own car exactly as if a cosy chat is about to ensue."

"With all four, I don't think it would have raised any suspicions in Petar if their hand had gone round his shoulders or down the back of the front seats. He would have been at ease with all of them."

"Ah, yes, it's just a nice cosy midnight chat about this and that, there's an arm coming round the back of Petar, a friendly gesture, and then suddenly it turns into something else. It would have happened very quickly. It must have done; the murderer would have needed Petar relaxed and unsuspecting."

"Matey injects the insulin. Petar's not a stupid man. He would realize immediately that this is something serious, that there is intent to kill. Who knows, maybe in that instant a few things fall into place for him – whatever. Petar does what I suspect anybody would do in those circumstances – gets straight out of the car and heads off into the safety of the club, finding himself very wobbly on his legs as he goes. Matey, realizing that the final part of his plan has been thwarted and that he'd better get out of the area, hops into the driving seat and pulls away without realizing that this 'W' girl is close by. He leaves the car in a side street where it's later taken to the police pound."

Stanway pursed his lips. "And what if Petar hadn't got out of the car?"

"Sir?"

"Petar's sitting in the driving seat. The murderer can't drive the car with a dead man behind the wheel."

"He doesn't need to, sir. Plan 'A' is that he gets out of the car and legs it. He's well covered with the hood and rather helped by the fact that the meeting is in such a place. It hangs together, sir."

"Yes, yes it does. Well, it's a good theory as far as it goes, Angie. There's just one little sticking point."

Angela sighed. "Yes, I know. Who was the person in the hoodie and how do we get the proof?"

"The Crown Prosecution Service tends to be hot on this detail." Stanway riffled through the papers on his desk. "Is this the only sighting you've got from that time? The 'W' girl?"

"Oh yes, otherwise known as Michelle Davies. She was the fan wandering around the area in a high dudgeon because she'd had a row with her friend."

"Hmm." Stanway looked through the statement. "The defence would make mincemeat of this testimony. No sign of Petar's mobile?"

"No, sir; it's probably at the bottom of the Thames by now. Either that or smashed into little pieces somewhere."

"Yes, yes, a non-starter really; the perp knew what he was doing. What about dabs on the car?"

"Stewart's, more or less everywhere. He'd driven the car on several occasions, as had Danny and Lavinia once or twice. Nearly everybody in the group who went to the restaurant had been in the car at one point or another. Still, at least we've got all their fingerprints on record now in case something turns up in an unexpected place."

"Well, that's always useful." Stanway smiled. "I'm not without sympathy, Angie, but I'm afraid there's only one thing for it."

Angela grimaced and nodded. "I keep digging."

"Indeed you do." Angela got up to leave but as she reached the door Stanway spoke again. "I think you're doing a good job, Angie, but be very careful to keep all your options on the boil. One of them is going to emerge as the front-runner."

"Yes, sir," Angela assured him as she headed out into the corridor.

"So, do we lean on them, then, Angie?" asked Jim some time later, in the incident room.

"No, you leave the suspects to me for the moment," replied Angela, not allowing Jim's comment to cause even the mildest flutter of irritation. After her meeting with Stanway she had called them all together and they'd been batting her theory back and forth for the past half-hour.

"In the case of Stewart," said Jim, "he's been sha... er, going out with this Candy Trueman lately, hasn't he? She'd have known if he went out during the night."

"Not if she's anything like my mum," said Derek. "My dad reckons she'd sleep through an earthquake." A light-hearted laugh went around the room.

"Naturally that occurred to me," said Angela, "and there's a reason why I haven't looked into it yet. I keep getting this elusive memory of something that's already been said which answers that question. Rick, you and Jim go through everything we've got on Candy. I'm sure it's in there."

"OK," said Rick.

"And then what, Angie?" asked Jim.

"We'll carry on in the best tradition of police work – we'll proceed with caution. We'll keep our minds open and we'll continue to gather all the evidence we can." She looked at Gary. "No sign yet of repetitive strain injury with you, is there?"

Gary grinned. "I don't think so, guv. Do you want me to take some more notes?"

"Mmm. I rather fancy rattling Mr Bickerstaff's cage a little."

"You're not worried that he'll moan to his mum and dad and they'll complain to 'Stanners' about it?"

Angela laughed. "Well that would be a result, of sorts. Come on, young Houseman, let's get going."

Angela was aware of a certain buzz in the air when she arrived back at the club a short time later. A quick check on the scores gave her the reason for it. Stewart had won his fourth-round match and a place in the quarter-finals, where he would play Philip Turnbull, if Philip also won his next match.

Philip's fourth-round match was scheduled for later in the day, so the British fans would be on tenterhooks for a while yet. Angela gazed up at the scoreboard with mixed feelings. Stewart and Philip were the last two British players left in the men's draw, and only one of them could win their next match. She thought back to Philip's dejected, frightened face at their last meeting, and her own shoulders slumped sadly as she thought about the weight that he was carrying on his.

Oh dear, she thought, and hadn't realized that she'd said it out loud until Gary said, "Guv?"

Angela looked at him, shaking herself out of her reverie. "Oh, nothing, Gary. Come on; let's go and find Stewart."

Stewart sat opposite Angela ten minutes later looking rather pleased with himself. *As well he might,* she conceded. She tried to keep an open mind but it was impossible to un-hear what Philip had told her, and very difficult not to imagine the outcome of his next match and the reason for it. She congratulated Stewart on his fourth-round win through not quite clenched teeth.

He received her congratulations with a pleased smile. "Thank you. It looked a bit tricky in the third set when I was a break down and my serve seemed to desert me for a moment. Happily, it all came together and I was able to get back on track."

"Yes, indeed," said Angela. "However, pleasant though it is to talk tennis, that's not why I've asked for this interview."

"Of course."

"Petar's car was seen outside the club in the early hours of Monday morning."

A frown creased Stewart's brow. "Oh, really?"

"Do you not think that's odd?"

Stewart shrugged. "I don't know where he went after he left the restaurant. Perhaps he came back to collect something he'd left here."

"Maybe," agreed Angela. "Somebody answering your description was seen sitting in the front passenger seat."

He raised his eyebrows in surprise. "Now *that's* odd. Very odd."

It was no more than she expected. "Was it you, Stewart? Were you sitting with Petar in his car in the wee small hours of Monday morning?"

He didn't even blink. "Is this an accusation, Inspector?"

"No, it's a straightforward question. And I have another one for you."

"Oh yes?"

"Did you kill Petar Belic?"

Thunder gathered behind Stewart's eyes and he gave the impression he was having difficulty controlling himself. He allowed a small pause to develop before speaking in a very sombre tone. "I hope you're making a very bad joke, Inspector," he said in a deliberately slow voice. "If not, that's outrageous."

"So is murder," answered Angela levelly, aware that she was supposed to be intimidated by his show of fury. She stared into the smug face opposite her. *Get a grip, Angela*, she told herself. *You might not like the man and you certainly don't like the way he's treated Philip, but that doesn't make him the murderer.*

"I would like you to know that I take the greatest possible objection to the... *question*." He took a couple of deep breaths as if he was having difficulty in speaking. "I'm outraged," he said, staring down at his hands.

"Why so?" asked Angela in a reasonable tone. "If somebody says they saw a person answering your description in a particular place and time relevant to our enquiry, the police have a duty to follow it up. We can't dismiss it on the grounds that Stewart Bickerstaff is a nice bloke and the witness must therefore be mistaken."

Stewart snapped his head up and met her gaze. *Aha!* Angela's heart gave a small leap. A look of chagrin had flashed across his features as he suddenly realized that his show of anger had been hasty and he'd now put himself on the back foot. She could see him considering his position.

He opted for injured innocence. "Yes, well. Of course I see that. It just gave me a turn, that's all. This is a very difficult time, Inspector. My great friend and mentor has been killed at a time when I needed him most."

Angela played it straight. "I do understand, Stewart," she said. "And believe me, I sympathize. My job isn't always a pleasant one."

Stewart nodded and gave the smile of one who has allowed himself to be mollified. "Yes, well, I'm afraid I'm unable to help you. I don't know anything about Petar's car being seen near the club. Is that all you wanted to see me about?"

"For the moment, yes. Thank you for your cooperation." There was a hint of irritation in his face as he picked up on

Angela's suggestion that she might not have finished with him, but it was gone almost as soon as it appeared. He wasn't going to let himself be caught out again.

"He's a cool one, isn't he?" remarked Gary after the door had closed behind him.

"As a cucumber," agreed Angela. She felt depressed. She could see no way forward. "Look, Gary. I want to sit in the sun with a coffee for a while. Meet me at the car in half an hour, OK?"

"Sure thing, guv," answered Gary.

Angela immediately felt better when once again she found herself sitting at a table in bright sunshine amidst a host of enthusiastic, excited tennis fans. She let her mind be invaded by the chatter and hum of the many conversations going on around her and regretted that she wouldn't be able to sit there for longer. She had closed her eyes for only a few moments when someone called her name and she looked towards the source of the voice. Edith Charlton was coming towards her through the constantly moving crowds.

"Hello, Angela," beamed Edith. "I'm so glad I saw you. I was hoping for a word."

Angela had wanted to spend a little time on her own and would have found some polite excuse about needing to be elsewhere, but she was puzzled by the site of Gracie lagging behind her friend with a hesitation in her step and what Angela could only describe as a reluctant expression on her face. Gracie met her gaze and dropped her eyes sheepishly. Edith bustled forward, gathering a couple of chairs from other tables as she did so and pulling them to the one where Angela was sitting.

"Come along, Gracie. Angela's a busy woman, you know. We're lucky to have caught her." Edith plumped herself down on one of the chairs and waited as Gracie took the other one.

"Edith, please," Gracie demurred.

Edith looked at her friend. "Now come along, Gracie. We've had all this out and we agreed."

"But…" Gracie cast an agonized glance at Angela before appealing to Edith. "Perhaps I should speak to them first, and – "

"Pshaw!" snorted Edith. "Don't be such a silly goose. The thing is," she continued, turning her attention to Angela, "she's somewhat invisible in the house, so people are not as careful in what they say and do in front of her as they should be. And Gracie doesn't always know how to interpret things. But I can put two and two together without any problems, d'you see?"

Angela nodded, hoping that she would in a minute.

"Oh dear," muttered Gracie. "This is all so worrying. I hate the thought of being mixed up in this. It isn't nice."

"Gracie!" Edith fixed her friend with a very firm expression. "Think of that little flat in West Ealing."

Angela suddenly got an angle on where this conversation was going and slowly started to rise. She didn't want to get caught up in a discussion of the dispositions of the late Margaret Bickerstaff's perfectly legal will. "Actually," she said, "I've got to meet my detective constable in the car park." She continued to move slowly so as not to seem eager to get away, but Edith's eyes didn't waver from her face.

"You remember me telling you that I've been reading up on the case since I came back?" she said. "And with what Gracie's got to say, I think we may be able to help you."

Angela had a sudden memory of Gracie telling her that "most of Stewart's tennis friends" had come to the house on one occasion or another.

Intrigued, she sat down again.

Chapter Twenty-four

When Angela finally rejoined Gary in the car she was flushed and slightly breathless from rushing. "Sorry I took so long to get here, Gary. I got held up."

"No problem." Gary misinterpreted what he was seeing and looked at her with concern. "Er, are you OK, guv?" he asked.

Angela smiled. Gary couldn't know that inside she was tingling with excitement. "Oh yes. I'm feeling absolutely fine," she replied. "I've been having a most interesting chat, and I've now got a new angle on this crime. I'll tell you all about it back at the incident room."

"Ah," said Gary as he started up the engine. "Well, we certainly need something, don't we?"

It didn't take long for Angela to relay to her team the gist of her conversation with Gracie and Edith. While she spoke she watched their interest become engaged. Her excitement animated them. Quite apart from whatever progress might be made, any new line of enquiry was going to be better than the stalemate of the past few days.

"OK, everybody," she called above a buzz that was going around the room. "It's now quite late and we're all tired. Well, I know I am. And we really need to get stuck in tomorrow. I want you all here first thing, bright-eyed and bushy-tailed."

"Sure thing!" they chorused cheerfully in response. The atmosphere felt energized. Jim and Rick were trying to persuade the other three to join them at a new pub they'd found in Wimbledon Village. She could almost see the spring in their steps and could tell they were glad to have something to get their teeth into.

The next morning, Angela had just sent Jim and Rick to take a statement, Leanne and Derek had set off to gather evidence and she was about to ring Stanway when the telephone rang and she picked it up to hear the D.C.I.'s voice.

"Oh, sir, how amazing! I was just about to ring you."

"Ah, good. My office in five minutes, if you please, Angie."

"I'll be there, sir." Five minutes later, she was sitting opposite him and wondering if his inscrutable expression meant that he was in a good mood or a bad one.

"You first," he said in a neutral tone of voice. Angela took a breath, marshalled her thoughts and, once again, recounted her conversation with Gracie and Edith. Stanway's eyebrows rose to his receding hairline several times as she spoke and he made a couple of notes on the pad in front of him. He remained staring down at these after she had finished speaking.

"Hmm," he remarked at length. "This is most interesting, Angela. If it pans out it could be the solution. I presume you've set the team hot on the trail."

"Yes, sir. They're all scurrying to their posts."

"Good, good. Don't lose sight of the other threads, though, and keep me closely informed."

"I will, sir."

There was a pause.

"Sir?"

"Yes?"

"You wanted to see me about something too."

"Ah, yes." Stanway cast another look down at what he'd written on his pad. "Hmm… I've had a complaint about you."

Angela's stomach gave a lurch. "Sir?"

"Yes. It was a beautiful evening yesterday, if you remember, and I was enjoying a gin and tonic in the bar of my golf club when Julia and Stephen Bickerstaff asked me if they might have a word."

"Ah." Angela's pulse suddenly raced and she felt herself go hot.

"Mmm. They seemed to think their son had been more or less accused of murdering Petar Belic and they're rather upset. They don't want him put off his game, you see. Surely I could understand that at a time like this Stewart shouldn't have any outside disturbances at all, etcetera. That was the gist anyway. I'm hoping, in the manner of these things, that whatever you said to Stewart has been changed along the way into what his parents now 'think' you said."

Angela gave herself a moment to breathe deeply. "I can assure you I didn't accuse him of anything, sir."

Stanway cocked his head to one side and raised his eyebrows.

"I did, however, *ask* him if he'd murdered Petar. But I asked him politely."

A fleeting smile passed across Stanway's face at the incongruity of this. "That's how I thought it would have been, Angie."

"Are they going to lodge a formal complaint?"

"Oh, no. I don't think that was ever their intention. They'd find that a bit common and wouldn't see the need when they're such good friends with 'Stanners' at the golf club."

"What did you tell them, sir?"

"I told them that Detective Inspector Costello is a very experienced and competent officer in whom I have every faith. I explained that sometimes in a murder enquiry it's necessary to ask unpleasant questions and that Stewart shouldn't worry himself unduly about it; it's just part and parcel of the sometimes uncomfortable duties you're obliged to carry out."

Angela thought she saw the corners of Stanway's mouth twitch. "Sir, is that the police version of 'diddums'?"

He smiled. "Well, I didn't like to say, 'If he's innocent he's got nothing to worry about, so tell your son to grow up and get over it.'"

Angela smiled back. "Of course not. Were they reassured, do you think?"

"I think so. They thanked me for putting their minds at rest, anyway."

"That's good."

"Yes, indeed." Stanway looked down at his pad again. "In any case, if this new line of enquiry proves to be fruitful and if the evidence is sound, we've got far more important things to be thinking about, haven't we?"

Angela rose. "We have indeed, sir. I'm on the case."

"Check every detail twice, Angie."

"I will, sir. Thank you."

The incident room was strangely quiet when Angela returned to it a few moments later. Most of her team were out fulfilling the tasks she had assigned to them. While they were all busy she had to play a waiting game. Then it would be for her to add the last piece in the jigsaw. She decided to go to the club. Apart from the convenience of being on the spot, she might just get the chance to watch some tennis. She suddenly remembered that she still didn't know how Philip had fared in his fourth-round match. By the time he and his opponent had got onto the court the previous evening it was quite late, and the game had been stopped because of bad light, with each player having won a set.

Almost the first thing she discovered on returning to the club was that Philip had just won through to the quarter-finals. This meant there would definitely be a British player in the semis and Angela could imagine what the sports media were making of this, already anticipating the possibility of Stewart getting to the finals. On impulse she hurried over to where the winning players were interviewed after each match. She managed to time it to perfection. She was almost the first person Philip saw on coming away from his interview. She caught his eye and gave him a thumbs-up sign. He gave her a small, sad smile.

"You're through to the quarters, Philip," she said, with what she hoped was an encouraging smile. "What a result; well done."

Philip glanced down at his feet and sighed. "Yeah, thanks."

They had kept moving as they spoke and Angela realized that there was nobody within earshot. "Philip," she said, lowering her voice anyway, "you can't live like this. You've improved enormously, you know you have, and you've got the potential for a really good, possibly brilliant, career in tennis."

Philip brought his eyes up to hers. "Yeah, I know you're right, but…"

"Even if you're banned, it won't last forever and he can't tell on you without the whole story coming out, and that's going to make him look bad. I can't believe Stewart would want that; he's jealous of his own reputation."

Philip looked at her, narrowing his eyes as he listened. "Am I still on your list of suspects?"

"Wow, I never thought the day would come when someone would bring up being a suspect as a way of changing the subject."

In spite of himself, Philip gave a small grin. "Shame it hasn't worked."

Angela smiled and pressed home what she prayed was her advantage. "Call his bluff and take whatever consequences come," she urged.

"I wish I could," he said. "But it's more complicated than that." He looked at her appraisingly. "How come you're so easy to confide in?" he asked. "Is it part of police training?"

Angela laughed. "That's just the way it is," she said. "What's more complicated than calling Stewart's bluff and going for your shots?"

From his face it was clear that this was more distressing to Philip than being thought a suspect. "The thing is," he began,

"Tessa and I have become very close and it's going very well. I feel… well, I feel that this is – could be – 'the one', as they say, you know? She's a very special lady."

Angela smiled. "That's great. I'm glad for you and I hope it works out, but why does that make things worse?"

"Well, I – I really love her, Inspector. I daren't tell her about – about Stewart and all that. How it started, I mean – the party. I wouldn't want to do anything that would jeopardize our relationship."

"Good grief! She wouldn't hold that against you, surely?"

"Well, I don't want her to find out about it. She thinks I'm as anti-drugs as she is. I am, of course, but if she gets to know about that party, well – I don't want to risk it. She's, you know, like I said before, she's not like most of the others on the tour; she's a churchgoing person – Mass and stuff."

Angela remembered the book *The Imitation of Christ* that had been found in Tessa's locker during the search. "All to the good," she responded in a matter-of-fact voice. "Do you know what 'stuff' means?"

Philip looked at her, puzzled. "What?"

"It means she has an angle on the need for forgiveness and acceptance of human weakness. If she hasn't, then she hasn't been paying proper attention on Sunday mornings."

Philip's brow wrinkled. This was clearly a new thought for him. "You think so?"

"I know so," Angela assured him.

"Oh, I'm not sure," he replied. "I couldn't bear the thought of her leaving me and… She doesn't get involved in… I mean, don't get me wrong, she's a lot of fun and we have a great time together, but… well, she's clean-living and all that. She's so good, you see. Lots of people say so, not just me."

"Nonsense," said Angela, allowing a brusque note to creep into her voice. "That's a malicious rumour. She's a flawed person just like the rest of us. You ask her and she'll confirm what I'm saying. If she doesn't," she continued, "refer her to my earlier comment about not paying attention." Philip laughed out loud at this and it was pleasant to see his whole face light up for a moment. "The thing is," said Angela, "you need to get the sugar coating off this romance and get stuck in. Your relationship is going nowhere fast unless you're prepared to trust each other. I bet Tessa would be shocked, and probably not too pleased, if she heard the assumptions you're making about her."

Philip was silent as he pondered this. "I hadn't thought about it like that," he said eventually.

"Take a risk. Lay your burden down."

Philip raised his head, a quizzical look on his face. "Are you telling me off?"

Angela laughed. "Yes, I suppose I am."

A chuckle escaped Philip's lips and then his face became thoughtful. "I suppose I have put her – well, my tendency is to put women on a pedestal."

"Not a comfortable place to be. Take it from me, Philip!"

Philip shook his head as if amazed at something. "Thanks, Inspector, you've been really helpful. I'd better go and find my coach now. He'll be wondering where I've got to."

Angela made her way to the police room. Just as the door closed behind her, she had a call. It was Jim.

"I think we've found your elusive memory, Angie," he said.

"Oh yes? Tell me."

"Yeah, in your interview with Candy Trueman… Ah yes, here it is." Angela could imagine Jim scrolling down the computer screen as he read. "'I don't know if I ate something in that restaurant that disagreed with me but I woke up feeling awful. I couldn't get going so I'm a little hazy about the time.'"

"Oh, bingo!"

"He could easily have slipped something into her cocoa that put her out for the count, couldn't he?"

"Absolutely. Unfortunately we've still got the same problem…"

"Yes, I know, proving it. Even if we had enough evidence to ask her for a blood sample, whatever she took would have passed through her system by now."

"Still," said Angela, determined to look on the bright side, "at least Stewart's alibi now looks a bit dodgy. I didn't like the thought of him as the only suspect with one; it didn't seem fair somehow." She paused. *Go on, Angie,* she said to herself, *be generous. Credit where credit's due. Show a bit of mercy.* "Well done, Jim," she added.

She could hear the smile in his voice. "No probs, Angie. We'll keep digging. You never know."

As soon as she hung up, the telephone rang again. She sat up, alert. Derek had been sent out on an errand with Leanne, and Angie had told him to ring her at once with any news. "Yes?" she said, eagerly.

"It's as you said, guv."

"Fingerprints?"

"They check out."

"And the samples themselves?"

"One hundred per cent H_2O."

"Bingo!" Angela punched the air.

"Also, guv, there's something else."

"Oh yes?"

"FI have been back to us about the Bel-Mor company finances." Derek's voice became muffled as he turned his head away from the phone. "Have you got those details, babes?" she heard him say, followed by an affirmative mumble from Leanne.

"Great stuff, Derek; put Leanne on, will you?"

Chapter Twenty-five

Angela made Leanne go through the information the Financial Investigation Unit had come up with, and then went over it all again with her. After she'd finished the call, she sat staring at the wall for what seemed like ages before dialling another number.

"Good morning, Bel-Mor Sports. May I help you?"

One thing was certain. This pleasant, welcoming voice didn't belong to Tara Simpkins. Angela wondered idly where she was.

"This is Detective Inspector Costello. I'd like to speak to Danny Moore, please."

"I'm sorry, Inspector, Mr Moore isn't in the office this morning. As a matter of fact, he's on his way to Wimbledon."

Angela left a message asking him to contact her at Wimbledon. *Of course, why wouldn't he be here?* she told herself. *He's an ex-pro and he runs a sports promotion agency. The wonder of it is that you got him in his office last week.*

Half an hour later there was a knock on the door, and it opened to reveal Danny standing behind a uniformed constable.

"This gentleman says you left a message for him to contact you, ma'am."

"Yeah, yeah, thanks, Constable," replied Angela, standing back and indicating that Danny should enter. "Thanks for responding so quickly," she added as he came in past her. "Take a seat."

"No problem," he said. "I got the message just as I was coming through Putney. What can I do for you?"

"I'll get straight to the point," began Angela. "Our investigation has thrown up some interesting information about the finances of Bel-Mor Sports."

Danny stared at her in silence for a few seconds.

"That little cow!" he said eventually.

Angela hurried on to deflect attention away from her informant. "When a murder victim was involved in business, as Petar was with you, it's normal to look at the finances," she said.

Danny didn't seem to be listening. "She's on her way out, you know. We'd extended her probation as part of the softening-up process but I'll cut with all that now. Her feet aren't going to touch." He looked at Angela. "I presume it was Tara who blew the whistle."

Angela tried to steer the conversation away from Tara again. "Mr Moore, it's normal in these cases – "

Danny stared into the middle distance. "It doesn't matter anyway. I know it was her – spiteful little mischief-maker."

"Mr Moore, I need to ask you about – "

Danny cast a brief, unseeing glance at Angela before continuing. "She tried to seduce me. Can you believe that? She's only a bit older than my daughter, for goodness' sake. Then she starts flashing her boobs and her legs at me – talk about setting her stall out; as if I haven't met the type before – cash registers behind her eyes! She must think all she's got to do is offer a bloke a good time and he's going to give her his PIN number or something; stupid little bitch."

Danny moved his head and focused his eyes on Angela. "I know you have to look into company finances in cases like these," he said, with a nod of acknowledgment. "I also know that you'd find our books are in perfect order."

"This is true."

"Yeah, completely kosher, everything hunky-dory." He gave a mirthless smile. "But you're here talking about interesting information regarding our finances, so it's back to our soon-to-be-unemployed whistle-blower."

Angela reminded herself that Danny Moore had a very

astute brain. "Obviously I can't involve myself in your personnel issues, Mr Moore."

He laughed out loud at this. "No worries, Inspector. Let's cut the crap. Your auditors have turned up a big movement of money recently, right?"

"Yes."

"There was a huge financial haemorrhage which, if not replaced, would have left Bel-Mor and me very deep in the poo."

Angela realized that *she* was now being interviewed, but as long as she got her questions answered she supposed it didn't really matter. "Yes."

"Well, your information is correct. A huge sum of money disappeared from our company account."

"What happened to it?"

"It got swallowed up in a scam – flushed down the toilet."

"Ouch."

"Yeah." The colour faded a little from Danny's face as he clearly recalled the shock he'd felt when he'd discovered the mess he had been in. He held his hands up in a gesture of surrender. "Big-time… It was me. I completely messed up."

"Ah."

The ghost of a grin. "Yeah." Danny's eyes suddenly became pink and moist.

"I need to hear about this," said Angela.

He flicked a red-rimmed glance towards her. "Yes, I know you do." He took a couple of deep breaths. "You've no idea how good Pete was about it," he said after a moment, his eyes fixed resolutely on his fingernails.

"So tell me," she said.

"I loved him like a brother, Inspector. Even before all this. There's no way I could have killed him. Even if he'd let me sink and wound up the company, I couldn't have done it."

Angela waited.

"I took a gamble," he said eventually. "It doesn't really matter what it was. The point is, I used company funds. It seemed such a sure thing; well, these things do, don't they? I pride myself on my business sense and I thought I'd looked at the whole thing inside out and upside down, but I was taken to the cleaners. I – ah, what the heck. I thought I'd be putting all the money back, and more besides, within a few weeks."

"And, of course, it didn't work out like that."

"No." The embarrassment and shame of his miscalculation were obviously still very present to Danny.

"What was Petar's reaction?"

"I don't know."

Angela's head jerked up, her eyes widening in disbelief. "You don't know?"

Danny gave another mirthless grin. "By the time I'd plucked up the courage to tell him he already knew, so I can't tell you what his initial reaction was."

"How was he when you did finally tell him?"

"How was he? He was Pete."

"Meaning?"

"He already had a contingency plan in place."

"He bailed you out?"

Danny let out a very long breath. "He bailed me out."

"My goodness."

"Yep, he forgave me. He had mercy on me."

There was silence for a few moments. Mercy was another thing Angela remembered the nuns at school telling them about. "That's really quite something," she said at last.

"Oh yes. Mind you, I didn't get off scot-free. I had to do my bit."

Angela raised her eyebrows in query.

"I no longer own a holiday home in the Dordogne."

"Ah. Still, compared with what you could have lost... We

don't get too much emphasis on mercy in police work. Wasn't he even angry? I mean, how could he let you off so lightly?"

"He said, 'OK, Dan, you have been very stupid, but we are good friends and we go back a long way. Let's see what we can do.'"

"Wow."

Danny looked at her. "You don't get it, do you? He was a diamond bloke."

"I can see that, and as a one-time fan of Petar I'm very pleased to hear it, but didn't he want any sort of restitution?"

Danny looked at her as if he hadn't truly considered the question before, and was silent for a long moment. Finally he spoke. "I suppose, really, he could show mercy because he was receiving it."

"Receiving mercy – from whom?"

Danny looked at her. "From Una. Yeah, that's it." A note of wonder had crept into his voice. "He'd done to his marriage what I'd done to our company; not financially, I mean, but…"

Angela nodded.

"He'd really screwed up with Una. Neither of us was a model husband at first. My Heather had quite a bit to put up with. We were like a pair of teenagers until well into our thirties, even though we were married. But Pete messed Una around a lot, and then he left her and I know he hurt her really badly. I think he realized quite quickly what an idiot he'd been but he wouldn't admit it and toughed it out at first. He pretended he was having a high old time but he wasn't really happy. I think meeting Lavinia must have been a kind of catalyst for him."

Angela nodded, remembering that Una thought much the same thing. "OK, I have another question for you. Have you ever been in Margaret Bickerstaff's house?"

"Bickerstaff? Is that some relative of Stewart's?"

"His great-aunt; well, late great now."

"Ah. No, never been to her house, nor, as far as I can remember, ever met the lady."

"Right, there's just one more thing."

"Yeah?"

"Somebody answering your description was seen in Petar's car in Church Road, just outside the club, at about half-past midnight to one o'clock last Monday morning."

Danny looked very puzzled. "My description? Pete's car?"

"Yeah, wearing a hoodie."

"I've got a couple of hoodies but I wasn't wearing one last weekend. I was smart casual in the restaurant."

"I believe you were in *Da Camisa* until around midnight."

"Around then; I just paid the bill and we went out to our car. To think he was so close. It might have been happening then." Danny's eyes became moist again and there was a suggestion of a lip quiver.

"Were you with your wife the whole time?"

"What? Oh, yeah, yeah. Heather was with me throughout the evening."

"OK, thanks for coming in to see me, Danny. That's all for the moment."

Danny recovered his composure. "No probs, Inspector," he said, standing up.

"Are you going to the show courts now?" she asked him as he headed for the door.

"No, I've got my eye on a couple of the juniors. One of them is from Petar's hometown."

"Ah, bit of sentiment there?"

Danny shook his head. "Nah, I can't afford to be sentimental about tennis talent, but he's looking like a very good prospect."

Angela was lost in thought for a while after Danny had left the room. She wasn't a very sentimental person herself but she knew genuine, raw emotion when she saw it and she felt convinced that Danny's grief for Petar had been real. However, he was still a contender. Further digging by the Financial Investigation Unit might reveal more discrepancies and Danny was an astute businessman. She wasn't prepared to cross anybody off her list of suspects until she was absolutely certain.

She was just about to leave the room and head for home when her phone rang.

It was D.C.I. Stanway. "Angela, I've now received everything from your team. It looks as though we have a case."

Angela's heart gave a small leap of jubilation but she kept her voice steady. "Yes, sir, I think so too."

"In spite of how conclusive this looks I hope you're still keeping everybody in the frame."

"I am, sir. You just never know, do you?"

"Indeed not. I shall be contacting the Crown Prosecution Service first thing in the morning, so watch this space."

Angela gave a big smile, punched the air and didn't bother to hide the pleasure in her voice this time. "Great, I'll let the team know."

Chapter Twenty-six

When she entered the house that evening, Angela draped herself against the kitchen door jamb watching Patrick in silence as he pottered around the kitchen putting food onto two trays. After a few moments he turned to look at her with a quizzical expression.

"The pose is definitely seductive but the smile isn't nearly vampish enough," he said, coming over and kissing her. "Fortunately, I find you sexy anyway."

"I wasn't trying to be seductive. I was trying to create suspense in the atmosphere."

"Consider it done. Why am I now suspended?"

Angela laughed. "Stanway is going to the Crown Prosecution Service tomorrow, so we're waiting to see if we get permission to make an arrest."

"Oh my! You have been busy. Here, take yours. You can tell me all about it over dinner." They settled themselves and Patrick switched on the television.

"Right," began Angela. "Oh, hold on a minute, Pads," she said as a picture of Joanna Clarke flashed onto the screen. "Let's just see what's happening here." They heard the voice of an announcer.

At the Wimbledon Championships, British player Joanna Clarke retired during her fourth-round game today because of ill-health. It was a sad end to what had been a very promising revival for Joanna, who has been playing very well here. In an interview later she spoke very positively about the situation and made a most unexpected announcement.

"Oh?" said Patrick, looking across at Angela as the scene changed to show Joanna sitting in front of the familiar backdrop used for the post-match interviews. The interviewer must just have asked her how she was feeling because the clip cut straight to Joanna's answer.

"Oh, I'm feeling much better now, thank you," she said. "I'm just grateful that I was fit enough to get this far. It's shown me what I can really do and I'm hopeful of my chances when I come back into the game next year." The interviewer was clearly nonplussed by this answer and suggested that it sounded as if she was planning to have some sort of injury time out.

Joanna gave a gentle laugh. "Sort of, I suppose. The thing is, I'm expecting a baby."

There was a pause from the other side of the microphone and it was obvious that the interviewer was stumped for a response.

"Er, did you say… er… you're pregnant?"

Joanna smiled and nodded. She looked supremely confident and at ease. "I know that it's not the best of situations, being a single mum, and I wouldn't really have chosen that, but there it is. I'm in a very fortunate position because my family are being really supportive. The baby is due January and after that I'll be practising very hard to get my game back."

"Er, er… congratulations," said the interviewer, rallying. "I'm sure you're aware of the rumours that you and Stewart have split up?"

"Oh yes, we have," replied Joanna. "Obviously, if Stewart wants to have a relationship with his child I won't deny him access but it's true that we're no longer together. He's with Candy now and I wish them every happiness." Joanna didn't say "And as far as I'm concerned she's welcome to him" but she didn't have to. It was etched into every line of her delighted expression.

"Does Stewart already know he's to be a father?" asked the interviewer.

"Oh yes," said Joanna and smiled pleasantly.

Even sitting in their living room, Angela and Patrick

could hear the unasked questions buzzing around inside the interviewer's head and, in spite of Joanna's definitive statement, were able to make very educated guesses about the headlines the following morning. *Joanna Clarke Expecting Stewart's Baby – Is This Why They Split?* or *Joanna Carrying Stewart's Child – Will They Now Get Back Together?* Even, *Joanna Pregnant by Stewart – Did Candy Know?*

Sitting in front of the camera, Joanna seemed blithely unconcerned with what anybody might be thinking. She looked radiant as she smiled and thanked the interviewer. The scene cut to the anchorwoman in the studio who expressed her amazement at the news, segued smoothly through the mention of one or two famous female tennis players who had done well after becoming mothers, and continued into the round-up of that day's play.

"My goodness," said Patrick. He looked across at Angela. "Never thought she'd break the news in bombshell fashion like that."

"Yes, that's toughing it out and no mistake. In a way I'm sorry she's out of the tournament, though. She's been having a very smooth pregnancy so far but it must have caught up with her today."

"Hmm," Patrick nodded. "Louise was like that when she was carrying Maddie; felt as fit as a flea and loaded with energy... OK," he said after a few moments, once the scene had switched to a mixed doubles match. "I've been aware of all the frenetic activity. Your team have been haring off collecting samples and checking fingerprints and it all sounds very like you're moving to a conclusion."

"Absolutely. That's why Stanway's pushing. He's going for a face-to-face interview at the CPS hoping to get the application fast-tracked so that we can wrap it up before the end of the tournament."

"You mean we might get to watch the finals with this behind us?"

"I sincerely hope so, Paddy."

"You have done well," he said.

Angela demurred. "We all have, Pads; I'm part of a team."

"Indeed you are and as a team, from what I can see, you've all pulled together and worked well, but…"

"But?"

"How many of your team would have stepped outside the police officer role to sit and have a sandwich and coffee with that elderly lady, er…?"

"Gracie."

"That's it, Gracie. Being prepared to engage with that woman has reaped huge dividends with you on this case."

"Oh, I hadn't thought of it like that."

"And then there's young Philip Turnbull. *Most* interesting information from him."

"Ah, yeah, but I knew something was bothering him and it was going to nag at me until I got to the bottom of it."

"My point exactly, Inspector Costello; you step outside the box. I didn't hear about Jim or Rick being aware that something was bothering him."

"Well, to be fair," countered Angela, "I'd probably sent them off to do something else."

"Point taken, but I've always noticed that you've got a particular interest in the human angle and that's what's paid off for you in this case. You know," he said, drawing his fingers gently across her brow, "you've got a very talk-to-able face. I've thought that right from the first moment I met you."

"Aw shucks," smiled Angela. She leaned into him for a kiss.

"Yes, I still think you've done well," he answered after a few moments. "And, of course, your main suspect was a little careless."

"Aren't they always, when it comes down to it?"

"Yes," he agreed. "There's invariably some small point they haven't covered, and thank God for it. So now it's a waiting game with the CPS."

"Yeah, it could take a few days but that's no bad thing. It will give us a chance to make sure we've got everything sewn up and all our paperwork's in place."

"And still keep your eyes peeled for anything you've missed on the way?"

"Oh yes, definitely that. The file remains open on every suspect."

"Talking of suspects, have you seen the papers today? The press are going loopy about the first all-British quarter-final in years, and I must admit I'm looking forward to the spectacle tomorrow."

Angela nodded. "I know what you mean. I've got very mixed feelings about that match. I just wish Philip could somehow get an injection of gumption or whatever it is that he needs to play on top of his game but I'm not holding my breath."

"Are you going to the club to watch the match?"

"Oh yes. I'm definitely taking advantage of my position for that."

Patrick grinned. "Good for you," he said.

A different kind of atmosphere could be felt in the air at the club now, or so it seemed to Angela as she entered it the following day. On day one of the tournament every player could harbour a hope, however far-fetched, of walking away with the trophy. Today, most of the players had been knocked out. The expectations of the crowds had necessarily narrowed and were now focusing on the few who remained in the contest.

It was a rare treat for the home fans to have two British players still left in the draw at this stage, and the fans and the media were making the most of it. Angela found herself surrounded by the buzz that the match was stirring up. She encountered it constantly on the television, on the radio, in the press and on the lips of people around her. The fact that Stewart and Philip were playing against each other today tempered a little, but not much, the pleasurable anticipation that there would definitely be a Brit in the semi-finals.

For many it was a foregone conclusion that Stewart would prevail. Angela had seen the headline on the sports pages of a few newspapers already that morning: *Stewart Sets Sights on Semi-Finals*. It was an expectation that was probably shared by many around the court, Angela thought, and she couldn't wonder at it.

They were already on court and warming up when she arrived. Using the police pass issued to her the previous week, she made her way to the court and managed to find somewhere to sit.

She found herself wondering how Stewart's strategy against Philip worked. Surely it would look suspicious if Stewart won too easily. But then, she reflected, Philip's game had only really developed within the past year or so, and they hadn't played each other much in that time and not at all in any high-profile match. Angela wondered how aware the self-absorbed Stewart was of Philip's improvement. In any case it was academic, she thought with sadness. Philip, in his own eyes, couldn't afford to let himself win against Stewart.

Finally, play got under way. Stewart and Philip walked to opposite ends of the court as the excited noise from the spectators stilled to an expectant hush. The first few games went with serve, but the way they were played was a very clear marker as to the possible outcome. Stewart won his games easily, sending powerful serves across the net which generally went unreturned. In his own games, Philip struggled to hold himself together and his movement seemed, to Angela, somewhat stiff.

There was a worried frown between his eyes and he gave off a general sense that it was all a huge effort.

In the fifth game, Stewart's serve, he sent four of his trademark aces across the net to win it in easy points. He had a "business as usual" strut in his step as he walked back to his seat at the changeover. By contrast, Philip's shoulders slumped and he hid himself under his towel. His head was still down and his expression grim as the umpire called time.

Philip served well in the next game and the two men got into a couple of very long rallies. The score went to deuce and then advantage a few times, the two players taking it in turns, it seemed, to have the upper hand. Finally, just as Philip was sprinting to get to a cross-court pass, he slipped and the ball landed on the line to the sound of a sympathetic "ooohhhh" from the crowd.

Poor bloke, thought Angela, watching Philip get up and brush himself down. *He must think even God's got it in for him now.* Whatever he was thinking, he didn't put up much resistance in the next game and he very quickly lost the set after that.

Angela became aware of an almost palpable sense of disappointment rippling through the spectators. There couldn't be a person present who wasn't aware of the match history of these two men but the commentators, though their money had been on Stewart as the prospect of this meeting had become more and more likely, had spoken with optimism of Philip's improved game and skill at returning. They had at least hoped he'd make a match of it before losing.

Angela began to feel a bit depressed. Philip remained under the cover of his towel whenever he sat down. The seat Angela had managed to wangle for herself wasn't too far from the box in which the players' teams sat and a sudden sound from that direction made her turn round just in time to see Tessa Riordan slipping into the seat beside Philip's coach.

As Philip made his way out onto court again for the second set, Angela saw him look up at the players' box. He gave an almost imperceptible shake of the head and didn't raise his eyes again as he made his way round to the service line. The next three games had just about every stroke in the tennis manual. Stewart's superb serves were met by good quality returns.

But they fell just short of scintillating.

There were drop-shots, cross-court passes, forehand and backhand drives and a couple of stunning lobs. Philip demonstrated every stroke in his repertoire. But there was no fire in his belly and it wasn't long before the score was three-nil to Stewart.

The sense of the crowd straining to encourage Philip, to egg him on to make a fight of it, was almost palpable. Angela watched him with a mixture of sorrow and frustration. She knew better than most that the real battle on court was being fought inside Philip's head. It was equally clear that he was losing.

As play progressed, Angela became aware of another issue. She had the definite impression that Philip kept his eyes averted from the players' box. She glanced up to see Tessa's face fixed intently on Philip as if she were willing him to look up at her.

Finally, as Philip emerged from under his towel and came out for the fourth game, she prevailed. It seemed he could hold out no longer. He glanced up at his girlfriend and held her gaze for a moment, his face grim as he stepped up to the line.

Suddenly there was a change. Just a small one. Nobody who wasn't watching Philip as closely as Angela would have noticed. She glanced quickly across at Tessa and caught an unmistakable surge of hope in her face. So she had noticed too. From her seat at the side of the court Angela leaned forward more intently.

Philip was just settling himself to receive serve when he held up his hand to indicate he wasn't quite ready, and turned to the back of the court. It took a few seconds only; he bent down to adjust his trainer in some way, jumped up and gave a couple of skips as if to test it and turned round to face the court again.

Angela's heart gave a small leap. Philip's shoulders were back and his head was up. The impression of defeat had lessened. *Go for it, Philip,* thought Angela. She wondered what was going through Tessa's mind right at that moment.

Stewart approached the line and prepared to serve. He was gearing up to send another ace to his opponent.

With a resounding crack, the ball left Stewart's racquet and cannoned across the net in the direction of the "T". Experience had taught him not to expect his serves back from Philip, so he had relaxed a little and had already begun to move towards the other side for his next serve when there was an involuntary gasp from every spectator in the place.

Stewart's stunning serve had been gathered up onto Philip's racquet and sent spinning back to him to land with an ineffectual little bounce at his feet. There came a collective "oooooh!" of admiration followed by applause as the crowd realized that this match could turn into a competition worth watching. Angela looked up to the players' box just in time to see a huge beam of approval stretched across Tessa's face, and both her thumbs sticking up towards the sky. Philip also glanced up at the players' box and gave a huge smile, the first one Angela had seen from him that day and, if nothing else, she was certain of one thing. He had enjoyed that. He had relished doing what he had known for some time that he could do, and from the new set of his shoulders and the angle at which he now held his head there was to be no turning back, no matter what the consequences.

Philip Turnbull had served notice on Stewart Bickerstaff.

Chapter Twenty-seven

It took Stewart a little while to realize it.

He had nothing more than a slight look of irritation on his features which disappeared as he prepared for his next serve. He produced another superb shot, just brushing the "T" as it landed. Philip was ready for him, however, and reached out, despatching the ball with a decisive backhand. It came back to Stewart so quickly he didn't have time to get into position, and a reflex movement had his racquet flailing away at the air as the ball landed just inside the baseline.

His next serve had all the hallmarks of the thundering smash that it was no doubt designed to be. In just three seconds, Philip's forehand drive had whipped it back across the net straight at Stewart's feet.

A whole new atmosphere could be felt around the court now. People were straining forward, eager to watch what was becoming a match.

Stewart was love–forty down, a scoreline he hadn't expected, especially on his own serve. His brow darkened but judging by the look he cast to his opponent at the other end of the court, he still hadn't quite grasped the implications of what was happening. He seemed more puzzled than anything else. Angela thought he had the sort of look which said, "Hey, what's going on? This isn't how it's meant to be."

Stewart planted himself on the service line, looking grim. He took his time. The toss was high and straight, textbook stuff. He stretched up; his feet left the ground. The crash of ball on taut string heralded another thundering serve hurtling towards Philip's backhand at astonishing speed.

Philip bent his knees, twisted just enough, moved his racquet, and the ball was sent whizzing back before Stewart had even straightened up. The return, however, went wide and Stewart gained his first point in the game.

Angela cheered, ooh-ed and ah-ed with the rest of the crowd, and a part of her wished she could be watching on the television or listening to the radio; she thought the commentators must have been going wild with excitement.

Stewart's next would-be smash went into the net and his softer second serve drew forth a rally of several nail-biting strokes. It was clear that each man was hoping to run the other out of court as they sent each of their shots as deep into the corners as they could. At first it looked like a tennis clinic; each forehand drive repulsed by a backhand. After several of these exchanges Philip managed to wrong-foot his opponent by directing the ball straight into Stewart's body. Stewart was quick enough to step back and send up a lob which allowed Philip to get into a good position. Philip was ready for it. He leapt up to take the ball in the air but unfortunately misjudged it and it overshot the baseline. Thirty–forty.

The tension palpably heavy in the air now, Stewart came to the line to serve again. He'd got back into the game. But saving break points on his own serve hadn't ever been part of his plan against Philip. Afterwards, Angela found herself wondering if this was the point at which he finally woke up to what was going on.

Stewart suddenly paused and straightened up. He cast a speculative look across the net, which turned into a threatening glance as he took the maximum time allowed. To Angela it seemed that he was trying to warn Philip of what he could do to him. Then he served a 120-miles-an-hour smash. It came back at 125; he had no way of getting his racquet to it, and the gasp of the crowd was audible across all the neighbouring courts.

Stewart Bickerstaff had lost his serve.

He'd lost all power over Philip.

A high lob from Stewart on the first point of the following game was put away with a contemptuous backhand that gave Philip fifteen–love up and demonstrated beyond all manner of doubt that this wasn't a fluke.

Now Stewart started to become very angry. He stretched the time between the next few points as much as he could and managed to stand and look menacingly towards Philip on each occasion. It was all to no avail; at no time could he catch Philip's eye.

The two players traded shots and the games were close. The score stood at deuce in the ninth game and the two men were in the throes of a very involved and gasp-inducing rally. Stewart sent a cross-court pass deep into a corner but Philip managed to catch it on the run and send it back. The ball seemed to bend in flight and land just inside the baseline a split second before Stewart reached it. Stewart was finding the pace increasingly hard to match.

Having disabled his opponent's serve, Philip set about demonstrating a superior ability at making shots. Cross-court passes were sent flying, forehand drives were blocked and returned and Stewart's backhand, his weakest shot, was treated without mercy.

Within twenty minutes, Philip had taken the second set to level the match. As they took their seats for the changeover, Stewart stood still briefly on the court and cast a truly thunderous expression on him. He found himself ignored. The message was clear: "From now on, if you want to beat me you'll have to do it by playing better tennis than I do."

Angela sat forward in her seat, impatient at the break.

Stewart tried another threatening glare as he and Philip passed each other to go to their respective ends when they came out for the third set, but it was a wasted effort. Philip didn't meet his eyes; his shoulders were back, his head was up and he had a spring in his step as he made for his end of the court. This was a new Philip, one that Angela hadn't met before. She liked what she was seeing. Every so often he cast a glance up at the players' box and on each occasion, Angela saw him get a thumbs-up sign and a smile from Tessa.

So he's risked more than just his game, thought Angela with delight, as she settled back down with several hundred other spectators to enjoy the rest of the match.

Once he realized that he was going to have to fight for his place in the semi-finals, Stewart knuckled down, got on with the job and showed how he had earned the British number one spot. But Philip had thrown away all his previous inhibitions. The games went with serve for most of the third set. Stewart put up a good fight and at one point the third set score was level at four-all, and it looked as though it could go either way. It went to Philip. Then Philip broke Stewart's serve with another scintillating return that again left the crowd gasping. He then held his own serve to take the third set. After that, Stewart resembled more and more a drowning man trying desperately to hang on to a piece of driftwood, and Angela was reminded of Danny Moore's assertion that he had peaked.

More tellingly, the triumphantly expectant cheers of Stewart's T-shirted followers had become cries of encouragement; their customary whoops of delight and yells of "Yay!" had turned into "Come on, Stewart".

The fourth set was a complete whitewash; six-nil to Philip. The final shot, a forehand drive from Stewart, went out of court. A huge roar rose up from the crowd and Stewart smashed his racquet to the ground in rage.

Even as the loudspeaker was intoning the name of the winner and giving the breakdown of the three-sets-to-one victory, Stewart, his face registering a mixture of disbelief and anger, came forward, gave Philip and the umpire a perfunctory handshake, collected his things together and sped back to the locker rooms.

Not many people noticed him go. They were too busy cheering. The player who'd started out as the underdog had won. The spectators gave a noisy, jubilant standing ovation to Philip, who leapt for joy and threw kisses up to Tessa and his sweatbands into the crowd. A huge beaming smile spread across his face all through the time it took to collect up his kit, sign autographs for the fans, write his name on a television camera lens and all but dance off the court.

He'd just disappeared out of Angela's eye line when her mobile vibrated, on silent mode in her jacket pocket, causing her to jump. It was Stanway. The hubbub of jubilation was still strong around her as she hurried away from the court, the phone pressed close to her ear.

"Sir?"

"We have lift-off, Angie."

Angela's heart skipped a beat. She stopped outside the court to orient herself among the throng. Stanway continued, "I've alerted the rest of the team and we're all on our way. We'll be there in five minutes. Stay close to our target and keep me informed of your whereabouts."

"Will do, sir."

She put her phone back into her pocket and gazed all around. Where to go? The locker rooms, she thought the obvious answer, or the nearest entrance to them. She set off.

Within a couple of minutes she came upon a group of people gathered round a radio and could hear the excited voice of the presenter: *"We knew there would be a Brit in the semi-finals but nobody expected it to be this Brit. Let's join him now and see what he's got to say about his victory today."*

"So, Philip," began the interviewer. "Congratulations on your win. Tell us about the match."

Angela could just imagine Philip schooling his expression into that of someone about to give a businesslike recap of a challenging match. She reckoned it would last for about a nanosecond before the beam came back and split his face in two again. She knew she was right from the tone of his voice. "Thanks. I knew it was going to be a tough one and I'm very glad I was on form." Angela smiled; he was trying, and failing, to make it sound like just another day at the office. The interviewer was speaking again. "So, take us through it. The head-to-head score between you and Stewart is undeniably in Stewart's favour, and in the first set…" The voice continued on as Angela became aware that someone else had joined the little knot of people around the radio. She looked up to find Lavinia Bannister standing nearby, intent on the interview. Their eyes met.

"I suppose you wouldn't know…" began Lavinia, then she shook her head as though she thought better of asking.

"What?" asked Angela.

"Er, I don't suppose you'd know if he's got representation."

I can't blame you for being an opportunist but I don't think you stand a snowball's chance in hell, thought Angela. "I wouldn't know," she said.

Just at that moment there came a muffled buzz and Lavinia jumped, put a hand into her bag, pulled out her mobile and held it up to her ear. "Yes?" she said, and listened. "Yes," she said again, and then, "No, no, don't do anything. You're overwrought. We need to talk. Where are you?" She started to move off. "OK, I'll meet you there," she said, and put the phone back into her bag.

Ah, thought Angela, remembering Stewart's hurried departure from the court. *This might be a better bet.* She let a few seconds go by before following her.

Lavinia didn't look back. She teetered along on her Jimmy Choos, her flimsy top – Versace, Angela guessed – fluttering out at the sides as she hurried through the milling crowds. Had Angela not already known that Philip had won the match, she would have discovered it on this journey. She constantly heard people talking about it, calling to each other and exclaiming over the news. "Hey, guess who won the match between Stewart Bickerstaff and Philip Turnbull?" "No!" "Say what?" "Philip – in four sets?" It was clear from her head movements that Lavinia was registering the same comments, but she didn't slow down or stop. Eventually Angela realized where they were heading and fell back further as Lavinia came to a halt at the place where Stewart's car was parked.

Angela watched. The driver's door opened. Stewart got out and stood up. Angela, keeping out of sight, circled round the cars and came to a halt some distance from them. She remained still as she texted Stanway with her location.

An intense, lively debate took place between Stewart and Lavinia. He gesticulated wildly, angrily. Whenever she could, Lavinia got hold of his hands and drew them down to his chest as if to calm him. Each time he allowed this to happen for a moment or so and then the arms would flail up and out again.

Angela bent down behind the cars and edged a little closer, the better to hear what they were saying. They didn't seem to be aware of her.

"He knows the score, Vin; he knows the score. Why choose today of all days? He's going to be sorry. He's going to be *sooo* sorry."

"Stewart, Stewart, listen! Calm down."

"Did you see him? Did you see him? That was supposed to be *my* victory."

"OK, OK, so you lost," soothed Lavinia. "There'll be other matches."

"Other matches! Other matches! I want this one. This was important to me, Vin; you know it was."

"Yes, but – "

"I'll ruin him! I can stop him playing for a long while – you know that. I could probably even get this result disqualified."

Angela's heart jumped. She had seen Jim approach from the other side of the area. She half-stood and waved at him. Alerted, he ducked down and she saw his bobbing back moving round other cars in her direction. Then she was aware of another back bobbing and weaving towards her. If she was right about the jacket, Gary had arrived. She suddenly became aware that two constables in high-visibility jackets were hovering in a seemingly casual manner near the exit to the car park. A figure came from behind to join Angela. She looked round to find D.C.I. Stanway squatting beside her, looking rather flushed.

"Everything OK, Angie?" he asked.

"Yes, sir. Everybody in place now?"

"Yes."

"Just thought I'd give it a minute to see where their conversation goes, sir."

"Absolutely."

Stewart was still speaking but he was a little calmer now; calculating. "I can do it – you know that, Vin. I can get him suspended from the game."

Angela saw alarm flare up in Lavinia's eyes and she grabbed Stewart's hands again. "You're not thinking straight, Stewart; you're not thinking straight. Let's get out of here so that we can talk properly."

"Ah," said Angela looking at Stanway, who returned a nod.

"Your cue to enter from car park left I think, Angie."

Angela licked suddenly dry lips.

Stanway gave her a small encouraging grin. "We're right behind you, Inspector."

Angela stood up and strode forward. Stewart and Lavinia hadn't seen her. Lavinia was still trying to reason with Stewart. "Look, it's a match. OK, it's Wimbledon, but there'll be other Wimbledons. Nobody's died."

Stewart opened his mouth to speak but the voice they heard belonged to Angela. "Have you forgotten already?" she asked, as she moved closer.

They swung horrified faces towards her.

"What are you doing here?" Stewart, quivering with rage, had found a new target for his anger.

"You're having a heated discussion in a public place," said Angela mildly. "You're lucky there aren't any journos here. They'll be looking for you soon enough."

Stewart stepped back as if to avoid a blow but Angela's shaft had gone home. From the look on his face it was clear he was recalled to his duty. The tournament wasn't quite over for him; not yet. At some point he would be expected to face the cameras and explain in regretful but manly tones that he was disappointed at the outcome of the match but he congratulated his opponent and wished him well in the semi-finals. Right at this moment, he looked very far from regretful manliness.

Lavinia drew herself up to her full height and tried to look down her nose at Angela. "OK, so our voices were raised but this is still a private discussion and has nothing to do with you. Oh, and of course I hadn't forgotten. I'll thank you not to be so flippant."

Angela ignored her. She fixed her eyes on Stewart. "You might think you can ruin him," she said, "but don't forget, you can't bring Philip down without bringing yourself down."

Stewart's eyes widened in alarm for a moment before calculation took over and they narrowed again. "I don't know what you're talking about," he said. "In any case, don't you have a murder to solve?"

"Just think about it," said Angela. *That's as far as I can go in helping Philip,* she thought to herself. *Right now I've got something more important to do.* She was facing Stewart and, looking beyond him, she could see her team standing up and emerging from behind the cars. She saw Stephen Bickerstaff come into view. He moved towards his son. Angela fixed her eyes resolutely on Stewart.

Unaware of all the others, Stewart bestowed a derisory smile on Angela. "Have you come to accuse me? Let's face it, Inspector, you haven't got a shred of evidence, and if you persist in persecuting me in this manner you'll find yourself facing serious disciplinary charges. I promise you I'll take it to the very highest level."

Stephen Bickerstaff reached his son. "Indeed he will, Inspector." Spotting Stanway nearing the group, he cast a stern look in the D.C.I.'s direction and then addressed Angela again. "Your job could be on the line. I suggest you think about that."

Angela was suddenly aware that her palms were sweaty; she could feel beads of perspiration across her top lip. She took a deep breath to keep her voice level and looked at Stewart.

"Stewart Bickerstaff, I am arresting you on suspicion of the murder of your great-aunt, Margaret Bickerstaff."

Chapter Twenty-eight

There was a stunned silence. Angela was to clearly remember it later. They could have been in a soundproof room. There were no sounds of cars from the road outside, no birds, no planes going over. It was as though every person present had been turned briefly to stone.

A gasp of disbelief and shock from Stephen broke the spell. Angela kept her gaze fixed firmly on Stewart. She saw the colour drain from his face. A look of horror and fear came into his eyes.

"You were witnessed withdrawing insulin from the cartridges in her home and replacing it with plain water; this led directly to the hypoglycaemic coma which caused her death."

"*Bitch!*"

"You don't have to say anything," continued Angela calmly, "but it may harm your defence if you don't mention, when questioned, something which you later rely on in court. Anything you do say may be given in evidence. Do you understand?"

There was a strangled sob from Stephen. "Aunt Margaret – Stewart?" He moved towards his son but it seemed his legs wouldn't carry him. Stewart started to lunge at Angela but quick movements from Rick and Jim on either side checked him.

"*Biiitch!*" His face was a mixture of fury and anguish as he struggled against the grasp of the two officers.

Now, thought Angela to herself. *Now, or it might be too late. Go on, risk it, you silly woman.* "And the insulin you'd taken – Petar Belic," she said simply, almost as an afterthought.

"I had to, you stupid cow!" Stewart, so caught up in his own overwhelming emotions, took the bait without thinking.

He spat the words out at her. "He was going to ruin everything. He thought he could stop me. Me! Who did he think he was?"

Angela was aware of feeling both anger and elation; she couldn't have said which emotion was the stronger. *I'll tell you who, you bastard,* she thought. *He was ten times the man you'll ever be, and you killed him.*

"Stewart, I don't think…" In spite of what he was hearing, Stephen retained enough sense to realize the implication of Stewart's words and tried to caution him.

"Too late," Angela muttered, but Stephen Bickerstaff didn't seem to hear her. He gazed with horror and disbelief at his son. He opened his mouth again and tried to speak. This time, no words came out.

Angela nodded at Jim and Rick and they edged the still-protesting Stewart away. Stephen was left, standing forlorn. He raised unseeing eyes towards Angela and Stanway.

"Aunt Margaret – I don't… I can't…" He shook his head in bewilderment. After a moment, he took a deep breath that was more like a sob. "Of course," he said, his voice unsteady, "we'll get him the very best representation."

Angela nodded. "Yes, Mr Bickerstaff."

Stephen stared around him. He seemed to have aged ten years in the previous few minutes. He shook his head again. "Aunt Margaret… I don't understand. She doted on him. We've always done our best for him. We always gave him everything. I don't under… I must find Julia."

He finally found enough strength in his legs to move and he disappeared in the direction he had come.

Angela let out a huge sigh of relief. Then suddenly she felt weak. A supporting arm came round her back, helping her to stay upright. She turned her head and found herself gazing into the sympathetic face of Stanway.

"Well done, Angie," he said.

"Thank you, sir."

"Nice little rider that, at the end. Just the mention of Petar's name, no accusation."

"Yes, sir. Well, as far as Petar's murder goes, he was right. We had no evidence."

"Indeed, indeed. We don't need it now, do we?"

"No, sir."

There was a brief silence and then Stanway spoke. "Well, you might as well get off home now. We have a lot of paperwork waiting for us tomorrow."

"Thank you, sir. Goodnight, sir." Angela moved away. It seemed so strange, after all the emotion and tension; she'd just arrested a murderer and now she was going home after a day at work. *Job done,* she thought.

"OK," said Patrick, the following Sunday afternoon. "Let's get this open before the match begins." There was a gentle pop as its cork finally left the champagne bottle. "Oh, very nice," he said, as he poured the golden stream into the two glasses Angela was holding out to him.

"So," he said, relaxing back on the sofa. "He ended up accusing himself out of his own mouth."

"Hmm, he blurted it out without thinking. It's funny, you know; we're all aware that criminals often forget some small detail and that's what nails them in the end. But in this case, it was me that overlooked something."

"What was that?"

"When Gracie and I had a sandwich together the first time, and she was telling me about Great-aunt Margaret. She said it would be most unusual for a person to be as old as Margaret Bickerstaff without having some sort of chronic condition and I didn't pick up on it. It didn't occur to me that she could have insulin-dependent diabetes."

Patrick smiled at her. "So you're not superwoman, you're just a regular cop."

Angela grinned and joined him on the sofa. "Mind you, I still would have had the same problem of linking the facts to Petar's death."

"Yes, indeed. What Gracie witnessed turned out to be the linchpin of the whole case. You don't think she'll retract her evidence – family solidarity and all that?"

"Oh no. She saw what she saw and there isn't any doubt about it. It's true that she's not happy to be giving evidence against a member of her own family. It's all very distasteful to her; a case of what she was brought up to call washing your dirty linen in public. But then, Margaret Bickerstaff was family too. And Gracie also has a very deep regard for the truth. And, of course, there's the business of the will."

"Yes, run that by me again. You were getting so excited, talking about sending the team off to collect what was left of the insulin cartridges and gather fingerprint evidence, that I think I missed it first time round."

"Well, from what I gather that's what triggered everything in the end – the solution, I mean. Gracie and Edith were having a glass of sherry at Edith's place. Gracie was bringing Edith up to speed with all that had been going on while Edith had been in Australia. Edith was commiserating with her about the new will and saying what a rotten trick etcetera. Edith has no high regard for Stewart and didn't mince her words whenever she mentioned him, apparently. She talked about how she had watched him worming his way into the old lady's affections for a long while, fetching and carrying. She had no doubt it was all to curry favour."

"Yeah?"

"Yeah, so then Gracie said, 'Oh, he's even helping her out with her injections now,' and Edith's ears immediately pricked up. She's right, Gracie seems to have led a sheltered life. The thing is that Margaret was completely *compos mentis*, had been dealing with her own injections for years and didn't need any help."

"Surely Gracie knew that."

"Oh yes, Gracie wasn't so naïve that she thought Stewart was actually giving the injection. She'd seen him handling the insulin cartridges, though, and simply thought that he was tidying them up or putting them in the place where Margaret kept the next one that would be needed."

"Ah."

"But, of course, Edith, just back from Australia, was hearing all about the death of Margaret *and* the death by insulin of Petar Belic all in the same information chunk, as it were."

"I see, so she immediately joined up the dots."

"Well, to be fair, even she didn't like to make the ultimate leap at first. She hesitated to think Stewart would stoop so low but she was alerted enough to make Gracie go very carefully through what she had seen. And what Gracie told her didn't leave a lot of room for doubt."

"Well, Stewart might have found an argument to explain it, I suppose, but you said Derek and Leanne found cartridges still there that had been tampered with and were full of water."

"Absolutely, and he very kindly left us fingerprints. And what with Gracie's evidence…"

"Oh," said Patrick, slapping his head. "I'm being a bit slow. I was just about to say, 'So where does the will come in?' when I realized – of course. If Stewart is found guilty of Margaret's murder, that invalidates the will naming him as beneficiary and the previous will is the one that goes to probate."

"Yes. So Gracie'll get her little flat near her friend and a pension after all."

"Well done, Inspector – and your team, of course," he added quickly as he saw her open her mouth to speak. "But I still say you found out the pivotal information because you're talk-to-able."

Angela smiled. Patrick put down his glass and moved closer to her.

"You're very something-else-able as well," he said. Their kiss lingered until their attention was drawn to the television screen by the sound of cheering which announced the arrival on court of the Wimbledon men finalists.

"Do you know anything about these two players?" asked Patrick.

"Not a thing, but I reckon the Slovakian must still be knackered after that five-setter with Philip, so my money's on the Argentinian."

"Yeah, shame Philip didn't quite make the final, but it was so close that things bode well for the future."

"They certainly do," agreed Angela. Just at that moment, the camera, panning round to find famous faces in the crowd, had located one.

There's Tessa Riordan, said the voice of the commentator. *Fresh from her victory in the ladies' final yesterday.*

"My goodness," said Patrick. "It was a victory and a half, wasn't it? She blasted Candy off court."

"Not half," agreed Angela. "But I think Candy's mind might not have been wholly on her game. She's been trying to disassociate herself from Stewart ever since he was arrested. I even saw in one of the papers this morning that she's quoted as saying that they were already drifting apart and she was beginning to think that he ought to sort out his relationship with Joanna and take responsibility for his child."

"Ha! The words 'rats' and 'sinking ship' come to mind."

"Don't they just." Angela sipped at her champagne and wondered idly if Stewart would be able to watch the match in the remand centre where he was being held. She even felt a stab of sympathy, but a picture of Petar Belic lying dead flashed into her mind and it passed.

The cameras panned back to Tessa to show that Philip Turnbull was sitting beside her. The commentator continued, *I'm sure Tessa Riordan must be looking forward to the ball tonight. While it's certain that she'll dance once or twice with today's winner, there can't be any doubt that her escort will actually be Philip Turnbull. What an impressive fight he put up in that semifinal match. Who knows? Maybe he'll be the champion next year. It's entirely possible.*

Contents

Handbook of microscopic anatomy for the health sciences

1

Primary tissues

The unit of structure and function in all living organisms is the *cell*. The cells that make up the human body are descended from a single multipotential cell, the fertilized ovum. During the first few weeks of embryologic development, the outlines of the main tissues of the body appear. These cells will subsequently differentiate in size, shape, and arrangement; structure will adapt to functional requirements. Aggregates of cells that are closely related in structure and function thus form the *tissues* of the body. The cells of a tissue may be closely packed or they may be widely scattered within a noncellular matrix, which contains specialized ground substances, fluids, fibers, or inorganic deposits. The noncellular materials present in a tissue are synthesized by the cells of that tissue. However, tissues are not ordinarily found as isolated units. They are integral parts of organized structures in close relationship to other types of tissues. It is customary to refer to a structurally organized group of tissues that subserves one or more specific functions as an *organ*. Each organ has a characteristic arrangement of component tissues, that is, a characteristic architecture that correlates with its function. A group of organs that function together toward a common purpose constitute a *system* (for example, respiratory system, digestive system, endocrine system). Tissues, organs, and systems make up the fabric of the complete living individual. They form the basis for the study of microscopic anatomy.

All the tissues of the body can be classified as one of four primary types, each of which has its own structural and functional attributes. These are epithelium, connective tissue, muscular tissue, and nervous tissue.

EPITHELIUM

Epithelial tissues form the covering membrane of the body (skin) and the inner membrane linings of body cavities and organs (serous and mucous membranes). Epithelial membranes are adapted for protection, absorption, and secretion. More specialized epithelium forms most of the glandular tissue and some sensory receptors of the body. Specialized epithelia will be discussed under the relevant headings in the chapters that follow.

Epithelial membranes have the following characteristic features:

1

1. They line free surfaces.
2. The cells are closely packed, held together by tiny attachments between adjacent cell membranes (desmosomes and terminal bars).
3. They are avascular (contain no blood vessels) and are dependent for nutrition on the materials that diffuse into them from blood vessels in the underlying connective tissue.
4. Epithelial membranes rest upon a thin supporting noncellular layer, the basement membrane.
5. Since they cover exposed surfaces, the cells are capable of regeneration and repair.

Epithelium that consists of a single layer of cells is said to be *simple;* if it consists of more than one layer, it is *stratified.* The simple and stratified epithelia are classified as *squamous, cuboidal,* or *columnar,* according to the shape of the cells on the free surface of the tissue; that is, in stratified epithelium, the shape of the cells in the superficial (topmost) layer determines how the tissue will be classified. On the bases of shape and single or multiple layers, there are eight types of epithelium:

Simple epithelium	*Stratified epithelium*
Simple squamous	Stratified squamous
Simple cuboidal	Stratified cuboidal
Simple columnar	Stratified columnar
Pseudostratified columnar	Transitional

Simple squamous epithelium is composed of a single layer of flat irregularly shaped cells resembling scales. The *mesothelium* of serous membranes and the *endothelium* of blood and lymphatic vessels are examples of this type of epithelium. It is also found lining the alveolar sacs of the lungs and is a vital component of the respiratory membrane.

Stratified squamous epithelium (Fig. 1-1) occurs in the epidermis of the skin, the external orifices of body cavities such as the mouth, the nose, and the vagina, and the lining of the esophagus. It may contain many layers or only a few. In the skin, the outer layers are composed of cells in which the cytoplasm has been replaced by a hard, insoluble substance (keratin), and the nuclei have disappeared. Usually, only the cells of the basal (innermost) layer of stratified squamous epithelium are capable of proliferation. These cells may be cuboidal or even columnar in shape.

Cuboidal epithelium is approximately cube shaped; the height of the cells is equal to the width. Columnar cells are somewhat taller; the height of these cells is greater than the width. *Simple cuboidal epithelium* (Fig. 1-2) is mainly found lining the tubules of the kidney. *Simple columnar epithelium* (Fig. 1-3) lines the gastrointestinal tract from the cardiac end of the stomach to the anus. Cells of heights that are intermediate between typical columnar and cuboidal often occur in the body. Where cells of unequal heights occur side by side in a single layer, a false appearance of stratification may result. This type of epithelium is called *pseudostratified columnar epithelium* (Fig. 1-4). It is found lining most of the respiratory tract. Stratified

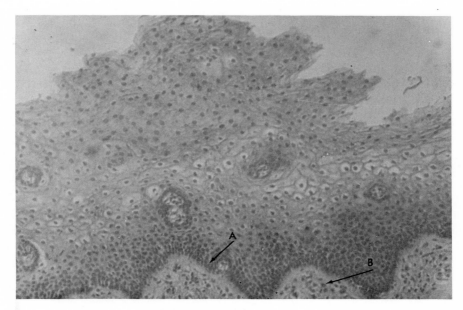

Fig. 1-1. Stratified squamous epithelium. (×100.) *A*, Basal layer, *B*, papilla of lamina propria.

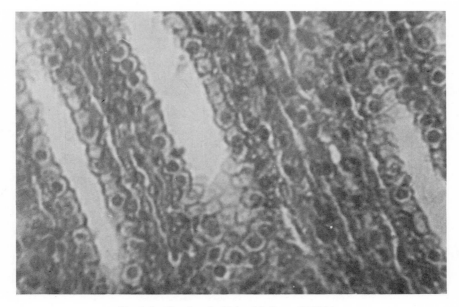

Fig. 1-2. Simple cuboidal epithelium. (×100.)

Fig. 1-3. *A*, Simple columnar epithelium; *B*, goblet cell. (X100.)

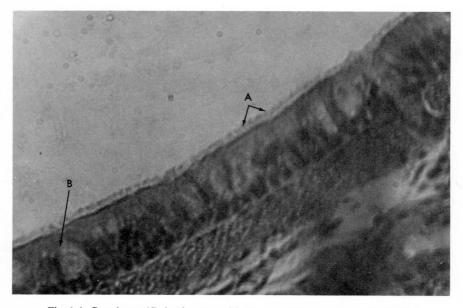

Fig. 1-4. Pseudostratified columnar epithelium. *A*, Cilia, *B*, goblet cell. (X400.)

cuboidal and columnar epithelia are mainly two-layered tissues and are not very common in the adult. *Stratified cuboidal epithelium* is found in sweat gland ducts and the female urethra; *stratified columnar epithelium,* which is difficult to distinguish from the pseudostratified form, is found in some areas of the larynx (voice box) and pharynx (throat).

Transitional epithelium (Fig. 1-5) is a special type of stratified epithelium found only in the renal pelvis, ureters, urinary bladder, and the upper part of the urethra. When these organs are empty, that is, not distended with urine, the epithelium resembles a stratified squamous or cuboidal type. The surface cells are, however, unusually large and dome shaped. They can thus be stretched considerably without breaking away from one another.

A characteristic feature of epithelial cells is the occurrence of specialized structures on the free surface of the cells. These include microscopic fingerlike projections of cell cytoplasm such as *microvilli,* and motile hairlike structures called *cilia.* The function of microvilli is to increase the surface area of the cell for absorption. These processes, formerly called "striated borders" or "brush borders," are abundant on the luminal surface of absorptive cells of the intestinal epithelium and the proximal renal tubule. The so-called *stereocilia,* which occur on epithelial cells lining parts of the male reproductive tract, are now known to be very long microvilli. Numerous "cell hairs," or cilia, are found on the pseudostratified columnar epithelium of the respiratory passages, where their function is to move foreign particles in inspired air away from the lungs.

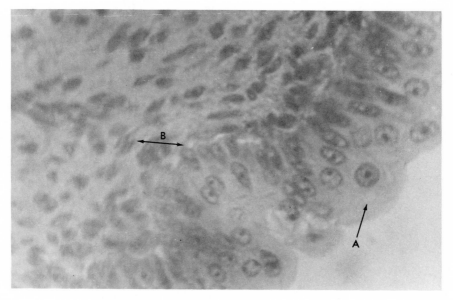

Fig. 1-5. Transitional epithelium. (X400.) *A,* Dome-shaped surface cell, *B,* connective tissue lamina.

Some columnar cells may become modified to form unicellular (one-celled) glands, or *goblet cells*. These cells are found throughout the gastrointestinal and respiratory tracts. The lubricating fluid, or mucus, that they secrete accumulates in a large globule in the upper portion of the cell, giving it the appearance of a rounded wineglass with a narrow stem.

CONNECTIVE TISSUES

Connective tissue is the most abundant primary tissue found in the body. It is actually a complex of different subtypes that exhibit a considerable amount of structural and functional diversity. All connective tissues are derived from mesenchymal cells of the embryo. They form the supporting framework of the body and its organs and function in transport of substances (blood), storage (adipose tissue), and immunity (reticuloendothelial system, lymphoid tissues, white blood cells). With the exception of cartilage, connective tissue is very vascular, that is, extensively permeated with blood vessels.

The connective tissues can be classified as follows:

Connective tissue proper	*Specialized connective tissues*
Loose connective tissues	Cartilage
Mucous	Hyaline
Areolar	Elastic
Adipose	Fibrocartilage
Reticular	
Dense connective tissues	Bone
Dense collagenous	Spongy (cancellous)
Dense elastic	Compact
(regular and irregular	Bone marrow
fiber arrangements)	(hemopoietic tissue)
	Blood
	Lymphoid tissue
	Reticuloendothelial
	system

The connective tissues proper will be described in this section, together with two specialized connective tissues, namely, cartilage and the so-called reticuloendothelial (RE) system. Other specialized connective tissues, such as lymphoid tissue, bone, bone marrow, and blood, will be discussed under separate headings in subsequent chapters.

The predominant cell found in connective tissue proper is the *fibroblast,* a spindle-shaped cell with a centrally placed oval nucleus. Other cells that occur are as follows:

1. Fat or adipose cells: distended round cells filled with a single large fat vacuole. The nucleus is pushed to one side, giving these cells a characteristic signet ring shape.
2. Reticular cells: stellate (star-shaped) cells with large pale-staining nuclei and cytoplasmic extensions. They are found particularly in association with reticular fibers in lymphoid tissues.

3. Mast cells: large ovoid cells crowded with cytoplasmic granules that are markedly basophilic. The granules contain heparin, an anticoagulant, and histamine, a local hormone that plays a role in allergic reactions. The granules of mast cells closely resemble those of the basophil leukocytes of the blood.

4. Various blood leukocytes and plasma cells that have migrated from the bloodstream to the tissues.

Unlike epithelium, the cells of connective tissue are generally spread out in an intercellular material, or *matrix*. In most connective tissues, the matrix is a semisolid gel. However, it may also be fluid (blood), semirigid (cartilage), or rigid (bone). The matrix consists of a ground substance in which variable numbers of collagen, elastic, and reticular fibers may be embedded. Connective tissue cells, notably fibroblasts, synthesize and secrete both the ground substance and the fibers. Flexible, strong *collagen,* or *white fibers,* are the predominant fibers found in connective tissue proper. The substance, collagen, is a protein that softens in boiling water to form gelatin. In tissue sections, bundles of collagen fibers appear as slightly wavy threads. *Reticular fibers* are specialized, very thin collagenous fibers that occur as fine network, forming the support (stroma) of lymphoid organs, bone marrow, the liver, and other organs. Reticular fibers are called *argyrophilic* fibers because of their special affinity for silver stains (Fig. 1-8). *Elastic fibers* are branching fibers that have, as their name indicates, elastic properties. In aggregate, they appear yellow.

Mucous connective tissue is composed of rather primitive fibroblasts and a soft mucoid matrix in which collagenous fibers are embedded. It is an embryonal tissue found in the umbilical cord. It is usually called Wharton's jelly.

The most frequently occurring loose connective tissue is *areolar connective tissue* (Fig. 1-6), which forms the packing in and around most body tissues and organs. The matrix contains mainly a loose array of collagenous fibers, but elastic and reticular fibers are also present.

Adipose, or *fat tissue,* always occurs in close proximity to areolar tissue, and appears to be a modification of areolar tissue. Large fat cells predominate, surrounded by the fibroblasts and matrix of areolar tissue (Fig. 1-7). Routine histologic processing dissolves the lipid in fat cells, and they usually appear empty.

Reticular tissue (Fig. 1-8), consisting of reticular cells and reticular fibers, is limited mainly to lymph nodes, the thymus and spleen, other lymphoid tissues, and bone marrow.

The dense fibrous connective tissues consist of closely packed bundles of fibers with scattered sparse fibroblasts (Figs. 1-9 and 1-10). *Dense collagenous tissue* is found in the dermis of the skin, the fibrous capsules of organs, and in the tendons binding muscles to muscles or muscles to bone. In elastic ligaments, of which there are only a few in man, elastic fibers are the predominant component of the matrix.

Cartilage is an avascular connective tissue with a semirigid matrix that is chemically a complex protein-polysaccharide. The matrix is secreted by large specialized cartilage cells, or *chondrocytes* (Gr. *chondros,* cartilage). The cells characteristically lie in small

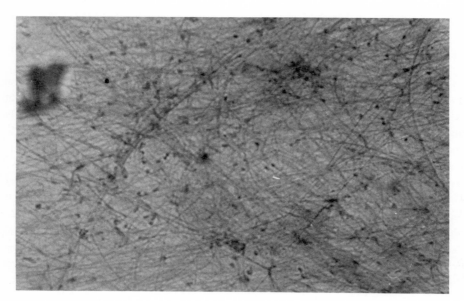

Fig. 1-6. Areolar connective tissue showing mixed fibers in matrix. (X100.)

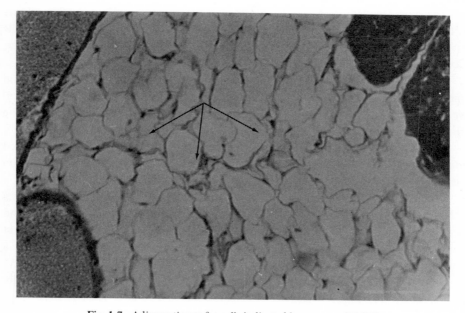

Fig. 1-7. Adipose tissue; fat cells indicated by arrows. (X100.)

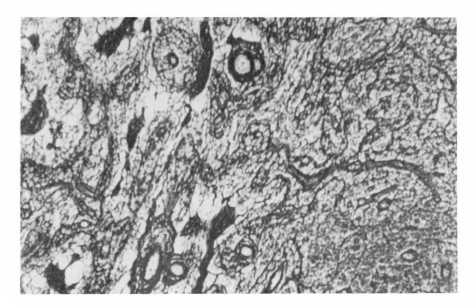

Fig. 1-8. Reticular connective tissue; reticular fibers (black) impregnated with silver. (×100.)

cavities, called *lacunae,* in the matrix. Cells enclosed in lacunae are also a prominent feature of bone. The commonest form of cartilage is *hyaline cartilage* (Fig. 1-11), which forms most of the fetal skeleton and covers the articular surfaces of bones in the adult. The matrix of hyaline cartilage appears clear and glassy (Gr. *hyalos,* glass) and is usually basophilic. It contains fine randomly distributed collagen fibers. *Elastic cartilage,* a more flexible type of cartilage, contains elastic fibers. It is found in the external ear and in parts of the larynx. *Fibrocartilage* (Fig. 1-12), which has dense collagen fibrous components, is found in association with the fibrous tendons and ligaments of joints. The intervertebral disks are the best examples of this type of cartilage.

The *reticuloendothelial system,* or *RE system,* is a term used to denote a group of ameboid, phagocytic cells that are present in tissues throughout the body. They are distinguished by their ability to engulf colloidal and particulate material, and obviously function as part of the immunologic mechanisms of the body. RE cells are exemplified by the fixed and free macrophages (histiocytes) of connective tissues, the Kupffer cells lining the sinusoids of the liver and the reticular-type macrophages lining blood sinuses in other organs, and the phagocytic microglia of the brain and the spinal cord.

MUSCULAR TISSUE

Muscular tissue is composed of large, elongated cells (also called muscle *fibers*) that have the ability to contract (or shorten) in response to stimuli. The three types found

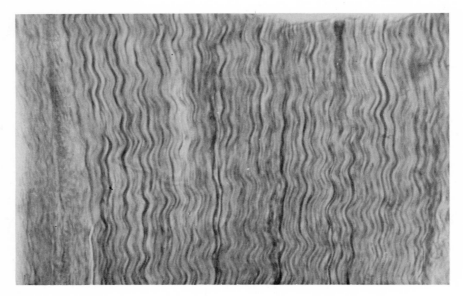

Fig. 1-9. Dense fibrous (collagenous) connective tissue. (×100.)

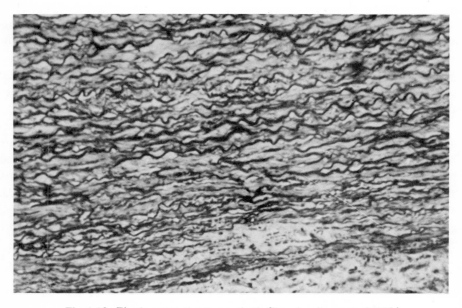

Fig. 1-10. Elastic connective tissue; elastic fibers in a ligament. (×100.)